FIRST OF EMBERS

EMMERSON ALLEN

Table of Contents

Acknowledgements

*Loyalty and love
for those who matter most.*

My special girl with her little marshmallow. You are my inspiration. Never, ever doubt how amazing you really are.

My Boo who has constantly interrupted me, begged me to go riding and generally made my life nothing less than the best adventure yet!

The other two. You have forgiven all my numerous mistakes and let me grow with you. You both taught me patience, love and fear! I am so glad you both still like me because I messed up so many times.

Well, what can I say but thank you to the big ADR. No matter what you have always ridden shotgun in love, life and all my crazy chaos!

To Sarah, Aunty Marg and my cousin Mark that read this book and gave me love, advice and honestly, I am forever grateful.

Chapter 1

I know the agony that comes. I have spent my life and hers preparing for it and I am helpless to stop it. The darkness gathers even now drowning the light and I have no other choice but to surrender to it.

Pain swells in my chest.

I know this is only the beginning; the start of a firestorm that may destroy us all and I can do nothing but pray.

I have been her lifelong protector; her shield and I have vowed to ensure her protection until death; hers or mine.

I am the reason she lives, and I will sacrifice everything to ensure our legacy.

Even in this misery, this sadness that grips at my chest I look across the span of armies before turning to see her at my right.

She stands so tall, so magnificent, brave and beautiful in the sunlight; so innocent to the horror that is about to unfold for her.

Made in my image she is, without doubt, the centre of our universe. The reason I have lived and the reason I will die, and I will die peacefully, knowing she lives.... because she is all that can save us now.

Chapter 2

Moments splinter into fragments of time. Light and balance fill the air around me as I shake with adrenaline from lifting my sword over and over, endlessly fighting for my world. I rage fiercely in the heart of the battle smiling viciously at my enemy as I kill, laughing at their screams as my sword drives deep into flesh and bone all the while I celebrate the cries of death surrounding me.

I am Everly Regla Mas Alta, Princess of Axis. My place is proudly at the right hand of my father, Solomon the First, Ruler of the Axian Realms. We are the First family of the four foundation families of Axis created by Axis herself.

My father rules the realms with integrity, honour and kindness. He is the shield that protects while I am the sword at his side that defends and together with my brother Tallon we defend the light and balance of our world ensuring the safety of our people.

But this day has brought war to our doorstep.

An unfamiliar enemy has come marching through our gates, an enemy that has access to our world without permission and wears no flags of identification, but my father and I are vigilant in our duty and they will only learn defeat for daring to attack us.

With precision and focus, I leave a trail of destruction in my wake and as I fight, I wait.... I fight patiently, purposefully, in the growing ruins of our enemy waiting for our salvation. The salvation my father will deliver to show once again our dominance is without question and unrivalled! Then, together, we will celebrate yet another victory.

It can be no other way. It is our family legacy, a history of power and protection that stretches out over more than a millennium. I know my place, my faith in my family and my world absolute and this is why I will never stop fighting.

My world, Axis, lay at the core of our realms. It is the light and balance of my world that gives our realms life and it is the strength and power of my family's abilities to secure and manage the light and balance that protects us all.

Every blow of my sword is for Axis and I fight with everything I have understanding always the cost of failure.

Blow after blow of swords strike in ceaseless ringing waves across my shield. The blood of my enemies flows in rivers down my face, yet it only gives me strength as I know in my heart the end must be but moments away.

In the chaos of blood and the constant clash of steel I hear the ever-increasing screams of death but do not falter knowing they are the price of war and accepting that it can only mean defeat for this enemy.

I raise my sword again and at the same time draw the light and balance from the air around me but unexpectedly feel nothing! The light and balance in the air of Axis give me power, strength and invincibility. Although I have drawn their essence to me throughout the battle it strangely does not flow to me now!

I pull at the air with greater aggression knowing it will cause ripples, but it is as though there is none left, and I cannot use it to help me! I have no time to wonder, nor worry at what this could mean for us. I must continue to fight.

Moment's pass and casualties increase and still no call from my father. I fight through the burn of fury tearing through my chest, not understanding why he has let this fight go on for so long. He must act quickly, even I cannot sustain this fight without the strength I draw from the light and balance. He surely must feel their absence and know without them we will be weaker.

Between soldiers, swords and shields I see nothing but chaos in every direction. I cannot see a single ally around me and realize I have somehow become isolated in the battle. I fight towards the centre of the city in the hope of finding allies but even as I fight fear blooms as more and more time passes, and nothing happens, and I weaken. Even in my fear, I will forever lift my sword, deadly and unstoppable to protect my world. I have no other choice but to live, to survive, and to win, regardless of my fading strength.

My momentum falters as I glance to my left and, as if directed by the hand of Axis herself, I watch as enemy soldiers clear in the fray and I stagger in shock when I see my father on his knees, his sword in front of him, kneeling silently in the mud.

A path of unforgivable violence sears through my blood-soaked brain rebelling in defiance of what I have seen. This is impossible! He is too strong to submit! It would be unthinkable! I must be mistaken! So, I try again to draw in the light and balance to save us, to find him, to finish this... but it is pointless. Only a void of nothingness surrounds me, empty and barren and I am afraid.

Maybe it is a ploy I am not part of, a plan or strategy because it is inconceivable that he would surrender for any other reason, so I continue to fight. I have faith in my father, so I will not fail him now.

This enemy streamed through our gates from a world beyond and fights us in the heart of Axis where we are strongest and if my father is unable to rise, I can do no less than fight for us all.

Desperate to seek the truth, I turn to seek my brother. I can hear his roar in battle like a beacon and move towards his bellows. I cannot initially find him in the fight and search in every direction until the shine of his amour catches my eye. Relief crashes through me until I see he is not in position! Terror slams against my chest as I watch him fighting some distance away and know it will be impossible for me to reach him.

"TALLON!" I scream trying to gain his attention, but he is focused on the enemy and violent in his fighting. I scream his name into the fray over and over as I struggle to creep closer with each slash of my sword to where he stands. If only he would look at me! If he only knew he was out of formation! My strong, powerful brother fights in isolation and it only fuels my fear.

My arms are heavy, and the flow of enemy soldiers is relentless. It is as if I fight multitudes with each step. I want to scream at the world around me! Tell whoever hears my cries that this is all wrong, but I can do nothing more than move in small brutal steps, carving a path of death towards hope.

I lift my head as I reach closer to my brother's position and see he still lives and fights. He is indomitable in his strength, my mighty warrior brother. His golden features are clear and focused in the blood and dirt of battle. He is a warrior of legends and I grin with relief at him as he finally catches my eye but strangely, he looks at me with some surprise before he shakes his head at me almost sadly and then, to my shock, turns away!

I see the sweep of a sword stroke come towards him and tell myself this is why he leaves me. He has time to defend but maybe this is the reason he chooses to move away. He will defend and I see, from the side of my vision, as he stabs his sword viciously into the soldier's neck. Maybe he knows. Maybe it is my brother who will save us. I can only pray my brother is strong enough to defend us. I do not have the strength to save us without the light and balance to continue without end in such intense fighting can only mean death.

I call to him desperately again, pointlessly, through the fray, worried. As I turn to try and find him, I am knocked to the ground and stumble in the mud falling onto my hand as a sword cuts deeply into my hip. Annoyed that I have let myself become so distracted I rise and turn, using my sword to sweep low, gutting my enemy. It is with growing weakness I fight through the dawning realisation that within this disarray help may never come.

I cannot see my father. My brother has moved away leaving me alone to fight amid chaos and this enemy appears in even direction around me as if their numbers are never-ending!

This is not how it is meant to be! We never fight in isolation! We rise together, we fight together, and we win together...every time, until now, but I must fight on determinedly. I have no choice. I fight for my world; my people so I cannot let this chaos distract me or this fear drown me. I must find a way to draw the light and balance to me. I need to fight my way towards my father and brother to regain our lost combat formation and then this battle will be done.

I throw myself closer, deeper into the fray in the direction I last saw Tallon, desperate to get to him but am rendered helpless to move forward as enemy after enemy soldier slows my steps and I can do nothing more than defend, their swords slashing towards me in ever-increasing endless numbers.

I am frantic as my body slowly begins to grow numb with weariness. I cannot use my power without the light and balance and if it does not flow, I cannot save anyone, not even myself.

There is no other way. Our allies must be waiting for my father's call as I cannot see any sign of the gold Aurelians, who are the second wave of fighting in this battle, but I also still cannot see my brother. I cannot stop the panic that begins to drown me as I struggle to stay alive, to find my way to safety or some hope in all that surrounds me.

I fight without strength, slashing and moving, clearing a path driven only by fear and desperation. I scream across the nightmare of savagery on every side, calling my brother's name over and over. I pull and pull searching the air for the light and balance knowing I leave ripples around me, but I cannot feel anything, and the terror of the void left in its place drowns me in icy waves.

A flash of gold catches my eye and I look to find my brother again fighting closer but still too far away to reach. I am boosted he is still alive but then his shine is blocked by the sheer numbers of our enemy and I am alone again.

I fight on endlessly, without emotion and it is as though I am caught in a nightmare that replays in endless loops. The blood flows, the ground at my feet is slush and still, I fight. I drop my sword slightly as I take a few hurried steps forward through a rare break in the soldiers surrounding me and as I turn to fight again, for a moment everything slows... and in infinite agony, I watch my enemy clear and I see my father... on his knees with a sword pressed against his throat.

My scream is of horror, of anger and despair. This cannot happen! Is my brother blind to the unfolding nightmare around us? To my father's capture? Where are the Aurelians who are meant to protect us? But even more...what is this void that steals the source of our power? This complete desolate emptiness where there should be light and balance in abundance.

I look through the battle towards my father, but I see nothing but death and acceptance in his face and I am enraged that he would concede so effortlessly. He has not moved! He has done the unthinkable! He kneels silently in the dirt; his armour covered in blood and watches me through tears as I continue to fight.

I can hardly do more than repeatedly defend my position as I struggle to focus, struggle to fight with what little strength I have left. I know I cannot die even for his failure and my heart tears in pieces as he watches me with unwavering sadness on his face.

"FIGHT!!!" I scream at him. "STAND!!! GET TO YOUR FEET AND SAVE US ALL!!!" The words tear from my throat.

He is power personified, yet he kneels as if he is helpless.

This battle is nothing but an easy victory against an enemy with no strong strategy or power, he told me so himself, yet he watches me sadly as if he has lost everything and has nothing.... from on his knees in the blood-soaked dirt.

I don't understand! I cannot fathom what he has done! I cannot see his reasons! Lost in the confusion of uncertainty, for the first time in my life I am alone. I do not have any choice at all but to fight on determined this is not the end. I will not let my people fall or see my world defeated. Not while I still have breath!

Even as my body shakes with weakness, anger fuels my fight. The void of light and balance means I have nothing else to offer but the rage of my sword. Righteous in my blows, I am furious when he continues to watch the battle from his knees although I fight valiantly in his name. I scream at him again as I ensure enemy soldiers fall to the ground dead. I beg him to rise with every breath but still, he does nothing but watches me with such sadness as if everything is already lost.

I will not let them take my hero from me. I will not let my world fall into chaos without a First. I am not ready for him to leave me. He will rise to fight beside me once he realises the folly of his actions. He will not die in the mud on his knees, it is not the way of heroes so if he refuses to rise, I will fight to save us all!

"RISE!!" I scream above the noise "RISE FATHER!!! FIGHT!!! FOR AXIS!!!" I try desperately again to draw the light and balance through me, it is all I need to save us... but it is still gone! Only the same ominous void in the air in every direction around me!

My sword whips at a frantic pace carving through countless soldiers and destroying line after line of attack but I do not seem to be getting any closer to my father's position. He does not move. He does not answer my call. I can feel the air around me bow and change as if warping in some way and I quickly draw at it hopeful but only gain a scant trace of light and balance, enough for a second of relief before it disappears again.

I look to see my father remains silent on his knees while the noise of the battle swirls around him drowning out my screams of rage. My sword grows stronger as my anger swells. I sweep towards countless soldiers and know they see only death in my face. I am determined to end this in victory regardless of the odds against us but within a strange shuddering heartbeat an eerie quietness suddenly spreads in every direction around me as soldier after soldier stops in the fight and steps away from me, I know the finality of my father's capture has been realised.

I look in every direction for my brother but cannot find him. I have faith he lives knowing he would be too stubborn to die, even for our father's sake!

There is little left on our side to fight for, little reason for enemy soldiers to keep finding death with every sweep of my sword. With our First kneeling in defeat, they stop, and I am enraged when they clear the area around me and step away thinking they have beaten us all!

I charge at them with my sword held high, but they will not fight. They will not engage me! They look at me warily but relieved as the shock and excitement at their victory reverberates in the air unspoken and for the first time, I understand the soul tearing pain of failure and the crushing weight of helplessness in the face of loss.

Outnumbered and surrounded I pause, as my father seems to finally find his voice. The air around me still a void I cannot draw on, so I turn towards him shaking with anger. As if the sound has suddenly been restored in deafening volume, I hear my father's voice screaming at me to surrender, to drop my sword to my side but defiantly I shake my head and stand still defensively daring them to try and take my weapon. His screams continue as the circle around me grows and although I am too weak to fight any longer, I cannot bear the thought of failure. I look in every direction for salvation, but it is pointless. This cannot be my end. This cannot be the end of my world. He screams the impossible at me and I can see no other way.

In shock and disbelief, knowing I do this only in the hope his life will be saved. I fall to my knees, placing my sword in the mud in front of me. On the ground I only feel rage, in the bloody mud I scream my frustration into the sky begging my world for forgiveness knowing my end must have arrived. I am ashamed. I am enraged. I will give my life to save him if only for the sake of this world.

As the darkness of what he has done burns through my bones, I look up to see the swords of this pathetic enemy surrounding me on all sides thinking I am weak. I am Everly Regla Mas Alta, the daughter of the First family of Axis, the strongest of my people and my father, even now, is the only person powerful enough to ever force my surrender! I would fight on for eternity for my world rather than kneel in the mud as I am now, surrounded by those who are unworthy of my defeat.

On my knees, tears' streaming down my face, I watch in horror as my defeated hero begs for my life while willingly sacrificing our entire world... and in the fraying doom of a single heartbeat, I know I am the reason he has betrayed us all. He cannot forfeit his life for mine! He is wrong. I cannot save our world without him! It must be him that lives.

"NO!! NO!!!! TAKE MY LIFE, NOT HIS!! KILL ME! I AM THE STRONGEST!!" I scream at them and he turns to me, sadly, beseechingly but I am cold to his expression. I do not look away. I am not ashamed to beg for the life of my father.

"Daughter...my precious daughter...I have not failed..." is all he whispers across the space between us.

"You have failed us all Father!" I scream at him in frustration "YOU HAVE FAILED ME!!! You must live to save us!!" But he does not respond, he does not protect us; he doesn't even try to save our people. He only looks across the distance between us and all I see is the acceptance of death in his eyes.

All is lost. This single moment of time marks eternally the depth of our defeat.

It is as though my soul is breaking apart when he looks into my face to nod his last goodbye and I scream back at him in righteous unforgiving anger. I will never forget this moment, the sliver of time my father doomed our entire universe and sacrificed everything for nothing.

"USE IT!!!" I scream desperately "SAVE US ALL!!! DO NOT DO THIS!!" but he shakes his head and it shatters what is left of my already shredded heart.

"It is you, Everly. Only you! You are what is needed." He calls desperately to me. "The darkness..." he begins but it is too late. The hooded soldier who towers over him lifts my father's hair and takes his head with a single swipe of his blade and I cannot breathe any longer, I cannot think, I can do nothing but scream in agony as I am dragged to my feet and carried across the battlefield. I feel the grip of dragon claws around my bound arms, but I cannot look away.

As my father's head rolls away from his body the light and balance flow once again, saturating the world with such strength it is suddenly overwhelming, but it is too late.

I am a lifeless rag in the dragon's talons, uncaring of my world, lost in shattering pain as the dragon slowly beats its wings and takes to the sky.

My agony never-ending as my eyes remained fixed on my father's lifeless body and I watch what is left of my hero kicked in the mud of what is unforgettably our final battle.

I do not look away. I let the pain overwhelm me, drowning me as if it will tear me apart. I did not cower in fear, as I am carried higher and higher into the sky but hang limply, not caring whether I live or die. I do not see anything other than my dead fallen hero, my beloved father and when I can no longer see him I draw every ripple of light and balance in the air roughly towards me, uncaring of the damage it will bring, and as I scream into the sky an explosion erupts and the world around me shatters into a million pieces of light more powerful than I ever thought possible and I fall into the darkness of oblivion with the whisper of realization echoing in my head.... that in the end.... it was all for nothing.

Chapter 3

I hurry towards the last room terrified I am too late. I glance back at the destruction that has laid this place to waste and I know what this room must hold. She has saved us all but not before it destroyed her too and I understand her love but even she may not have survived this explosion.

It is as if I have walked through an apocalypse. There is only snow and cold now. The buildings are gone and, in every direction, all that remains of the great city Samara is rubble and fire.

I have walked towards this house near the edge of the city, alone, for more than an hour. The explosion has detonated from this point and I recognise the unmistakable flow of light and balance.

Another blast suddenly comes from within the house, blowing outwards in ripples of such pure power. I brace, accepting the pain it brings as its intensity scorches deep within my bones and watch as the world around me lights up in white once more. I feel the pressure of power against my chest and pause, waiting for it to pass.

It should not be possible!

This level of power should not be able to thrive within the realms. It has brought death to an entire city and I know without a doubt what I must do.

I am the only one strong enough to save us now, to save Axis. And as I see the source of the destruction, I freeze unable to move, unable to breathe. Destiny has arrived and in this singular moment, my entire life changes and I know the price to save us will be everything.

Chapter 4

We are the First family of Axis, Alta Axian. Our world is the core of all life within our universe. Axis sits at the dissection of all seven realms that make up our universe. To protect these realms there are four foundation families of Axis. Each of the four families is critical to our survival.

My family is the most powerful, until now, we are born to rule and control the flow of light and balance that originates on Axis itself and sustains all life. The other three families are spread across the realms and ensure our future, our defence and our accountability.

Each world is accessed through gateways located at the centre of each realm and controlled by the First. Not even the other families can help me now. At the death of my father the gateways would have closed to all. Only me, all that is left of his blood, can open them again. But worse of all, the closing of the gates signal to the realms he is dead and the Last has been triggered and they will not open again until the next First rises.

I feel coldness seeping through my armour as I lay not knowing or caring about time or place. My mind in disarray, my body in agony, I pray death is upon me for I remember only the impossible and do not want to face the truth of all that has happened.

It cannot be real, and should it be, I want no less than death. The pain of it all tears at me. The harshness of the cold and the ache of my injuries burn in the aftermath of the explosion and keep death at bay, but nothing stops the torment in my head. I long for oblivion, hoping for an end to this reality but like a cruel joke, it is my mind constantly reliving the agony of our heartbreaking defeat that keeps me grounded to this fate. Death will not let me escape this easily.

It must only be hours since I had foolishly gloried in the magnificence of my life. Since I stood on the roof of my family's royal house, the one place in my world I thought was untouchable... and had unknowingly faced my doom.

I had looked across at my family with such blinding ego and arrogance, as they stood on both sides of me ready for war and ruthlessly, foolishly I had smiled in anticipation of an easy victory because I believed in the infinite hero that stood boldly in our midst.

My father... why? Why would he have done what should be impossible? Where is my brother in all of this? The dragons? The Aurelians? In an instance, it is as if everything has disappeared, vanished and I am alone.

With such fierce pride, I had surveyed my world from lofty heights and saw nothing but all we had achieved and all the power that was ours. I gave myself glory for the innocence, purity and goodness that defined my world and gloried in the knowledge we were above all others and that my place was protected and safe from harm.

I had stood proudly in the heart of that battle and had looked across at the sweeping gold plains that lay just beyond our city walls ablaze in their splendour filled with the lethal precision of our allies, the invincible Aurelian army.

I looked to the skies at the darkness of night that heralding the force of our mighty dragon protectors and leading it all shone the iridescent alluvial gold armour that bleeds to the purple of my royal line blazing unmistakably at the centre of it all, ready for war.

With such conceit, I looked across towards my father who stood proudly next to me and I smiled knowing his incredible power, appreciating his abilities and thinking he was invincible. The king, the First, the unmistakable leader of our realms and all I saw was everything he was and all I one day longed to be. My ego sang to be made in his image and to be reminded of his fierceness by others when they looked into my eyes.

He was the embodiment of heroes and he represented all that could surely only be found in the best of men. There was no army within the realms that he had not defeated. No evil he had not banished. His protection of us all was absolute. This timeless defender of the balance and light of Axis had proved over and over his brilliance in leadership and his indomitable strength.

I had spent my lifetime at his side. He was my teacher and my mentor but most of all he was everything I dreamed to emulate. He had honed my brother and I in every way and we fought believing in all he represented, proudly at his side.

With this confidence resonating zealously in my heart I had run forward into war with the assurance of my abilities and my powers bolstered by the strength of my father and brother on each side of me. I boldly lay claim to the death and destruction I left in my wake and smiled with the smug audacity of knowing my father would be proud and glory in the sword I wield and the trail of blood that followed relentlessly in my steps.

The harmony of our fight was the secret to our success, and it was everything our father had instilled and trained us to be. With the exceeding confidence of numerous victories, I moved with arrogance and assurance against those who thought, in their stupidity, they stood any hope of defeating my family and destroying our universe.

The ring of swords and the clash of armies was a seamless dance of little consequence, it was triumph beyond battles of old or stories of victory as armies of gold, black and blue who came together to drive back this foolish enemy who sought to claim our world.

The adrenaline of pure credence drove the intricate battle of death and I was at its core...until it shattered in disarray around me and my world changed forever.

My body aches and tears fall with the pain of memories down my face. With nothing left and my future gone I lay in the dark, injured, afraid and without pride.

My father dead is unthinkable, and I do not know my place now.

I lay, in the dirt, begging death to take me so I might find peace with the hero I loved endlessly. I am not strong enough to face what is left of my life. I am not strong enough to face this destiny so soon and I keep my eyes closed refusing to confront what comes next.

Chapter 5

Ripples of light flood my world and I can do nothing but wait. I cannot fight what is innocent. I cannot hold what is volatile. I cannot comfort what is unique with the familiar.

I stand patiently waiting for the burn in my bones to slow. For the white light to dim. For the universe to settle.

It is pure and good. There is no malice in this action only innocence with perhaps a touch of defiance.

The pain subsides and the light slowly fades away and I only see sunshine and perfection.

I raise my head for a moment to the sky and beg Axis for her help.

She knows. I know she waits. I know the destiny that unfolds for me and the suffering we both must face, but we agreed long ago. Our universe is not yet ready for such change without understanding sacrifice. We cannot bring salvation to those who do not believe they are lost. But I am ready to honour this gift and knowing the beauty of it only brings me joy.

Quietly, I move to the source and let the light and balance flow through me. As I touch what I must protect I feel the strength of power surge towards me. It is as if I am a magnet to its detonation, but it is only because this is mine, so I let it draw towards me.

With care and kindness, I tether myself to the light and shield it from harm and as the shield locks into place I look into the eyes of our future and I am calm.

Knowing I will protect my greatest treasure regardless of what comes and no matter the cost.

Chapter 6

I open my eyes to a clear night sky, the majesty of the universe shining brightly above me as if it watches to see what happens to me next. I can feel my injuries are numerous. I know the pain in both legs from sword strikes and my back aches with the impact against what feels like rocks beneath me.

I lay silently, muted by pain and watch, for a moment, as the stars gently twinkle in such contrast to this dark day and I don't know whether to embrace the rage and frustration of everything that's happened or fall apart in hopelessness and let fear consume me.

But I know death is not for me, not yet. I know Axis would not let it be so, not now. I know what it means for us all, more than any other at the death of a First. I want to rebel against what comes but know I will do want is required of me. My father's death will signal the beginning of the Last, a ceremony to crown the next First so the rage or the fear must wait.

I want to scream at the unfairness of everything that has happened! I want to point at someone other than my father and blame them for all that has transpired but my heart will always know the truth, regardless of the blame that lingers with the pain his death has brought.

Echoes of screams followed closely by cheers in the distance break the quiet of the night. My body shakes as another tremor of pain rolls agonisingly across my injuries and I gasp in the cold night air willing it to subside.

I try to slowly push myself up to sit, stopping midway as the pain makes my head swim and my stomach threatens to vomit in protest at such movement. I focus on breathing, slowly and carefully, taking measured shallow breaths, calming myself, waiting for the pain to ease just so I can be sure I am actually able to move.

The echo of screams followed by cheers breaks the quiet of the night repeatedly and it guts me to recognise the sounds of torture. It is yet another heartbreaking reminder that in my world everything has changed. Within such a small space of time, our future is uncertain, I don't know who is left, my allies are gone, and I am alone. But those screams echoing across the night only make it obvious I need to move!

I need to move NOW!

As uselessly hopeful as it seems, given the gripping pain wracking my body, I am at least relieved that my body seems to be mostly intact. Maybe it's only cuts and bruises, I assure myself as the screaming pain runs down my back before shooting through my legs in sharp spasms as if to prove me wrong.

The screams rise again and with their increasing regularity I know I cannot lay here waiting for rescue when my fate would likely only be capture by what sounds like a cruel enemy!

I grit my teeth and I use my hands to push my body up into a somewhat unsteady sitting position. My teeth clench together as the pain makes my head swim, but this is no time for self-pity, and I force myself to fight through the pain. Struggling to stay conscious I lower my head and focus again on breathing carefully until I am able to lift my head with fear of passing out. Every breath, every movement brings screeching, stabbing pain and I pause again and again as I am overcome with agony, but the sounds of those screams keep me focused and I pant in shallow breaths before eventually getting my body upright enough to figure out where I am.

I am trained to survive, to thrive in misery but this is raw and somehow feels different. It is almost as if the air hurts as it brushes against me and I wonder at the sensation. During the battle the air felt so void of light and balance but now it feels overfilled and is strangely electrifying, almost painful to touch.

But the screams come again, and I force myself to stand, gritting my teeth stubbornly, knowing the importance of freedom. I must survive. I must do what is necessary to save us all and I must find my brother. I did not see his end during the battle so I can only hope and pray to Axis that he lives.

The cheers rise again and as I gingerly stretch my sore body upright, I turn towards their noise and freeze immobile, suddenly very aware of where I am. I stand on the lower levels of the mountain that overlooks our capital city, Amara Arcelia, were the battle took place. I creep towards the edge of the outcrop and my eyes fill with tears at the sight beneath me.

My Amara Arcelia, the jewel of Axis! The city, which only hours ago was my home, is filled with the armies of this unknown enemy. Soldiers celebrate in every direction across the city as they revel in our defeat. I look at the destruction, the fires burning, the smashing and destroying. I look at the royal house and notice throughout the courtyard prisoners are huddled in pitiful groups while rows of dragons, our allies, sit chained and subdued and it is then terror truly grips me, and I cannot believe my eyes.

They would undoubtedly consider all that is left the spoils of war, but the soldiers are contained within Amara and it is this sight that leaves me confused. Other than the seven gates of entry to the realms the real treasures lay outside the city and it hits me...I must seal the tomb!

My freedom puts their victory in jeopardy, and I smile at their mistake or perhaps my good fortune! We can still rise from this and face the Last and if my brother is their prisoner my freedom will keep him alive. They will know it can only be me who protects and completes what is sacred.

I search but cannot see any sign of Tallon amongst the prisoners or crowd, at least not from this distance and it gives me hope. I will save us ... I promise the dark night as a tiny bit of faith grows within me.

I drag my eyes away from my beloved city to look at the chaos around me. Soldiers and dragons, that were my capturers, lay in almost a circle from my position dead. I painfully limp over to the nearest dragon and lay my hand against its head knowing sadly it is too late but feeling the guilt of its capture. I reach to pull the chain from around its neck, to at least let it find freedom in death but shards of pain shoot through my hands at the slightest touch making the chains impossible to remove. I can do nothing more than sadly stoke its neck hoping it found peace before rising again.

I look back towards Arama as the cheers sound out across the night once again and see a large bonfire flare to life in the centre of the city; its shadows flicker and dance in every direction from the huge flames. I follow the crowd to see what captures their attention and at the top of my family's home stands a group of people with their fists raised in victory.

I watch angrily as they celebrate. Chanting and cheering they call out until the crowd of soldiers move with excitement. It is in this frenzy the crowd parts and I see lines of prisoners brought forward and the cheering horde swells in anticipation. I cannot watch. This is not merciful. I cannot do anything to save them. I am helpless, even without injuries I could not attack the city against an army of that size. A sudden heart-wrenching cry of agony pierces the night and I look away across to the battlefield outside the city, unable to bear the suffering that bonfire brings.

The plains sit still in the night, so eerily quiet after the chaos of the battle and I know what my eyes seek. As if the burning cries of prisoners echoing in the night do not break my heart enough, I look again for the inevitable truth of it all. I find the first waves last position and run my eyes across the line stopping when I recognise the armour of the body that lies exactly where he fell amongst the filth. They have left him in the blood and mud with no regards for all his goodness, his place as First, his history of greatness, no; my father's body lays in death, forgotten. His armour clearly glints in the dark and I sink to my knees unable to look away.

"I will honour you," I whisper quietly into the night. "I will burn a pyre for you. I will never forget your sacrifice, your love. You will be honoured my father, now and at the Last. It is with your teachings I will rise never forgetting what they have done." I promise him, vowing each word vehemently in the darkness, letting the tears flow, knowing that I have to ensure he is remembered into the next life and avenge his death.

His death changes everything. I will be forever hunted. They do not understand the destiny they have set me on, nor do they grasp the balance of their fate. His body represents more than victory. In killing him they have changed the course of our universe. They have not just conquered and destroyed an army; they have tempted the wrath of fate. Destiny will remind them soon enough that this defeat puts the balance and light of our entire universe at stake and for this, I know destiny will make them pay.

Until the Last is completed our world will be shut to all. Not a single person will be able to travel on or off Axis. Our realms will lie quiet in the aftermath. They will know. They will wait. Our realms will be venerable, the dust slowing rising without the balance and light which cannot flow again until the crowning of a new First.

Deep in thought, and still searching for my brother's armour in the city beneath me, movement catches my eye and I stand to watch two squadrons of dragons rise into the air. As I look, I am shocked to realise the dragons carry soldiers! This cannot be! Dragons are not slaves in our world! They are not transportation!

The dragons are allies, revered, honoured and I watch horrified at this humiliation of them, but it also explains the soldiers and dragons on the ground around me. Could we possibly have lost a more powerful symbol of the strength of Axis? Creatures so extraordinary, so vital to our lives have been captured as if spoils of war and treated this way! It seems impossible to think but their fate is clear.

I am still standing immobile, stupidly, caught in the horror of this spectacle when see them gently arc in the sky and in this small moment I appreciate the beauty and magnificence of their flight until I see they change direction in that arc.... and the glint of chains at their throats catch my eye...those chains...they certainly must have powerful forces within them to be able to contain them. But even that seems impossible because they would need to chain each one to succeed!

I watch, deep in through, but before I can consider the implications it becomes clear they head straight towards the side of the mountain where I stand!

The dragons may be captives, but I have no doubt of what the soldiers seated determinedly on their backs seek! I suddenly remember I drew in strength through the light and balance in the air! If our enemy is powerful enough this will give away my location and by the look of the direction of those dragons, it is clear they are powerful indeed.

I scramble quickly, my injuries are forgotten as I begin to move with unyielding desperation down the side of the mountain towards the sanctuary of the thicker forest below. I am weak and injured, still, I slide and clamour needing to survive, and knowing my life and my brothers depends on it. I cannot be caught, even for his sake. It is likely he is their prisoner and I must do whatever it takes to save him, to protect our world and the realms.

I can hear the sound of dragons' wings as I reach the forest floor and run without direction ignoring the constant pain that gathers in my body, hoping to find cover or a hidden corner to collapse in! I refuse to look around or look back. I know what comes for me. My only focus is forward and escape.

A sudden rush of dragon fire lights up the world around me with blinding intensity. It leaves nothing in its wake, but a barren wasteland of ash and smoke where once stood the sanctuary of trees to my right. The heat of the blaze sears the air around me as scorching flames move with increasing speed through the canopy before roaring, in a downward cascade of heat and light to the forest floor.

I feel the burn of the inferno as it rages and devours, spreading in a huge arc of entrapment, its ferocity blackening and obliterating everything in its path. I cover my mouth as the heat steals the air around me, each fiery gush of choking hot air explodes in my lungs as I struggle to breathe while I run.

The noise of crackling and sparking flames is deafening as they ravage the trees and bushes in a flaming display of purgatory, licking upwards to rise high above the canopy in a wall of red and orange incandescent fury.

I find the semblance of a path amongst the trees in front of me. It is narrow and I only catch glimpses of it as I run through following its unknown direction. It is barely wide enough but nevertheless, with no other choice but death, I move as quickly as possible with increasing desperation, pushing forward with fearful determination, begging the universe for escape.

I call over and over to Axis for help! For salvation! I uselessly hope for a rescue from this hell all the while aware it's never going to come.

I cannot see them yet through the dense canopy of trees, only the destruction they weave in the fire surrounding and burning towards me. I choke, as the smoke continues to thicken, suffocating me. I feel the movement of air as if they encircle my position, warning me they are gaining and it may be impossible to elude them, but I have not survived in the most chaotic of battles, or this life of sacrifice and service to be so easily caught.

My eyes are stinging with the pain of the smoke, flowing with tears from the bitterness of ash and making it almost impossible to recognise anything around me, let alone navigate the path that lays in front of me or how much further I need to travel in the hopes of reaching safety. I know they will hunt endlessly. I know with my injuries I cannot run for much longer. I can only be thankful knowing I would have no hope of escape if hunted by a willing dragon but as slaves or captives they do not seem to be so willing to give me away.

I squint fiercely into the distance glimpsing nothing other than the thick forest of trees while behind me lay smoke and fire that follow my every step. I can barely navigate this path but nevertheless keep moving forward, I must.

The forest extends for miles in every direction and this path seems to move in a line towards its centre, deep into the thickest part of the canopy and trees. If I can make it to the centre, I may at least buy myself time before they hunt me again. I am alone and vulnerable against a force of darkness so powerful its ferocity is able to easily destroy everything in its path, but my only other choice is death or surrender and I refuse to consider either.

My hair whips savagely across my face fighting against the swirling air. I can taste the fire in every shallow breath and the acidic burn of its destruction as it rolls down my throat making it ache painfully. Each inward gasp for air is crippling as I trying to block out the embers by breathing through clenched teeth. I cough in panic as I begin to suffocate. As I beg for strength while dashing faster than I would have thought possible, seeking salvation in what increasingly seems like the impossible.

My frustration only increases as the chase seems never-ending and my legs ache and burn as they struggle to keep my upright at this hectic pace. My hands are gripped in fists so tightly I have lost feeling in my fingers and my knuckles are white, with the terror of stumbling or falling a constant dread.

I feel the danger growing, the fear of capture moving closer and the intense urgency of their hunt rides hard on my heels. Weakness grips at me and I use what little strength I have left to gently wrap the air around me, which will at least protect me from the fire and hopefully keep me on my feet but the blood flowing from my injuries is weakening me so I am unable to use it for anything more for fear of capture.

The violence and peril of where I am hammers in my head driving me to keep moving and all reason is lost as I focus on the need to escape.

I stumble and feel the blood flow down into my boots. A shudder of pain grips at me and I wonder if it will be dragon fire or blood loss that takes me first. I must move...but any motion is pointless as another spasm of pain grips me and I am rendered helpless as I crouch in agony on the soft grass on the forest floor. I cannot keep running. I look at the trees around me searching for a way out. I gently draw the light and balance in unsteady waves towards me but cannot hold them.

As the light and balance trickle uselessly away from me, I feel an electrifying pull in the ripples around me as if some pulls against my waves.

'Hear me, Everly! Do not stop! MOVE! I will save you." A voice urgently whispers through the trees across the ripples, breaking the turmoil that surrounds me on all sides and I focus on the direction of the call. I am vulnerable and weak and can only hope what calls to me is safer than the two squadrons of dragons carrying my enemy that think to burn me alive!

I can barely keep my eyes open and I am lucky to see what little I can ahead. I know I am running blindly following only a gentle whisper to what I can only hope may be a slim chance of safety.

My body aches and titters on the verge of collapse as I keep stumbling forward. I can feel the spill of blood from the wounds on my side and legs as it flows down towards my feet before soaking into the ground each time I step.

Within seconds of the whisper, a battle cry sounds, and I feel the rush of swirling air as they close in on my position. They've found me! The vibration increases with sudden voracity, almost with the fury of a small tornado that beats in motion with their wings. The air shifts and moves the trees so violently it fuels the fire stealing any scant breath I have left and makes the impossible smoky maelstrom worse. A thunderous roar blasts close to my position through the smoky night deafening my senses. I cry out as the pain of it resonates in my head, slapping my hands over my ears in an attempt to muffle the noise. I run on wildly forgetting about following the path as the motion of the air moves closer again and buffers my entire body, pulling at me, making it hard and harder to stop from falling.

I am trembling and the pain is overwhelming.

I squint my aching eyes upward to see which direction they come from but all that catches in the peripheral of my blinded vision is shadows in the midst of the fire and smoke. I am at my end, exhausted and weak. My body cannot take this! I'm battling to stand from my injuries and now from the fire. My eyes ache and sting with the density of smoke. My legs are shaking with exhaustion and at the point of collapse and are almost unable to hold myself upright any longer.

I fall to my hands over and over but get up again and again and keep moving. My ears ache and throb with the increasing noise that now thunders around me in quick resounding successive roars. The mess of knots and agony across my body escalates from trying to run while trembling. I slow to a walk, feeling the crushing despair of weakness but still stubbornly move forward.

"Surrender!" a voice thunders through the trees but I refuse to look towards it. I will not acknowledge them even as they begin to surround me.

"Not far Everly! Do not stop! Do not concede. You are strong and powerful. Do not let them capture you! Move!" the whisper comes, closer now. My body starts to spasm with the violence of pain and stress. I can feel the numbness spreading as the adrenaline fades and my injuries start to take over. My legs give from beneath me and I crumple to the ground. Not knowing what else to do I roll towards the undergrowth in hope of at least hiding for few seconds.

The whisper still calls urgently, begging me. I must move. I must not concede so I push to my hands and knees and crawl towards its promises. It is the best I can do. Tears flow freely down my face. If I am lost, then so too is my world. If this whisper that calls to me is death, then I am finished and so is my world and with this truth echoing in my head my body finally concedes. My mind shatters at the pain yielding to the blackness of oblivion and as the world fades, I feel hands grab my arms and drag me and I know the end rushes towards me as violent and bloody as my life has been.

Chapter 7

"It is difficult to accept, and I understand your struggle, but I must ask this of you. I can only trust you in this. I am sorry." I tell him hoping he understands the gravity of the situation.

He does not seem surprised by my request, which concerns me, and I wonder if he knew this was coming.

"I knew you would have no other choice and I accept that. I knew there would come a time when the truth was revealed."

I watch him walk the length of the room. I see the fear and uncertainly bloom as the implications sink in.

"We all know the choices you have made have had consequences. It was always destined to be her. I understand what you ask of me but is this the only way?" He asks aloud and continues to pace when he sees me nod in understanding.

He knows it is a difficult road ahead, likely more difficult than the countless battles he has faced. I watch him carefully. He is a good man, an honourable man. He looks at the world with the ability to assess a situation fully. He knows this time it is beyond his control, but I have faith in him.

"There is no question of what must be done. This is me pleading for your support, knowing what I ask and placing all I value at your feet. It is not an easy task. You must do this alone. No one can know." I remind him and he stops pacing.

"You think I don't know that! You think I would abandon my world?" he comes towards me angrily as if I have insulted his honour.

"I do not doubt your ability to face your responsibilities, but this is different, and you know it. This is love and care and protection above everything else. Our future depends on this."

"It shall be. You have my word." He tells me quietly and I see the truth of his vow.

Destiny calls to him in ways he is yet to understand and demands a price I wonder if he is able to pay but I will ensure it. He is my son in every way, but blood and I will guide his path. That is my vow to him.

Chapter 8

My mind seeks only oblivion in the darkness of sleep as it tries to keep the pain at bay. The deep recesses of dreams and nightmares that hold you captive as your body fights to recover from injuries together with that bone-deep exhaustion that overcomes everything other than the need for rest.

My body burns and aches, sharp stabs of agony running across my chest that seems to endlessly shift in waves across my body making me groan but the injuries to my body will heal.

Fragmented memories of the battle swarm in vivid reminders torturing me with death and destruction. The sense of dread, of failure, of unfathomable loss, overwhelms me and as the darkness starts to clear I lift my head to scream. Screaming in frustration at my uncertain future, knowing if they have captured me, they keep me alive only to serve one purpose, and I cannot face the truth of it. So, I give in and sink resolutely back into the blackness of my nightmares hoping they will leave me alone.

I surface again when my headaches with never-ending stabs of pain. A reprieve from the nightmares but a reminder of the injuries that I have to recover from yet. This weakness inside and out haunts me. I have been broken and weak and maybe I have even come close to reaching my end, but it is not the injuries that worry me. It is what comes once they are healed. I will recover but struggle with the reality I will face knowing as a prisoner I cannot save anyone.

I know my body suffers from the damage not just from the battle but also from smoke and ash and every limb shakes as I battle to heal. Each time I awake I am too afraid to open my eyes. Not yet. Not while I can feel the weakness of my body and feel so frustratingly helpless so again, I choose to sink into the darkness of my tortured dreams rather than face what comes next.

I cannot die. I cannot leave my world in chaos and I have no doubt this world will not let me go so easily. I cannot push aside the pain that forever wakes me and as my head clears once again I focus resolutely on the throbbing in my leg, using it as an anchor to stop the shaking in my bones as I accept death refuses me and my body is well enough to rise.

I struggle to open my eyes, to look at what surrounds me. The sense of foreboding chokes me. I must be strong. I must protect myself even in this weakness that keeps the light and balance from me. I have never back away from what is right or what must be done so even as small tendrils of fear wrap around me, I cling to the strength of who I am.

I remember gentle hands tending to my wounds and cold and heat presses against my brow as tremors shook my body. I have felt my bandages changed regularly and I do not struggle knowing that healing will only make me stronger. It seems I was cared for kindly although I imagine they only do so to torture me as they have done to my people. They must know the price of my death to work so hard to keep me alive.

I can only hope they know the full implications of what they have done because if they don't, we are truly lost.

The darkness will not let me linger and the world calls in ripples of light and balance around me almost taunting me to heal. I open swollen, sore eyes to see the fading light of the sunset blinking through the surrounding trees and pause, immobile, confused at the sight. This is not the cell I thought I would wake in! I cannot see the heavy stone of the cells beneath the royal house in Amara.

I roll to my side, leaning to cough and gasp, uselessly trying to expel the dirty black ash I can feel coats my lungs. I look with wonder at the ground beneath me and the forest around me when I expected walls and soldiers.

I have to move! This must be a trick. I lift my head, turning it in every direction possible but the pain beats me, I want to stand and run, to escape whatever this is but the weakness of my body renders me helpless. I lift my arm opening my hand to call my sword and through ripples of light it appears. Even in my weakness I am reassured when I feel the familiar steel touch my palm and I wrap my fingers around it comfortingly. It is my greatest treasure, a gift from my father. A sword of Axis herself that only answers to me and remains unseen, hidden by the light unless I call it. It can never be taken or stolen from me as it only answers to my light and now it is all I have left. The only thing they can never take from me.

Too sore to fight, too weak to stand I cling uselessly to my sword as I painfully lay back again resting my aching head on the cool ground and look around carefully. When there is no sign of soldiers or fire or even smoke, the tension I have held in my body finally releases a little and I breathe a fraction easier, inhaling the fresh forest air. I lay quietly wondering what this could all mean... it makes no sense that they would heal me only to set me free back in the forest!

It is within this moment, as my mind races with possibilities that I hear the gentle rustle of movement close by and roll towards it, clutching my sword, foolishly attempting to rise ready to fight only to find my body collapses and I cry out in the pain. Propped painfully, still pitifully lying with my sword gripped tightly in my hand I watch as a man quickly walks towards me.

I wait, not knowing what he wants of me, but he ignores my obvious terror and knees down beside me before gently cradling my shoulders, helping me to carefully lie back again. That familiar gentle voice from the forest tells me "Please be still Everly, you are still too injured to move. You have nothing to fear here." It is the whisper that called to me in the middle of the fire and I turn my head to look at him in shock.

"Who are you?" I rasp in a voice I barely recognise. I have no allies left...not now...not when my world is gone and don't understand why this man would help me. I feel vulnerable and guarded with everything that's happened and I need to know what he wants from me. I cannot be captured when I can only do the impossible as long as I am free.

"My name is Az.," he tells me simply, smiling kindly when he clearly sees the suspicion on my face "I am a friend. All I ask is that you remain still, or you will do even more damage to your injuries. We are hidden and you are safe from those who hunt you so sleep, heal and we will talk when you are able." He tells me, so I nod too weak to fight. I am pitifully at his mercy as he tends my wounds. What choice do I have but to trust the words of this stranger? I am too weak to disagree or run from him, so I let myself rest again closing my eyes. I release my sword before sinking back through the pain to the emptiness of sleep.

The warmth of the sun flickers across my eyes and I scrunch them against the persistent shine before moving my head away. I lay quietly for a few heartbeats before slowly opening my eyes to look carefully at the world around me. Soft grass beneath me, a gentle breeze and trees. Still in the forest. No burn marks around the immediate area from what I can see. No prison bars or soldiers. So far so good. It seems this man was not a dream and my injuries certainly feel much less painful and although I am grateful, I have much to do.

Determined to move I try to push gentle onto my elbows, but I am beaten by my own body and groan as pain radiates through my limbs. Perhaps not as healed as I thought, I tell myself annoyed, gritting my teeth together as I wait for the wave of pain to pass.

"Be careful." comes his voice again and I turn to see him crouched down next to me studying my reaction with concern. Gentle brown eyes ringed with forest green look at me softly as I take in his features. He is tall, with dark hair and wears strange armour I do not recognise. He looks my age, but it is the way he moves and the sound of his voice that seems...older and then familiar although I do not recognise him. He looks at me expectantly as though he waits for me to finish my assessment of him before he gently speaks.

"You have been badly hurt Everly and so you must give your body time to heal before you face the world. For now, you can find peace in knowing no one will harm you nor will they find you here. We are safe here. You must rest. Sleep. I will watch over you." He tells me and I hold my breath watching as his beautiful face breaks into a soft smile almost as if in the midst of all this hunting, killing and death he is trying to reassure me.

"I know you," I whisper as he moves to check my injuries. My throat is still sore from the ash and smoke. I watch as he gently lifts each of my legs and changes the bandages once again.

"I am Az." comes the simple answer in the strangest of moments. Confused at his response I look away from him to the injuries on my legs and the crisscross of bandages across my body. He is efficient as he wraps each wound using clean bandages and the well-organised array of medicine that sits beside him.

"Do you know what has happened Az? Am I your prisoner?" I ask quietly well aware of how this situation could change rapidly for me should he decide he is no longer a friend. I wait, listening to what his answer will be, knowing that with everything that has happened I will need to be vigilant. I will be under constant threat and I am very aware of the fragility of my current situation, as I lay there unable to defend myself.

"No, Everly you are not a prisoner and yes, I am aware of the battle. This world, the universe, all on Axis... knows who you are." He tells me calmly, smiling a little again and I cannot look away from his face. His brow scrunches slightly as turns his head and that familiarity hits me again. I must work out why. I look across his armour frowning, searching for any sign of allegiance but there is nothing. It is completely blank of any markings but strangely it is the armour of a warrior. "As for what has happened...where would I begin? I think, for now, it is best to focus on the present. You need to heal before you can do anything else."

I take in the details of his face. The gentle lines of his face hold the most perfectly shaped nose; beneath those eyes, his smile changes his face with its light.

I watch him as he moves and as he talks to me, explaining my injuries but I am puzzled at his reason for helping me. He talks gently describing my injuries and how I should care for them and I listen without hearing a word! I breathe in slowly the elemental gentleness of him that intrinsically seeps into every word he speaks giving the listener such warmth that I never want him to stop talking and I know this is not the first time we have spoken.

"We have met before." Is all I say and watch him looking towards me.

"Yes." He answers but I also see his body still.

"I don't remember your face as much as it is a feeling." I try to explain "The safety, the care...it is a kindness of family or friends, not strangers."

"You have always been very perceptive Everly." He smiles at me and although I wait patiently, he continues to discuss my health and care rather than answer my growing questions.

His kind countenance has me spellbound with each expression as he speaks. I have met beautiful men, intelligent men, rich men, clever men and many, many others but this man... is different. I hear the deep, soothing timbre of his voice as he talks, as he tells me how I must be more careful but I can only watch the warmth in his eyes, the shape of his lips as they form each word and in my embarrassment I realise he has stopped speaking and is watching me as I study him. I flush with embarrassment, but he only smiles. If he is aware of my curiosity he acts as if he is oblivious, and quietly moves away to a box of supplies he has resting on a tree nearby. I feel the loss of him and the warmth of his conversation. I struggle to steady myself as I sit wondering at my reaction.

"Our families are old friends?" I ask still struggling to fit him into my world.

"Yes, Everly...old friends." He answers but again gives me nothing more.

I gingerly pull myself more upright to rest against the tree behind me. I am suddenly too tired for evasive conversations and puzzles of strange men in forests. I look down the length of my body at the damage from the battle. My arms and legs have taken a beating and there are small burns in numerous places, a deep cut in my thigh and some superficial damage to my armour from taking in the mishmash of sword strikes and blows but thankfully nothing too drastic.

I flex my hands and point my toes trying to get circulation back into my aching joints. My body still feels tight and tense from all the running and I know even I have pushed beyond my limits and this has not helped my injuries from the battle in any way.

"My armour should have repaired most of these injuries by now," I say looking at the damage.

"It could not without the flow of light and balance. It is still repairing itself." He answers.

"Did you feel it too? As if the world was... hollow?" I ask hesitantly looking for answers.

"All on Axis connected to the light and balance felt it." He answers but does not elaborate.

"It must have been my father," I say aloud knowing only he could have had the power to hold it at bay in such a way.

"He was a very powerful First." Az acknowledges with a nod.

"It is not something I have ever known him to do. Even now I cannot understand why he did it." I pause still searching for a reason. "Had it flowed I could have saved him..." I trail away.

"Maybe he knew that is what you would do. Maybe it was not what he wanted." Is all he says.

"That makes no sense Az," I respond shaking my head. "I have gone over and over the battle in my head. It is all too confusing, too many things out of place...too many changes to our formation.... then I became separated ...and the dragons...how?? That in itself is unthinkable! My father captured! My brother disappears! The Aurelians nowhere in sight! I wonder whether I have imagined the catastrophe half the time as I still cannot fathom how...or why." I finish looking at him expectantly and he is watching me intently.

"It was certainly a battle that will not soon be forgotten. As to all your questions...I cannot give you any of those answers. I have too many questions of my own." Is all he offers gruffly, almost abruptly, and I wonder at his frustration.

"How long have I slept?" I ask quietly needing to move the conversation away from what consumes me.

"Four days." Comes his gentle reply.

"Undiscovered? For four days? How is that possible? Surely they have searched for me!" My broken voice rising in shock again, but he just smiles.

"They have searched tirelessly." He answers, again short, and again I feel frustrated when he doesn't offer more information.

"And they haven't found me?" I prompt, looking for more answers. It is not possible with the dragons at their bidding...surely.

"Everly, they will not find you here. I will keep you safe." Is his only reply and I'm not really sure what it means? To make it worse I feel tears filling my eyes as uncertainly grips fearfully at my chest. He is watching me carefully and I look at him surprised at the emotions that crush against me, unfamiliar and laced bitterly with such fear. Terror rises like bile in my throat and as if he sees it, his eyes fill with shock, but thankfully he does not speak.

My tears begin to flow freely as the enormity of my situation begins to become reality. I need to know more, to understand, to face what must be done next.

"How did you find me?" I gulp through unabashed tears. I am too caught in all the emotions that flood me at this moment, in this panic, to even care what he thinks, and it unnerves me that he watches me with such interest.

"I found you in the forest. You were badly injured," he tells me quietly moving closer to sit beside me as if wanting to offer comfort but then deciding to keep the space between us, likely because he doesn't know how to deal with a weeping, messy girl.

"Is there no one left? None of the Axians in the fight?" I ask knowing the answer but struggling to find questions that I don't want answers to.

"The dragons are captured. The Aurelians have disappeared. Axis is currently being burnt to the ground. There are deaths each day as they hunt for you. The dust has risen, and the light and balance are beginning to suffocate our world, but you know what needs to be done."

"I do." I whisper through my ceaseless tears. Our allies are gone. My world is slowly imploding on itself. The death and destruction are growing. No allies. Guilt, anger and fear drown me when all I see is our doom.

"We are not lost." His kind voice tells me, and I look up as he turns towards me. "We have you." He simply says as he smiles, and it only makes me cry harder at how stupid I would have to be to believe that! I cannot even begin to comprehend what he means. He doesn't understand. It is too much. I am weak, injured and alone with a strange man, hidden in a forest.... makes no sense. Maybe it is not me. Maybe it is Tallon who should save us. Maybe I am delusional and weak with blood loss trying to avoid the truth of what I must do.

"Does my brother live?" I ask needing to know.

"There is no proof your brother is dead." he answers.

"Is he their prisoner? He must be a prisoner, or he would have found me. I could not see his body on the battlefield." I mumble more to myself before looking at Az "Do they know he needs to get to the pAx? I need him beside me at the Last?"

"Everly, you cannot expect to be able to finish the Last. Not in your state. Even with your brother at your side you are weak...and alone. Although you need to do what is necessary to save Axis there are other options given your ...defeat...." And I look at him angrily.

"You think I don't know what you are implying? I know what needs to be done. I am not helpless or in need of assistance. I am Alta Axian. I have no choice! There are no other options." I tell him angrily.

"Maybe...but your place as First is...precarious to say the least." He simply states and although he may be right it leaves me wondering what destiny awaits my brother and me.

I am barely a survivor of this horrific battle but have no choice. If I do not complete the Last... my world, my universe is finished.

Without a First the intersection between realms that balance and light flow through misaligns, and our universe will slowly turn to dust and decay. Every realm and every person connected to the light and balance Axis brings is affected until the crowning of the next First.

The Last is always triggered by death but thankfully this usually occurs in old age and rarely in battle and certainly never in defeat! For Axis to be defeated is beyond the realm of possibilities...until now but it seems it will not affect the need for a First and only an Alta Axian can be First. It is my family's legacy as the first foundation family and now, with my father's death, I am the only Alta Axian left.

"Where are we?" I ask as I watch the wind move gently through the trees but cannot feel it against my skin. Az looks up at me carefully, measuring his words.

"We are safe." He tells me, looking up to watch the wind with me.

"Are you of Axis?" Realisation dawning. "Is that how you saved me? Is that why they have not found me? You are so familiar....and wear the armour of a warrior..." I trail away watching as he gently smiles and nods before turning back to watch the wind gentle move the trees around us.

"Yes, I am of Axis." Is all the answer he offers. I study his face again as he looks towards the sky wanting to know the answers to all my questions but finding myself hesitant to ask.

"You do not look Axian," I tell him as my eyes follow the line of his profile.

"Do all Axians look the same?" he asks smiling at my question and I cannot help but smile back at the foolishness of my question.

"How long will you help me?" I ask.

"As long as I am needed," I answer.

"Why?"

"So, you live." He smiles.

"I am dead as soon as I leave." I push at him, poking at his calmness.

"Only if that is your choice." He answers winking at me strangely comical as he stands and smiles before continuing. "Everly, you have not been healed to simply die. Axis has plans for you. At least do us both a favour and fight a little to live, I mean, after all the hard work I have put into healing you it would be...irresponsible to give in to death so quickly."

Surprised at his reply I can only watch as he moves to light a small fire. Lost in the confusion of this conversation and his weird sense of humour I watch as he efficiently prepares a simple meal. Focused on him I am distracted from the magnitude of what awaits me, and I sit silently too afraid of the answers he might give should I ask any more questions.

It is a moment of sanctuary before my reality returns and my fight begins. He is right I must survive. This was always going to be my future, even if it has happened in this unexpected way. It is time I stopped fighting against my world and started fighting for her. The light and balance of my world flows through my veins so I am not without power or defences. It is time I made plans.

Chapter 9

Perfection.

Strength.

Power.

Light.

Balance.

They do not see it.

They think themselves greater.

They search for the impossible and gather in the darkness.

They are fools.

You cannot change what is born to lead.

You cannot tempt fate nor fight destiny.

We can do not less than rise against the firestorm that comes for us.

When they see all I have hidden, when the truth is revealed, only then will they see how foolish their actions. How they have underestimated my legacy.

Only then...

Chapter 10

"It is not from knowledge that the righteous fall but from pride. Pride blinds you from the truth impeding your judgment." My father used to tell me and as any good daughter would do, I agreed with his wise words all the while having no idea just how righteous I actually was and even more so proud.

My father was powerful, tactical and decisive. He was loving and kind but did not expect anything less than the best from me in every way. He honed me in his image, training me to his exceedingly high standards until he ensured I fought at his side through every victory over the past decade. But my father also shielded me from the rest of the world. He would boast of my battles and praise my abilities but kept me close at all times. I had time after time proven myself in battle and in negotiation and it had only fuelled his pride.

But more importantly he ensured I understood the duties and obligations of my position and I righteously thought I already placed the needs of the many over my own. But it is safe to be magnificent and honourable when you go home to comfort and riches and never have to lose anything or pay any price for your decisions. I was Alta Axian. The First family of Axis. Born to rule. Untouchable. Protected by my father. Respected and feared and I stupidly took such egotistical pleasure in my position and never lost sight of the great and wondrous destiny I could confidently see laid out in my future. How could I be so naïve? My future only begins and ends with death, my father's death and even in death I must rise and when I am hunted and defeated, I must survive...for I am Alta Axian...the last, the Heir, the only one left.

"Everly, are you asleep?" I hear Az call to me breaking through the rising frustration and fear of my thoughts.

"Not asleep," I answer knowing it is time. Knowing that this moment of peace and safety is quickly coming to an end.

"It is time, Everly. You must begin." Is all he says, and I sit up and turn towards him. I can see him watching me carefully as if he is waiting to see me hesitate but I only nod. I have spent more than five days here and thanks to his abilities and my armour I am fully healed of my injuries.

"It is a shame we cannot travel together," I say hoping for an easier option, but I know it would be too dangerous to travel with others and this journey must be mine alone. I could have left earlier but have appreciated the time. Time to plan and savour this peace as I am aware that when this fight comes, and it will be for my life. So, I have remained silent in the hopes I can delay the inevitable.

"Axis requires everything Everly, you know this. You cannot complain or wish it easier for a task you have been trained in your entire life." He tells me walking closer and I turn towards him shocked at such abruptness.

"It wasn't meant to be like this Az. I was not taught defeat, or murder or running for my life in any of my father's instructions. I expected to complete this journey with an army at my back, not an enemy hunting me and I certainly didn't expect to have to do it alone."

"Life rarely goes the way we expect it." He looks at me intently. "But for you, there is no choice. You were born for Axis. You cannot run from it or hide just because it is harder than you ever imagined or were taught. This is it Everly. This is what is expected of you. There is no choice, no alternative...you were born Alta Axian....and for that...I am sorry." He is right and I know I have no other choice, but I am ready. I must be! I am ready to leave.

"I know. I am ready." I answer nodding and stand to prepare.

I am grateful Az has helped repair my armour, which I methodically check. My sword is ever-present, and I open my hand slightly calling it for reassurance before releasing it back into the light. I also carry a small pack of basic supplies that Az has given me for the journey.

"Everly?" he asks, and I ignore him pretending to concentrate on checking myself. "Where will your journey take you?"

"The tomb," I answer firmly. "The tomb needs to be sealed once I trigger the pillars and then I must go to Eos to the pAx."

"If this enemy knows about the pillars, they will be waiting for you." He reminds me.

"It is unlikely as the location of the Tomb is unknown, but I can defeat soldiers and formations easily. Axis is lost if I do not trigger the pillars. We are lost without salvation."

"I agree." He answers and looks at me intently.

"I will travel to the pAx once I have done this." And he nods in agreement knowing what I will face. "Thank you, Az."

"Always." Is all he answers bowing his head slightly in acknowledgment.

"It is not the first time we have meet is it?" I ask knowing I am right.

"No Everly, it is not." He smiles slightly.

"And we will meet again?" I ask, almost sad to say goodbye to my only ally.

"I will find you before the Last. Once you have sealed the tomb take the plains. I will do everything I can to assist you and will meet with you as soon as possible."

"Why are you helping me?" I ask knowing people rarely help others expect to benefit themselves.

"Axis is my home and you are born to be our next First." He answers simply and I cannot see any lie on his face.

I pull my long dark hair back, away from my face and focus on securing it in a long plait ready to fight.

"Everly, you must plan to fight to the end. You must succeed in reaching the pAx." He looks at me pointedly. "If you trigger the pillars and die before the Last, we are all doomed. You must live."

"I will not fail...my father would expect no less from me but what of my brother Az? Have you heard any news of his capture? Or escape?" I stop as I choke on my words scared of the truth of them.

"I have heard no news of your brother. You cannot think to search for him when your task holds the balance and light for the realms. He is a strong and brave warrior and will chart his own path Everly."

"I must find him."

"No. He must save himself. You cannot take that risk."

"What if he is killed?"

"Then that is his destiny. You will not sacrifice yourself for one person, not even him. This is for Axis and her realms Everly.... for billions. If he is worthy, then he will succeed in getting to Eos."

"He will succeed," I state determinedly knowing my brother is stubborn and also has many more years of experience than I. He will not fail me by leaving me alone.

"Axis will crown a First. You may think you have given everything of yourself already, or that your father has paid the ultimate price but now it is time to prove yourself. Axis has not been defeated in many millenniums. She only needs a First to hold our world together. The light and balance only need one to save billions. To save us all. Everly..."

"I am not my father, Az. You speak as if understand but don't." I snap looking at him annoyed that he places so much expectation at my feet without knowledge of the pressure.

"No, you have proven in many ways you are not your father. But now the damage to the light and balance must be fixed, the gates must be opened, and the realms saved and for that task, there is only you. Safe travels to Eos Nevaeh and to the protection of the pAx. The pAx will guide you." He replies and I turn to face him.

"The pAx are not allies Az. They are only holy men." I reply surprised that he has knowledge of such a secluded place but if he is Axian then it is possible he understands.

"They are more than holy men." He smiles at me. "They will ensure the Last is completed. They serve Axis in every way. The pAx will always remain." And I watch him for a second disturbed by the confidence of his words.

He turns to pack his things away and I watch his careful precise movements as he methodically cleans up any trace of us. I do not fully trust him...not yet. He, like every other person, would have his or her own agenda for me, a hope to use me for their own gain. It has always been this way. People come seeking friendship or kindness for their own selfish needs, even those that heal. It is a lesson I learnt very early in life.

"What do you want from me Az?" I ask wanting to find some truth now and watch as he turns in surprise to me. "Everyone wants something so just tell me what it is? No games. No wordplays. No cryptic riddles. Just speak your mind. I am open to discussion should our objectives align." I tell him honestly.

There are no politics left for me to play. No delicate negotiations or discussions. I have nothing left to lose and am past any kind of time-wasting diplomacy.

"Everly?" he asks looking at me confused.

"What do you want Az? It's not a difficult question. Everyone wants something, most for his or her own benefit. People are at their core are innately selfish and this generally drives their suggestions or ideals or even motivations to help others so let me ask again...what do you want Az?"

"I only want what's best for Axis..." Is all his says as he opens his hands at his sides as if he is neutral and this should answer all the questions in my head!

"I don't know who you are, or your motives but even a child of Axis wants for themselves...so what do you want from me?"

"Nothing other than for you to do what's right. It is not about you. It is about what you were born to do. The light and balance protect billions, Everly. You know there is so much more at stake here." He tells me holding my eyes with his as if daring me to accuse him of anything else. "This army you think conquered without thought would surely not come here just to destroy the most important place in our universe. They burn and kill but do you ever ask yourself why? Why they come here? Did they know what killing the First could do to our universe? And where are your allies? The Aurelians disappeared? And the dragons? You have no one left." Comes his quiet voice. "Besides, what else is left if you don't fight for what matters? What you have trained to do? What you know in your heart is your only choice. What hope is there for billions if you don't trigger the pillars and reach the pAx? This army who brings defeat brings uncertainty and fear, maybe you should ask yourself why. There has only ever been one family able to rule, should the First family cease.... are we all lost? Maybe they seek something other than your family's destruction? Maybe you live because there is another way."

I don't understand this man; he talks as if he knows my family and our place in the world but there are secrets. There are always things within families that must remain hidden for the safety of all. He asks questions that bother me; questions that I cannot answer. I know what is that destiny expects of me, but I do not know what he wants me to see talking of this enemy as though they may seek more.

"I am ready. Can you please tell me our coordinates Az? So, I can navigate to the tomb?" I ask and am pleased when he tells me the coordinates without hesitation; thankful the intensity of our conversation is gone.

I will travel to Eos Nevaeh but not today. I am strong now, recovered and can feel the light and balance flowing through me. It is time, and as I step forward, I draw the magic in gentle waves towards me, comforted by the familiarity of my world and set out to the tomb of my family to save us all.

Chapter 11

"It will change the course of our history."

"I am aware."

"It will require no less than your loyalty or death."

"That is assured. I would offer no less."

"I cannot do this without you, Tallon. There is no other I can ask."

"It is worth it."

"It is beyond our expectations."

"The light?"

"It has been contained. We will have to use the old ways to develop the flow of light and balance because..."

"I know. I saw the devastation."

"It is contained with my shield. It cannot happen again, especially in this you must listen. It cannot be a weapon. It will take all that we are to ensure our safety."

"And if I cannot?"

"We are all lost."

"I will not fail you."

"I know...if I ever need to contain it.... the air needs to starve."

"Who knows of her origins?"

"None."

"Who knows of the treachery that comes?"

"Only those to think to change our destiny."

"And the price?"

"Everything. It will cost us everything."

Chapter 12

The heat of the day hits mildly under the cooler canopy of the forest and it feels surreal walking through my world without an army at my back or at the very least an array of guards but hey, welcome to my new reality...alone. No more constant protection. No more comforts of home. No more advice, support but hey, no handcuffs or prison cells either. So, with a very sketchy plan and an army destroying my world I walk forward determinedly into my very, very unknown future.

I savour the coolness, the greens, the peace of the forest, for a second. The trees that reach endlessly into the sky, branches heavily weighted with whisper-soft mossy green leaves. It is a sanctuary in itself with the light of the sunlight filtering through and the shelter of the canopy. So different from the fire and smoke, hunting and terror that seems so distant now.

The purity of the air as it moves the leaves around me is filled with light and balance which intrinsically weaves through me and it sings through my lungs as I inhale deeply, feeding my body all the way down to my bones. It is life itself, sustaining and pure and I feel energised, grounded and whole as if the air itself reminds me of who I am.

I look back to see Az watching me. My eyes lock with his and he nods in acknowledgment before stepping back into the trees and disappearing. I look, for a second, at the place where he vanished and send a prayer of thanks to Axis. I am grateful to her for sending help and will always remember meeting this weirdly familiar stranger.

The intensity he brings is focused and serious. I have listened to his counsel and together we have discussed my plans, but he has also raised a lot of unanswered questions. Only time will tell whether I have the strength to face all that comes or even the courage to face some of those unanswered questions.

I focus on my plan. I must move quickly. Our conversations have given me much to think about ...later, for now, there is only the tomb. Some of our conversations have me struggling to understand how it will be possible to get to Eos. I face an unknown enemy in a time of uncertainty but simply because I have no choice I must succeed. I need to gather myself and work through what I will face crossing the plains to get to Eos Nevaeh and the pAx but for now, I need to light the night and close this chapter to trigger the beginning of the Last by calling the pillars.

My father brought me to the tomb many times over the years to remind me who I am and to show me the strength of those footsteps that have protected Axis. I will offer thanks and blessings and I will hope my father has also found peace in the long goodnight. It will be goodbye, for now, as it will likely be a long time before I ever see the tomb again, but I will never forget what it represents.

The growing weight of loneliness starts to take its toll as I walk further and further into the forest towards the mountains. Except in the quietness of my bedroom, I have never been alone and even then, I was surrounded by guards and staff and could always hear the whispers or conversations of the array of people who moved in the hallways around me.

The quiet and stillness start to crawl at my nerves. It makes me feel exposed and defensive. I am completely reliant on myself...a fugitive, spoiled princess who has never had to rely on herself for anything! The nervous edginess turns to panic as I constantly scan the area around me, and I realise my heart is racing and my breathing is erratic.

On shaky legs, I sit quickly leaning against the strength of a thick, tall tree as I try not to fall apart. This is ridiculous! My brother would laugh at me right now and my father would raise his eyebrow and cross his arms as he waited impatiently for me to pull myself together before lecturing me about how foolish I have been to let such trivial things best me.

I sit still, scanning the trees around me, and let the emotions I've been holding in release in quiet tears. The pain of losing my father makes me feel raw and exposed. I fear for the life of my brother like a constant worry that never leaves. Then to face the unknown of the Last, never mind the journey I must take to get there...and the reality of it all.... is too much.

I sit alone trembling as tears flow endlessly down my face. I will give myself this small moment but no more. I cannot contain the agony that screams in my head, but I will not let it drown me. I let the light and balance flow through me as my tears fall and it is as though they wash them away, but I cannot help but ask the questions that resonate in my head. The questions that Az asked of me and I could not answer.

"Why did my father surrender? Why did he let them destroy our world? For what?" I whisper quietly. Why would this enemy come and invade the impossible? We are undefeated and have been forever. It makes no sense...but then neither does sitting in a forest crying like this!

Disgusted with my weakness I stand quickly and wipe my face. This is not who I am, some quivering snot drenched girl huddled beneath a tree! My father would be shocked to see me now, the warrior princess of fearless deeds crumbling in self-pity in the middle of a forest when the world waits for her to do something! Pfft!! This is a waste of time; I tell myself angrily.

My sobbing done I take long slow breaths to clear my head. I will not let myself fall for the misery I have let in. An adult of age sitting in the dirt sobbing loudly at the universe! I am so ashamed. The first sign of defeat will not break me by those who think to bring chaos and destruction my world! I do not have time to sit in the dirt hopelessly waiting for someone to rescue me. I will fight because really, what choice do I have? What other option do they give me? I will not be a prisoner at their mercy. I will not beg for my life back.

I will be whom I was born to be.... then they will know. They will know the pain and suffering that comes for them next time they look at me. Well, at least I'll hopefully feel brave for the next five minutes if I keep telling myself this!

I lift my chin resolutely, brushing the leaves and dust from my armour before purposefully walk in the direction of the tomb knowing, for the next few hours, this is at least my path and that's all that matters right now.

I am relieved when the day passes with nothing but sunshine and quiet. It is coming towards dusk and the forest begins to fill with shadows. I am only an hour or so from the edge of the forest when I hear the slide of the sword from its scarab. Without hesitation, I call my sword wrapping my fingers reassuringly around its comforting steel as it settles in my hand.

It is only a second before the first soldier attacks, but it is already too late for him. My mind clears and my body moves fluidly as I defend quickly thrusting my sword into his stomach before moving to the next. They came individually before they try in pairs and then in small groups each time retreating or finding death on my sword. Their numbers are small, so the odds are certainly against them.

This is less than my daily training and is such sweet relief! Something to pass the time! A fight to the death is bliss against the tortuously boring quiet. Everything else fades but this battle and my blade. I do not need to think as I kill and it is a flurry of swords and screams, of metal scrapping and blood flowing. This is my element. This is where I thrive... in the death and the dirt of the fight.

"Stop!" A voice cuts across the fight and everything pauses. Soldiers quickly retreat back as I turn towards the voice to see a tall, well-built soldier emerges from the shadows and strides towards me. He is clearly a commander of some sort and smiles at me before coming to stand confidently in front of me.

"Your brother needs you." Is all his says and my heart leaps.

"My brother?" I asked stunned but his face remains friendly.

"He is a guest in the palace."

"A guest or a prisoner?" I ask as suspicion blooms at this strange change of tactics.

"A guest. We only ask that you accompany us back to the palace so you may speak with him." And with that, he turns and gestures into the forest as if I should lead the way.

"Yet you attack me..." I incline my head.

"Only to gain your attention." He smiles again as if we are friends, but I do not return his smile. He turns again as if we should move but I remain in place. I will not have this stranger at my back.

"You first." I smile sweetly at him, but I see him pause to look me over carefully before turning and striding into the bushes. I am suspicious. It is curious how enemy soldiers found me within hours. Stranger still that my brother is a prisoner because it is impossible to think he would be a guest. He is powerful and strong, as a guest he could easily have escaped, and I have no doubt he would have taken no time to find me, but I will play this game...for now.

I can feel I am surrounded on every side as we walk through the trees, although they keep a careful distance. I gently push the light and balance outwards and feel as it touches the hidden soldiers in the surrounding trees. Before long we arrive at a clearing and I can only gasp in shock, stopping abruptly. Dragons! I look at the formation of about a dozen dragons in front of me. They have not turned against us! They suffer. Even worse! Right before my eyes, hunched in agony is Abrastos, King of the Night Sky, my father's oldest friend.

"Abrastos..." I whisper and he raises his majestic head to look at me. Without thinking I step towards him.

"Be careful! They are wild." Comes the commander's voice as he moves to stop me, and I turn to him in shock.

"Wild?" I repeat in disbelief, letting my sword disappear as I look around at the soldiers. It is clear they all think the same foolish notion.

"Yes. Wild animals." He answers and I am stunned by his stupidity. I walk rapidly towards Abrastos.

"Old friend?" I ask quietly but he does not answer. He does not move. I look across his face before looking at the base of his neck at the thick, heavy silver chain and as I touch him the same electric yet slimly feeling of the chains on the mountainside rushes over my hand and I quickly step back. I can feel the dark magic that thickly coats the metal around his neck.

"I am so sorry old friend." Is all I can say stepping back to face him. Abrastos lowers his head to me and I raise my hands to greet him placing my hands on his face. I cannot feel his power! All I feel is the slimness of the spell that has them bound. It is as though he has been drained and as I sadly run my hands gently across the ridges of his face, I hear a soul-wrenching, gasping plea...."*Help*..." which reverberates in my head as he barely manages to whisper a silent plea. I look up quickly at him and he blinks, his eyes filled with pain and suffering. My brother will have to wait. Guest or prisoner, he is powerful enough to stay alive at least. I cannot walk away, and I certainly will not allow these fools to think themselves worthy enough to sit astride these dragons. It is sacrilege! These pompous soldiers will walk home or die. It will be their choice.

My hand lifts at my side as my sword connects quickly with my palm and a wrap my fingers firmly around my constant companion.

"Alta Axian you have no choice! You are alone! You have nothing left!" the commander calls at me with frustration. "Do not throw away our offer for animals!" He yells but it is too late. I turn and stride angrily towards them and smile at them viciously as they quickly scramble to draw battle positions. I do not slow my stride as one by one as they determinedly attack, and it only makes my viciousness more so as I see the hatred for me clearly in their faces and it is too soon when these pathetic enemies lay at my feet.

I look at the bodies without conscious. They think it their right to attack my world, but they will not find it so easy with me!

I look around carefully for their leader who seems to be unaccounted for and has undoubtedly fled like a coward in the chaos, as it is quiet in every direction. I keep my sword ready before running the short distance back to Abrastos. The dragons have not moved in this whole time and I can see the forced stiffness in their bodies. Whatever those chains do has crippled these amazing creatures in every way.

I test the chains at his neck, directing the light to break them but I cannot get close enough or gather enough force to do anything other than cause sparks. They lay so heavy, almost as if they are embedded painfully into their thick scales, and the more I see of this spell the more I know I must find a way to free them.

The forest in the darkness I am vulnerable to attack but cannot leave them! I will not walk away from this fight! I draw light and balance to me again feeling it swirl and lift the air around us. As the ripples gain more and more momentum, I move towards the chains again but am even more repelled, as my power seems to push in an opposite current to the power of the chains. So strange and clearly created by someone as powerful as they are evil. I clearly cannot use my ability to gather light and balance to break them but there must be a way.... They are made of metal.... Of course! My sword! It is metal from the core of Axis, unbreakable, unyielding and I quickly call it to my hand.

"Sorry old friend. This may not be easy on you." I tell him concerned about the pain I may cause but sadly he does not move nor respond.

I gently touch his face before moving to the chains around his neck. I point my sword towards the metal links holding it tightly between my hands and although it is able to touch them, I cannot push any further. Abrastos sweats at the pain as I try again and again before I step away angrily. No doubt the commander knew this was impossible so waits patiently hiding in the trees for me to give up so he can fly them all back!

I sit on the grass next to Abrastos refusing to admit defeat. I cannot leave them here. I cannot walk away leaving them injured and in pain.

I stand determined. Az is right. This is my world! I cannot be defeated here! These chains certainly will not defeat me!

"I can do this old friend," I tell Abrastos and he looks at me sadly. "Do not doubt me! I will not fail although...this might hurt!" I yell at him as I draw the light roughly to me stealing it in gulps from the air. I feel in swell through my chest as if it opens and grows. It cracks and sparks as I revel in the power it brings. I raise my sword, knowing I'm likely to be blown back into next week, and bring it crashing down with everything I have onto the chains. White light blinds me and although the blowback is intense, I somehow manage to keep my feet. The light fades and I look expectantly at Abrastos.

"*I do not know how you succeeded Everly, but I am glad.*" Abrastos's voice rings in my head and I grin relieved as I watch the chains sink heavily into the ground before turning a nasty rusted red. Only 11 more dragons to go...

Covered in sweat, bruised and exhausted I am relieved when the last dragon is freed. Dragging my sword behind me I to walk towards Abrastos before collapsing to the ground next to him.

"*I cannot imagine your pain, Everly. But you know what must be done.*" Abrastos's deep rumbling voice comes from above me.

"It will be done Abrastos. This is my world, not theirs. They will not succeed. I must travel alone. It will draw less attention." I answer too tired to look up.

"*They track you in the hope you will surrender. You must get to Eos Nevaeh.*" He continues.

"I know but you must go to the pAx, Abrastos. It is not safe for any dragon to be here while someone has the power to cripple you."

"*This enemy you face is very powerful. Very determined. Everly... There is something you should know...we have much to talk about...this journey is not going* to be easy for you. You must be very careful who you trust. There are those who bring the dark that have the power to destroy us all. This is not an invasion child this is more."

"Who has the power to design such misery that the dragons surrender?" I ask, pointing to the chains before turning my head up to look at him.

"It is a sacrifice to save what was most precious. It gave us hope. There was no other way Everly, you must trust me, trust Axis…. trust yourself." He answers.

"Who of Axis would design something like this? What would you sacrifice the dragons for? Abrastos this is sacrilege!" I stand and turn to face him angry but confused.

"No Everly these are the actions of those who are our foundation…" And I know, I understand when I see the sadness in his expression. It can only be one of the four foundation families of Axis. There are no others with such access to power and knowledge.

"Whoever it was must have been forced. No one would ever have done this of his own accord. Not against Axis."

Abrastos studies me carefully for a moment before answering.

"There is much to be guarded, Everly. Much to keep safe against this enemy." Is all he says.

"I understand Abrastos. I journey to the tomb now to secure it before seeking the pAx, but you must go ahead of me. At least ensure my final task is safe from our enemy."

"We have the cover of darkness to make the journey to Eos and the pAx. We are forever loyal to you Everly, just as we have been to every First. We will wait there for your arrival. We will be at your side for the Last."

"Thank you Abrastos. Thank you. Para Axis my friend." I bid him farewell in the old ways knowing I must leave. I have spent too much time in the forest and as I see the gentle light of the moon know I will not make it at the tomb until tomorrow.

"Para Axis child of Solomon. Everly Alta Axian, Right Hand of the First, Our Princess. Travel well." And he bows his enormous head slightly and the dragons begin to rise through the canopy. I watch until they disappear into the blackness of the trees above before I turn and move quickly into the forest. I am sad to leave my only allies behind, but I cannot risk the recapture of the dragons. It gives me the strength to see them saved, knowing even if they will be miles away, I am no longer alone on Axis.

This is my world, the place I am strongest. I will make my peace at the tomb and trigger the pillars quickly so all Axis may know salvation comes. I will face each day determined. I will step forward cautiously finding my future not in attacking great armies or saving the universe by sacrificing everything but in the small victories of freedom such as this. The freedom of those that matter, and I understand for the first time the capture of our dragon allies. It was not a choice but power that sealed their fate. This life, this world stands precariously on the edge of destruction ... and for me, I will fight, I will rise, and I will never surrender to this darkness.

Chapter 13

I hurry through the forest. I need to find shelter for what is left of the night and look around me carefully as I run. This is no doubt the first of many uncomfortable nights and when my hope of finding a warm house or luxury tent in the middle of the forest fades, I settle, reluctantly, for the base of a dying tree. The dying tree actually sounds very dramatic, as it is nothing more than a small opening near the ground of a tree large enough to at least protect my back.

I dig deeper into the soft dirt with my hands before trying to huddle into the lumpy groove determined to find some warmth if not little comfort. I watch the scant traces of night's light that flicker through the canopy across the forest and through the trees. I close my eyes, resting my head against the old tree and feel the comfort of the light and balance in the air around me.

The darkness brings noises and the scurry of animals that sound amplified in the dark. I breathe in the cool air as it settles at the base of the trees where I am huddled, and as the blackness deepens, my teeth add to the noise of the night with their chattering and the cold seeps through the forest reminding me of how cool the air gets close to the mountains.

I wrap my arms around myself and sit listening to the night time chirping and quiet movement around me. Probably not going to get a lot of sleep but happy to be at least resting after a day of jogging through the forest. I have travelled most of the way towards the mountains today without any further attacks although I have heard dragon formations fly over the canopy quite a few times.

I figure they must search for me but in the forest, the foliage is dense and will make spotting me almost impossible. I have not stopped since saying farewell to Abrastos and the dragons, only slowing my pace to pick at berries along the way.

I reminisce foolishly of all the food prepared throughout the day at home and how I never considered the effort that went into each meal...until now when I am hungry, and I feel ashamed. What I would give for a bowl of anything cooked in those kitchens right now and how grateful I would be! And as if on cue my stomach grumbles. I know it will only be a couple of hours before I reach the mountain tomorrow and after I have said sealed the tomb, I will need to make better provisions and plans before heading to Eos.

I try to relax a little knowing I will need every second of sleep, but it is only snatches of rest in the dark. It is in the middle of the night with the noise of the forest I wonder if I should have taken Abrastos's offer to travel together, at least I would not be alone in the dark or hungry. Such weakness! I scold myself shaking my head and pushing away those pitiful thoughts.

The loneliness is making things worse, but it is something I am determined to master. I hold myself together breathing through the pain that feels like a fist scrunching into my chest every time I imagine a life without my father. I sit lost in memories thankfully for the training my father instilled in me and grateful to have the skills to at least defend myself even if eating may be optional at this point.

If only my brother was here, and it saddens me to think he may be a prisoner of our enemy. I miss my brother. He is always so dependable, so good, so...everything my father wanted in a son and I needed in a brother. I can see his face smiling at me, always proud of my victories and successes, always needing to test the limits of my power so he could find ways to beat me. I can only hope he is surviving. It is all I can ask for after the savagery of the battle. No doubt he worries about me but must know to I will go to Eos as soon as I am able.

I wonder how I lost him in the battle and where he disappeared to when I was captured.

My father, I call silently to the sky above me, if only you were here for us to discuss this battle like we always did after a fight you could tell me your reasons and help me plan for this uncertain future.

There were so many things in the battle, which in hindsight, were out of place. The synchronization of our fight was always extraordinarily effective, and we never wavered from this plan of attack. We had stood together in our combat formation as always before it all began so it is curious as to how the formation broke but pointless to wonder at a different outcome when the only reality was defeat.... and death. But I need rest, not torment myself with what I cannot change so I close my eyes and focus only on the forest around me.

I keep my eyes closed as I feel the first rays of the day play across my face. It must be later in the morning than dawn as the light would not be able to penetrate this heavy foliage with its first rays.

I greet the forest around me, quietly checking in each direction before I dare move. It will not be long before I need to leave the safety of this canopy and start the climb up the mountain trail to the tomb. The trail to the tomb is wide and open and I do not imagine it will be an easy journey up the side of the mountain.

It is a trail large enough for a full combat formation, but I am hoping a lone traveller will be unseen against the rock wall that runs its length on the mountainside. I know once I reach the tomb, I should be safe inside. Well, at least that's what I'm hoping.

I stand stretching from my uncomfortable sleep, taking a minute to check for any sign of movement or possible attack around me. There is no point wasting any more time here, delaying the inevitable, so I begin the new day with as much enthusiasm as I can muster.

I move quickly and quietly through the last part of the forest. Within a couple of hours, the trees begin to thin and before long the edge of the forest comes into view. I am grateful to see the road to the mountains, which runs across the end of the forest from the direction of the Aurelian plains and towards the mountain trail, stretch out in front of me. Now, all I need is a little luck to cross the open space without being seen. Piece of cake right!

While travelling through the forest I have heard the formations of dragons flying overhead carrying soldiers. These formations pass in staggered intervals that seem to have no pattern or regular gaps so are hard to track or anticipate. It has been painful each time to know the dragons are slaves that carry our enemy, but it only increases my determination. I have run into no ground troops or formations of soldiers through the forest so imagine they search in the air because they would be able to cover a greater area.

When I reach the edge of the forest I stand quietly, watching, getting ready for what I know comes next. I decided, during my sleepless night, that given the length of the road from the end of the forest to the start of the mountain trail speed is likely to be better than stealth. There is no easy way to cross such an open space! So, after one last glance around me.... I run...focusing on the track I can see in the distance, that is the start of the mountain pass.

My injuries ache a little, but thankfully the rest has ensured my body has mostly healed. I do not look in any direction other than the wall of mountain on the other side of the track and I stride, without check, pushing harder and harder. If I am found I will hear them calling in victory as they descend and then I can turn and fight. I hope.

My adrenaline spikes in excitement at the halfway point when I can see my goal. Sweat beads and falls and my legs ache but I run. My body was warrior fit and this is not so much a physical feat as it is mental strength that weakens me with each step as my fear of capture increases. I dare not use the balance or light in the air around me in case the ripples are recognised.

While it has felt like hours it is only minutes later, I reach the end of the pass and throw myself against the wall. Laying in the dirt on the ground facing the open road I look in every direction with disbelief that I have not felt the pierce of an arrow or the burn of dragon flame but it is quiet, even the skies are clear and the road remains ominously desolate and I lay for moments against the coolness of the mountain wall catching my breath.

When my heart has stopped racing, I stand and brush the dirt from my armour. I shake my head annoyed at myself for such unreasonable panic and stupidity. I am a lone person travelling in a quiet area of our world, I am certain they would think I would head to one of the lesser cities for safety or the pAx which are in the other direction. That would make their lack of presence in this area understandable and with that comforting thought, I scan the road one last time before turning to start the trek up the mountain.

This will be another first, in what I can only imagine will be a long freaking line from here to eternity of things I've not done before, like walk up this trail. I jog the incline because if I'm going to start doing things differently, I may as well start with some enthusiasm. I refuse to become weak when my life will depend on my strength.

My jog slows to a walk as I near the plateau that holds the doorway to the tomb. I have stayed close to the side of the mountain as I ascended the trail, which has taken most of the day. The dragon formations keep flying across the forest, which I could see with increasing clarity as the trail reached upwards but thankfully none seem to turn in this direction. I am thankful they must not know the significance of the tomb.

The climb is steep, but it is still during daylight when I reach the plateau and see for the first time the beautifully carved doors on the far side. I solemnly study the shadows that fall in lines across the face of the doors before I stride the last few meters towards them. I have come here many times, reverently, sadly and with respect but never in all these moments have I felt the heart-rendering emotion of what I am about to do.

I pause at the door and stand, just for moments, in the quiet coolness of the shadows on mountain plateau finding myself hesitant, hesitant to take the last steps into the past and hesitant to face a future I never imagined. It is behind these doors that every First of my family quietly sleeps in death. My heart clenches as I realise this tomb will never hold the remains of my father. It sickens me knowing I will always vividly remember the sight of his body left to rot on the battlefield.

I shake my head clearing away thoughts that would have me drowning in sadness. There is no time for this endless pity. It was a risk to even come here and I cannot stand in the open like a fool lost in misery, worrying about what comes next.

I move determinedly towards the doors. My blood will open the tomb doors so with my sword I pierce my palm and place my hand against the centre to break the seal that holds it shut but as I can press my hand against the amulet the doors creak open slightly and I jump back, sword in hand as the shock of the open doors hits me.

It is impossible that the tomb is open! These doors can only be opened with blood, Alta Axian blood, and I am the only person left that should be able to open them! I grip my sword tight ready for battle, knowing that no good can be waiting beyond these doors. Only a member of my father's bloodline would have the ability to open the tomb and there is none left but me free to roam this land. I vow that whatever nightmare lay waiting in the place that is most sacred to me will meet its end here.

Cautiously but with increasing violence, rage burning through me, I push the door a little more until I can silently slide my body inside. As I clear the opening, I drop to crouch scanning the inside of the tomb. I can see no movement even as my eyes adjust to the dimmer light glowing gently, for eternity, around the perimeter of the hall but with the doors unsealed who knows what evil waits in the shadows for me.

The tomb travels for meters into the mountain and I can barely make out the end. I still see no movement; no noise just the usual cool quiet. I creep the first few meters down the centre waiting with each step for an attack to begin. I know each of the eleven Firsts by name and place within our family and as I silently move with cautious steps, I run my hand over each engraved pattern on the sides of each bier that sits beneath each ornate coffin. Their places in my history taught to me as a child and I draw strength in the knowledge of my heritage. "I am Alta Axian, the future of these Firsts." I tell myself, quietly focusing as I move forward.

In my increasing anger, I do not notice, until the third sepulchre that each First is missing a piece! Each First is entombed with their talisman displayed across their chest but as I turn to look at each coffin around me, I realise with horror; they are all missing! My anger violent, my sword raised to destroy I stand straight and sweep in a circle to check my position. Come for me now I beg enraged! Attack me!

How dare they!

I run down the length of the room needing to reach my grandfather's resting place while searching for those who would violate my family's legacy. It is meaningless to them, I know, but to me, I am ready to destroy this entire world for such sacrilege! Light and balance swirl around me as I call it to me violently, gathering more and more of it as I run. It is dangerous to draw it in such violent waves knowing that it will be felt across my world, but I will destroy this enemy here where they think to destroy me.

To think I was relieved to see everything intact! My anger rises as I pass row after row of missing talismans. What use could they possibly have for talismans only valuable to the owner? The light and balance I have drawn swirls in the air around me creating waves of colour and motion making the dim light of the tomb flicker before glowing brighter.

What possible use could they have for them...that they would steal...more questions gather as I race to the end of the tomb desperate to find who did this.... but any thought I have is lost...I am lost...the air explodes in bright white light around me before rushing to the tomb doors. I hear the distance crash as they explode open. It's too much...my entire body trembles in racks of horror, then rage, then grief. I cannot control the screams that tear from my throat in endless agony. My last shred of sanity disappears, and my sword falls from my hand and clangs loudly on the stone floor. Uncaring I fall to my knees, collapsing under the weight of my pain and beg the universe for peace, plead for this to be the end as I am fixed, unable to tear my eyes away from the mangled body of my father that has been dumped in a heap at the end of the hall next to my grandfather's resting place.

I would have thought it impossible for anything more to break my heart or change my world, but this feels beyond. My soul is shattered. I thought I could find peace here, but I know now the battle and his death...will haunt me through eternity. My life without his guidance seems less, his death pointless but to leave him like this is despicable.

Chapter 14

I cannot bear her pain but know I must do this for our future. I made this vow to my father and I will not fail her even know, when they keep me from her or when they torture her searching for her weaknesses.

The agony of her doubts and the coldness that she lets wrap around her stealing all sense and leaving only fear make me want to shake her. I want to show her they do this only to find a way to break her.

She loses her way so quickly.

The screams of horror called to me and I cannot answer.

They hunt her in packs, and I have cleared her way, killed over and over to protect her but they ensure I cannot get close to her.

I am beyond caring about anything other than her safety. I must do what is necessary to ensure the light.

I have vowed to protect her, defend her, and betray her but only to save her.

All that has ever mattered is our future.

For Axis. For our destiny. For me.

Chapter 15

The light and balance beat and hammer at me as I lay on the cold floor. I no longer bother to control my powers and I can feel the increasing pressure of the light rising around me but do not care. No one can get close to this level of power. Any person foolish enough to enter the tomb will not survive. I can only hope it consumes me. Maybe this is how I can find peace.

My enemy will feel and know without any doubt my location. Axis trembles under the weight of my agony as I release any control. I cannot imagine nor do I care about the destruction I reek. I want to tear our enemy apart. I want this world destroyed. I am beyond sanity and let the pain gather and drown me in waves of rage and violence and frustration.

I am lost to my rage when a hand gently touches my shoulder. I hold still hoping they bring death and close my eyes in the hope I feel the thrust of a sharp blade pierce my heart. Knowing that whoever has the power to be this close must strong enough to kill me.

"Kill me. Finish this." I tell them "Let me go."

"Everly."' his gentle voice pleads with me "Everly. Stop this. Stop or you will kill the innocent and destroy what is left of Axis. Control your power. You must let the light and balance return to the air. The whole world trembles in your pain. Please, hear me." He begs but I don't care.

"No. Leave me. Don't touch me. Don't comfort me. Just let me be." I savagely snap at him drawing in greater waves until the walls around us shake and the lights spark blindingly with my rage.

"I cannot let you do this. Everly, please. You will destroy us all." He quietly tells me.

"It is over Az. I am done. I don't want this world, this life. Leave. Everything they destroyed of mine I will repay a hundred times when the world shatters from my power. They will never have my world and I will never find peace so we will be destroyed together." Is all the response he gets. And I am grateful when I feel him move away from me.

I will lay here until death comes for me. I will find peace with my father in the beyond rather than living the agony of this life. The Aurelians will keep my brother safe if only because they need him, and I know he should be able to survive my power.

"Everly, we will honour him. This is what you wanted." His voice comes again urgently. Everything stills, pausing in confusion, as I smell the soft spice of burial incense burning.

The quiet descends as I watch him move what is left of my father's broken body to the top of my grandfather's coffin. The light and balance begin to gently fade away as I let it go focusing only on his actions, watching as he carefully lays my father into the proper burial position. He honours him with such care, and it breaks me and heals me all at once. The respect he shows as he handles my father's broken body leaves me quiet. I watch, unable to do anything but struggle to breathe, as he finds covers to shrine him in and he wraps him gently I push myself up and sit watching his actions.

The grip of heartbreaking agony loosens and weakly I stand before walking over to help him. I will do this for my hero. I will honour the person I loved above all others. Maybe Az is right. I cannot destroy the world my father loved. My father deserves this from me at least.

Together, in silence, we prepare my father for the ritual that has been part of our history for generations. We will honour his place in our world regardless of the violence or of the destiny that comes. We reverently place the rites of family and legacy in the proper manner around and across his body. A calm takes over me as we work without pause until it has all been prepared.

I stand beside Az quietly, reverently before touching my hand against the pyre, lighting the room with blue flames that cover him in a fiery display moulding his body to the coffin for eternity. It is the final goodbye I wished for and I live the moment in reverence and contemplation.

As the sadness and fury burn away with my father at the ashes gently glow, I reach for Az's hand in the dark and feel comforted as his fingers thread through mine. I stand without tears watching my dreams burn, my life change and accept the end of what I thought would endure forever.

As the fire burns, I feel the pull of power wrap around the space. I look at Az questioningly, but he looks as confused as I. The swirl increases as the pyre burns but I cannot see a source. I turn back towards the flames and realise the power centres in the heart of the flames. Flames suddenly rise furiously from my father's chest and his talisman rises through them and into the air above him. I step towards the pyre in surprise not understanding the significance of the flames. Talismans are laid across a coffin they do not rise from the fire!

"Az! Do you see it?" I whisper not taking my eyes away from it.

"This is impossible." He says quietly. "Reach for it. You will know if it calls for you."

Hesitantly I step closer to the flames and the light and balance increases, coming now in intense waves towards the talisman. The fire blazes but I am unafraid as I stretch my hand through the flames. I brace for burning but feel warmth instead. As my hand touches the talisman I am fascinated to watch as it wraps around my fingers before rapidly moving up my arm where it flattens, as if an amulet or part of my armour, against my skin. I touch it tenderly recognising my father's symbol although this only raises more questions in relation to the missing talismans.

I look at Az for an explanation, but he looks as shocked as I and stares intently at the talisman on my arm.

"It would seem your father left you a parting gift, Everly. Talismans have always been sacred, and it would appear that this is your father's final act. His gift to you."

"Talismans are not gifted Az. They forever remain with the First." I answer studying the talisman on my arm.

"I did not know they could be gifted either, but regardless it is clear this one was meant for you Everly." He tells me and my eyes fill with tears. Such a gift.

"Talismans are sacred. There are displayed with the First but cannot be used by another. Why would they take them? Why strip the dead of artefacts?" I say aloud but Az does not respond.

It is such a violation that they take talismans. It is part of the mystery of a First to never know the details of their personal talisman, which is why they are proudly displayed after their parting.

I watch my father's body as the last flames die away. He now lays forever moulded in the alluvial white gold of our family. I tenderly touch his face. He was extraordinary, not just as a First but as a father, and I will forever walk with his wisdom in my mind and his love for me in my heart. I press a kiss against his head before touching the cool metal of his talisman on my upper arm. If this is his parting gift, I will not let it be wasted I vow. I will avenge and put right what has been taken from us I silently tell him.

"What are you doing here Az?" I ask quietly.

"You needed me. I could feel the destruction of the ripples in the air." He answers me with honesty, and I understand why he came.

"It was too much. The shock...I felt weak in this Az. I have combat strength, but this is personal and the pain it brings..." I whisper to him vehemently "I cannot save this world alone. I am but one person."

"You do not have to be alone." He has told me this before and as before it annoys me.

"I am alone. Alone in this world. Alone as I walk through it not knowing who is going to try and kill me next. Alone, as I try to get some small amount of sleep without waking terrified, I may have been found. Alone, trying to work out what the hell I'm supposed to do now that everything I loved, everything I valued, everything I have ever known has gone!"

"Not everything is gone, Everly. You were raised with a purpose and that purpose still remains. What happens around you may change but you still have an obligation to fulfil what you were born to do."

"To become the next First. What good is that now? I cannot open the gates without it helping our enemy! I cannot protect Axis without an army at my back! Look around you Az there is nothing left! It is all gone!"

"It is not all gone." Comes his quiet reply sounding so reasonable so....

"What matters to me seems gone."

"You know the history of the foundation families?"

"Of course, I do! Light, balance, created by Axis herself, everyone has their role and they all lived happily ever after...until now."

"Everly it is not that simple you know this. A First isn't about light and balance it's also about their ability to shield and protect. Your family were not chosen they were born. It is in your blood this gift. The things that you think are learned and trained, are instincts that are buried deep in bloodlines that run with the purity of Axis herself. In your grief you did not focus, you instinctively drew the power to you to shield and protect you while you grieved. Your family has always been powerful, but gifts demand a price. You don't get a free ride, Everly. Those obligations you were raised expecting don't change just because the world around you does. Trying to ignore then will only end in disaster.... for us all."

"I am not running Az. I am surviving. I cannot fight like this. I am one. If my father could not defeat this enemy, then I have no hope."

"Nobody is asking you to fight. You are only being asked to remember who you are...a guardian of Axis and to complete the task you were born for."

"What are you doing here Az?" I ask again. "Why did you bother coming if only to lecture me?"

"The world shook with your pain Everly. You could have destroyed us all and I could do no less than help."

"Are you my guardian? Perhaps a knight in shining armour? Or spy for the enemy?"

"I would rather be your friend."

"And I would rather be home."

"You are home, Everly."

"I am far from home Az and way out of my depth."

And he looks at me sadly. I think he knows there is little hope. It is impossible to ask me to fight so he stays quietly beside me. He has no purpose in this other than to keep me alive.

"You freed dragons." He says surprising me.

"Yes."

"How did you do that? Did the chains yield?"

"The power lit up through my sword. It was strange." I tell him and he stops and studies my face for seconds.

"It takes powerful magic to hold a dragon, but even more to release it." He answers, but it means nothing. I have used my sword as a conduit before.

"Why do they need the talismans?" I ask looking again and again at the coffins angrily.

"Maybe they hold power?" Is all he answers and pointlessly I wait for him to continue.

"Will they resurrect the Firsts?" I ask when he remains silent.

"No" he smiles at the hope on my face "No power can resurrect the dead."

"What purpose would they have for such desecration then?"

"What happened with your father's talisman?" he asks.

"It wrapped around my upper arm." I look at him frowning.

"Can you feel it?" He looks at me and then at the gold on my arm. I place my hand across it tracing the edges, admiring the beauty of the blue that fades to a rich purple. I don't want to tell him what it did or how it feels. It was my fathers and somehow feels...personal on my arm as if it is a secret between us alone.

"I can feel it on my arm but only because it is foreign. I will get used to it I'm sure." I answer flippantly and stand as if to leave. He laughs quietly knowing I have not been truthfully but also knowing that is all the answer he will get from me.

"In time I hope you will trust me." Is all he says but does not push the point or ask any further questions instead he turns and faces me. "It is time Everly. You must trigger the pillars, bring salvation."

"I agree. I cannot do this alone. I know this now. I only hope I do not lead them into defeat or death, but it is time the four reunited." I respond and he nods solemnly.

I walk to the end of the tomb and stand in front of the star that represents the four foundation families of Axis. Taking my sword, a cut across my hand and place it in the centre and watch fascinated as the blood suddenly pours from my palm and traces the lines that represent the pillars of Axis. Once every line is filled the wall lights with power and the symbol blinds us in a flash of incredible energy before disappearing and as I take my hand away, I look at my palm to see my cut completely healed and there is not a drop of blood in sight.

"Well, that was impressive!" I hear a shocked Az say from behind me.

"It certainly was. I never expected it would be like that." I agree with him as we stand side by side looking at the wall. "Thank you, Az." I offer as I turn to leave, and we walk towards the doors in silence.

I am sad to have found my father and happy to have honoured him. I am definitely relieved to know the pillars have been triggered and now only have to worry about getting to Eos... but suddenly noise erupts as the small reprieve of peace is broken and I look to see soldier after soldier streaming through the tomb doors and running towards us. They line the walls and fill the spaces until there is only face after face of our enemy's fighters, swords drawn in front of us.

"There is nothing for us here Everly. It is done. We have been found." And I nod in agreement before he can continue.

"Then we will enjoy the fight!" I grin at him viciously calling my sword as I jump onto the nearest coffin and leap into the fray of my enemy as they converge on my position and the blood and sweat bring me sweet relief as I plough through those who thought to destroy my family only to die at the hands of a solitary girl.

Chapter 16

"You cannot ask this of me! You cannot stand here pleading and begging and think this makes it acceptable! I refuse."

"I do not ask this of you, I demand it as your husband and tell you it is done. It will not be any other way. It is final. I am sorry that it must be asked of you but it this is the way it should have been if I had not been foolish...." He trails off angrily.

I study him carefully understanding the enormity of what he expects even more than he does I suspect. He truly expects me to accept this without a fight...without consequences. This relationship between us has always presented challenges but I have always stood at his side proudly. I have done everything needed to bind myself to him. I ensured it was so and wonder if this is the price Axis has asked of me because of my schemes. It makes me rage that someone such as he is granted such greatness without anything other than being born to the right family but this! He has humiliated me.

"Why?" I ask, "Why would you do this? How could you? Why could you not be content with what you had?"

"Sidra..." He answers me tiredly and moves to sit in the lounge under the window. "Is this really the question you want to be answered? Because I can assure you the answers will not be to your liking. You ask me why knowing the answers, knowing it was never mine to be content without ensuring my legacy. I protected yours when I raised Tallon, I only ask the same of you now!" He pauses but before I can respond he continues "I do not want to hurt you any more than I have already done. I know what it is that I ask. I know the situation it places you in and I cannot stress enough the importance of this regardless of the pain this causes. It is done and I cannot change it, nor can I change the future that comes for us now. This is beyond you; this is for Axis."

His handsome features are shadowed, and I see the grief and brokenness he has suffered as I listen to his words the depth of his feelings clearly evident.

"Does she live?" is all I ask, and watch satisfied as his breathing pauses but for a split second before he calmly looks at me.

"I do not know." He answers as pain mars his perfect features, but he does not elaborate.

I know his honesty. He is a good man; righteous even and in this, at least, I am assured that this will be the last request he ever asks of me.

"This is all you will ever ask of me."

"Agreed. That is all I can hope for but Sidra, you will do as I ask in this without question." He threatens me and with that, he stands and walks out without any further conversation. I sit quietly understanding the implications of his request. He knows the truth for certain now. And for certain only war comes from this because I will never condone his actions and I will ensure his consequences.

Chapter 17

I wipe my sword on the inside of my arm and smile at him with glee! The blood disintegrates as it touches my armour leaving my sword clean. Magic and blood...and the beauty of a good fight. Ok, well, this one wasn't that good, but it was certainly a good way to burn off some steam. He shakes his head at my bloodthirsty ways smiling as I see him look me over for injuries.

"Such a vicious princess smiling happily while men lay dead at her feet! Really Everly." he pretends to admonish me while shaking his head and I look at him with fake horror.

"Says the man who helped put them there," I answer him enjoying a rare moment of friendship.

"I can do no less than protect you." He answers and then smiles at my indignation.

"Hmmm...protection. Are protectors are allowed to battle? Do they fight gleefully alongside the fragile princess trying to keep up with her sword?" I ask poking at his seriousness.

"I must surely be allowed to take whatever means necessary to protect you, so I battled fiercely to keep you safe." And his brow furrows as he continues. "Because clearly, you needed protecting..." he mutters, and I wink at him before looking across at the havoc left by the battle within the tomb. There is minimal damage to the coffins and thankfully most of the fallen lay beyond the door, but I cannot leave it this way.

"I need to clean this up before we leave, and I need to seal the tomb," I tell him and start to move the bodies out of the doorway, dragging each one beyond the threshold and onto the plateau before dumping them in a pile and I am grateful when I see him helping me with this at least.

"Why didn't you just surrender to the soldiers Everly? You have triggered the pillars. It may be time to find peace?" he asks as I watch him pull the last body through the door and I look at him, considering his question.

It bothers me that he is here. My family know of the tomb, but it is not common knowledge. It is a sanctuary for us and never attended by anyone outside our family nor can it be entered by anyone outside our bloodline, yet he has appeared again in a moment of need.

"I must reach Eos," I answer, and he watches me.

"Who would know you would come here? It must have been someone who knew you well wanted to leave his body within the tomb knowing it would hurt you. Did anyone else know of the pillars? Of Salvation?" He asks clearly concerned.

"I don't know." I answer honestly "My brother might, but he would never betray me. My father only told me of the pillars, and I swore an oath to protect them. I have never discussed any of this with Tallon nor anyone else...until you." I look at him pointedly, but he ignores my words and continues.

"They were waiting here for you." Is all he says. To me it seems stranger than after I have defeated formations so easily, they still sent so little and they did not cry out for capture, or try subterfuge, they fought knowing they would die.

"I didn't see them until after the pyre burnt so how could they be waiting?" I ask him confused as to why I didn't realise they were there.

"Maybe they were shielded." He response and it surprises me.

"So, our enemy may not be without their own powers then." I wonder aloud. "Yet they hide never having the courage to face me themselves. You would think that if they wished to capture or kill me, they would send their strongest. To send formations of mere soldiers is a mistake that only costs them numbers. It seems a poor tactic in a war."

"You may seem vulnerable out here...alone. They clearly underestimate your abilities to.... endure, I think. Maybe they have done what was needed. You were weakened." He tells me and I can see he's being careful.

"Yes, but I am also not easy to defeat. It will take more than a couple of formations."

"They will send more."

"I know."

"They will try and trick you."

"I know this too Az. I am not a child nor am I some newly fledged soldier. I know who I can trust even if it is very few. I have fought alongside my father for more than ten years now. Battle, fighting, tactics...these are the ways I excel in."

"They will know this."

"How?"

"The same way they knew you would come here."

"I don't think so. It would have been easy to track me here. The mountain pass is open, and I saw numerous formations patrolling the skies. It wouldn't have been hard to spot me from the air. The track up the mountain is so open. They may have waited shielded while I was inside but if that is all they send to capture or kill me then this enemy does not know me at all."

"I think it is time you had a better plan, Everly."

"What... as opposed to my 'no plan at all' strategy? What was wrong with that?" I smile at him "Az, honestly, I thought it was safe to come here. I would have had to come regardless. I had no choice. I cannot save Axis without the pillars. I just didn't expect..." I trail off not wanting to relive the memory of my father's body.

"I understand. My point is they did expect you to come here, Everly. His body was dumped here to devastate you. Someone knew the truth of the tomb. Who knows what their intentions were? Was it just to distract you? Break whatever was left of your heart? Weaken you enough so they could either capture or kill you? They cannot capture you by fair means or fighting so this is the length they will go to in an effort to find what makes you vulnerable. Whoever is hunting you knows they need you so I have no doubt there will be plans and schemes waiting for you. There is more at stake here Everly, you know this. They will not let you go quietly. They know the risk of your freedom. Maybe it is time to meet with them? To talk? You would have value to them." He tells me but this time I ignore him.

"I need to seal the tomb Az." I look at him searchingly hearing his words but not yet ready to confront what they mean. "I need the tomb sealed beyond my blood. I need it sealed so only I can open it, so I need you to leave." I look at him pleadingly.

"Of course, Everly." He tells me, nodding as if he understands my sudden change in conversation and I am grateful. He never pushes or demands. He only turns and closes the doors carefully ensuring they are held in place and I watch him begin the walk down the trail.

When I can no longer see him, I trace the edges of the door flooding them with light. I place my sword against the joint and use it as a conduit for my power. My powers usually thunder across the universe but this time I am quiet, careful and ensure they are intricate and lace with blood.

The glow of the seal is subdued and traces the line in blues and purples and when it is finished, I test the seal to ensure its strength and am pleased. At least this place should be safe, for now. With one final check, I turn and jog down the incline to catch up to Az.

"I will head towards Eos, to the pAx," I tell him as I reach his side and look across the valley towards the plains.

"Are the dragons you freed safe?" He asks me, falling into step beside me.

"In Eos? Yes." I ask hoping they made it given the danger of such a journey.

"So, they have been given sanctuary by the pAx and will await your arrival for the Last." He asks as if confirming my plans and I nod, as it is the truth.

"Az, I really hope that you don't turn out to be the world's biggest asshole. All this helpfulness usually means that someone is after something or wants to manipulate me somehow. I would hate to have to chop off your head if you ever thought to betray me or the dragons especially now." I warn him and he smiles gently at me.

"Let's hope not. I like my head. I've had it for many years and am quite fond of it." He replies and I look at him surprised. He is a strange man. I return his smile glad for his company and grateful for his actions in the tomb but still a little lost as to why he is so willing to help me.

"You told me you were my friend Az. Let's just hope for both our sakes you are... because funny or not I will hunt you down and kill you if you betray me...here or in the between. Clear?" I ask looking him dead in the eye. He looks at me intently for a few seconds and my stare does not falter until he nods his head in agreement.

"Take the east road Everly. It will be the path they least expect, and it is mostly deserted. A man named Hayes lives along that road with his family. You will feel the strength of his power as you get near to his home. He will not be hard to find. He is a friend and will, at the very least, provide shelter and food."

"You are not going to travel with me?" I ask surprised and maybe hopefully. I hate being alone.

"No, Everly. There is much that needs to be done. Our universe stands at the brink of catastrophe and many on Axis need food and shelter. I will help you whenever I can." he says and starts to walk down the mountain trail. "You are strong Everly.... maybe a little broken but strong. The pillars have been triggered now...you could just find peace but I can see you are stubborn so you have help along the way I can assure you....to make the right decisions...for Axis." And with that cryptic comment, he lifts his head and whistles into the air. Within minutes an admetos horse appears, and before I can even shut my mouth at the shock of such a sight, they disappear in rapid strides down the mountain, and I am alone again.

"Hey! How did you get an admetos??" I call out stupidly "You know you could have given me a ride!" I yell pointlessly to the air around me. Nice! I'll trek for two days down the East Road while he pops on a freaking horse and rides off in a puff of smoke! Whatever!

He is right. There are others that need help. This can only be my journey and I will reach the Last for the sake of Axis and if only to save my brother. And with one final look at the mountain that holds the resting place of my family I turn and start the trek back down to the forest, alone and annoyingly not on horseback!

Chapter 18

The air changes, charging with fire and light, with death.

My shield slips in the fray of emotion and I have no choice but to answer. I cannot bring death to what I must save beyond all else so I must protect others with life.

It takes seconds, which feel like days before I see the truth.

The blood. The light. The white flames. It is chaos and catastrophe. It is everything and nothing gone in an instant and I am in awe and terrified all at once.

I hold and watch unsure of how to stop the scorching circle.

There is none strong enough to do this and the joy of hope races through me together with the terror of all that can be lost if this is true.

I call to Axis. This time it is beyond me. I cannot hold the truth of us alone. This cannot be accomplished without the effort of us all and my answer comes quickly. The firestorm falls until it is spent, and I watch with relief as it is made right. The light recedes, the fallen rise, death is vanquished, and life is restored.

In the heart of the storm, I see the white gold of Axis threaded through blue and purple. It is not only strengthened, but it is also saved.

Axis knows the truth now more than ever...this is my legacy.

It is all that can save what has been destroyed. All that can defeat the darkness. The only one strong enough to face what comes and she is extraordinary.

Chapter 19

The east road is beautiful. Like a picture book, fairy-tale fantasy it stretches infinitely in both directions in vibrant colours and an array of patterns. Deep, rich soil with lush green fields on either side, filled with an abundance of crops. It is mesmerizing in its beauty, like the sweet newness of fresh clean air and growth and dirt and as I walk, I am reminded of all the trips on horseback where I didn't appreciate the sights around me in our largest farming area.

I have walked the road for two days. Camping at night off the track at the base of whatever tree was mostly hidden. My long walk has been surprisingly uneventful although the tension of my journey never fades, and I am always glad for the reassurance of my sword hidden in the light. I am tired, hungry and a little on edge.

Dragon formations still fly across the land, but I suspect they search the plains for me, as they seem to completely avoid this area. The Aurelian plains are the safest and most direct route to Eos whereas the east road is more isolated, and these are the only two paths to Eos. I expect they will turn to the east road soon enough in their search. With at least two days head start I'm hoping it will be enough.

My only real enemy here is hunger. I have gotten past the point of gentle belly rumbles. I am now consumed with the need to eat! All I can think about is food! I remember our last meal together before the battle. I remember our conversation. I remember sending back half-full plates...but I cannot remember what we ate! All that wasted food seemed so unimportant at the time but now it seems like everything should have been saved for now!

It is also impossible to hunt with a sword! It would certainly be difficult, but not impossible to throw it at a rabbit, or swipe at a fish, never mind taking down a bear with my blade and with many more days to come I have certainly considered that it may come to that! I wonder if I should have become more proficient with a bow at least then when the world fell in chaos and my life was completely destroyed...I may still have been able to eat!

I walked away from the tomb and down the trial with such focus and propose. After any victorious fight, there is a rush of confidence and that in itself carried me the entire length of the mountain and down the path towards the east until hunger kicked in. Maybe if I scream like a child with hunger pains to Axis, she may take pity on me and some lovely person will turn up and make me some food...Pfft. I must be going certifiably crazy more than hungry at the moment!

It makes me realise how many times I took the little things for granted! I never actually thought about the logistics of moving or travelling before now! My father could shift groups from one location to another or we could ride on horseback but walking for hours is completely foreign and although I trained in combat for hours each day between the walking and the lack of food I feel weak and disheartened and just a touch annoyed with this whole situation. I still haven't found the elusive Hayes yet and hope I haven't walked past his home especially if he knows how to cook.

It is hours on this road today before any sign of civilisation comes into view. The little white house seems so far away when I see it as a speck in the distance. It finally comes into view just as the sun starts to go pink on its journey towards the horizon. It would be a perfect setting with the day setting beyond the little white house if it wasn't for the death and destruction Axis faces and the possible soldiers who hunt for me. Even now I can see the dust in the air from the misalignment as my world waits for the crowning of its next First, it is slight but still sits ominously in the air so no time to appreciate my world's possible charms.

As I get closer to the house, I feel it.

This must be the home of Hayes.

Az is right, there is an unmistakable current that runs through the air like a spark of electricity. I look at the building waiting for anything unexpected but all I see it is a modest home, set back a little from the road, on what I assume is a working farm. There are no signs of neighbours and nothing other than crops in the paddocks surrounding it. It certainly looks innocent enough but before I even step two strides up the path approaching the door, I feel the air thicken and a sudden increase of power stops me as though I stand in front of an invisible barrier.

I test the strength of it with my hand and know I cannot get closer to the house without alerting those who live inside. I reach my hand out and into the air gently placing my hand against the barrier aware that it likely surrounds the house. My light sparks against the barrier as if it is testing my strength but everything stays calm.

I wait, knowing if I destroy the barrier, I will offend those who are safely protected by it, so instead I push a gentle pulse of light against the barrier as if I am knocking. I do not have to wait long for any reply and step back as the door of the little house is opened abruptly and a very, very large man steps out to stand in front of it protectively. He studies me suspiciously in the fading light and as I stand meekly showing no signs of aggression, he folds his arms across his chest as though he thankfully does not consider me a threat.

"I am Everly." I quietly tell him hoping for as little trouble as possible and when he doesn't reply I hurriedly continue. "Please. I only ask for a little food. It has been days..." I trail off when he suddenly strides towards me. Surprised at the suddenness of his movement I move, without thinking, into a defensive position and extending my hand at my side calling my sword. He stops when he sees my defensive position and I see the shock on his face as he looks at my sword. For a second, we face each other in silence before he recovers.

"Everly...Alta Axian...finally. Az told us of your travels. It is good to see you are safe." He says looking relieved as he drops to his knee in front of me and I have no doubt this is Hayes. Az is right; the magic around the house is unexpectedly powerful. "We have been expecting you for the last day. Come quickly inside, you must be tired." He regains his feet and looks beyond the barrier protectively before I feel it open and he gestures at me to come towards the house.

"Come Everly. Let's get out of the open." He beckons to me urgently and quickly turns and walks towards the house. He opens the front door and stands so I am able to enter before him. I walk cautiously, waiting for the unexpected, into the little house but am relieved when the door closes behind us and see the only other occupants of the house are a woman and two young boys. The woman drops to her knee in the same manner as the man.

"There is no need," I tell her gently. "I am grateful for your help."

"I am sorry...for your loss." Her voice breaks but she does not say any more.

"My apologies Alta Axian." Hayes intervenes putting an arm around his wife comfortingly "The events of the last few weeks have been a shock to us all. My wife does not mean to upset you. We have waited for news and were so relieved when Az called in on us to warn of your arrival." And he turns to his wife and gentle wipes the tears from her face "It is going to be alright love. She is here. Solomon's child lives and there is still hope. Come now, she looks half-starved and in need some of your good cooking." He gently tells her, and she nods, wiping her face before she hurries into the kitchen.

"Az has been here?" I ask surprised at the news.

"Yes, he was here this morning." He tells me. "But could not stay. Az has responsibilities far beyond Axis."

"I understand and appreciate your help." I begin but he raises his hand as if to silence me.

"There is no need for thanks. I am a son of Xiana, and your task ahead affects us all. As Axians we can do not less than help even in these precarious times." And I am grateful to know his place. A son of Xiana is a member of the second foundation family of Axis and although he may be many times removed from the Heir of Xiana his loyalties would be to Axis and therefore me.

"I am grateful. This enemy likely wishes me dead or at least safety imprisoned as a captive not travelling across the country determined fight for our world." I say. "And I am clearly easy to recognise so the risk of being found is always great. I appreciate the shelter if only for a night." I smile a little at him as if I can reassure him that everything will be ok, but I know he understands. There are four original families of Axis. Our family, the Regla Mas Alta or Alta Axians, are the First and the Xiana are the Second. Each family line is sacred and although my family can only produce a single heir the other three families have grown rapidly in numbers with many members found across the universe.

"There is no other in this universe you could be. I am sorry for what comes but it also gives us hope. We are loyal to Axis. The Xiana have always protected the light of Axis. We do as you and wait for Salvation, our pillar, to arrive. These are times when the darkness creeps in trying to destroy us all but the Xiana remain forever loyal to what is best for Axis."

"I agree. We must do what we can to protect Axis, every one of us. I am hunted, with no army, no allies but I will face the Last if only for the destiny of our world. These are dangerous and uncertain times for all of us, I only pray Axis guides our path true and the pillars have been triggered in time."

"I am sure she protects us and guides us all. An Alta Axian is hope and it is assured Salvation Xiana has heard your call. You are the only hope for our world, our future. We will know the will of our world even through this chaos. She will ensure we will rise again." And he nods as if he agrees with himself and I dare not tell this family living in the middle of my world that I fear the unknown and the destiny that comes.

"Para Axis" I quietly say not knowing what else he expects from me.

"Para Axis" he repeats solemnly bowing his head in acknowledgment and it clenches in my chest to hear the call of my world from another who no doubt loves it as much as I.

"The food is ready." A quiet voice calls thankfully interrupting such a serious conversation.

"I should not be so rude. I welcomed you into our home and yet in my relief to see you arrive safely did not introduce myself. My apologies. I am Hayes and this is my wife Abella." He tells me as he leads to way into the next room and we sit quietly at the table that thankfully is full of food. I try my very best to be civilized as I stuff as much food as politely possible into my mouth. It is possible that this is the best tasting food I had ever eaten, or it is more likely I was just hungry... either way I am appreciative and grateful for their generosity.

There is, thankfully, little conversation as we eat. A sense of awkwardness remains at my presence, but I am well used to stares and curiosity.

After the meal, I stand to help clear the table.

"No, please. Let me. Rest...while you can." Abella tells me and not knowing what to do I stay at the table. The two young boys, who have been surprisingly quiet the entire meal, scramble from the table almost with relief at their father's nod and I am left alone with Hayes again.

"I have met your father." He begins "He was a powerful First. Very much respected. We felt his loss across Axis and know the task that now rests with you. The dust gently rises; the crops have started to fail. This affects us all."

"I appreciate your respect and understand the struggles we face but this is a powerful enemy. Powerful enough to defeat our First." Is all I can manage.

It is difficult to sit at this table and hear another speak of my father when the wound from his death lay raw in my chest. I wait for the worst though, knowing it will come...

"And you brother..." He begins with some hesitation "Have you seen him? Did he also survive? I wonder at his absence from your side." he asks and watches me expectantly.

"My brother has his own destiny." I push out the words even in the hope of finishing this conversation.

"Perhaps they do not understand the importance of our families, even the critical ascension of the First, maybe these invaders do not have anything other than greedy and control in their hearts for something they do not have the power to understand. To attack Axis is easy to rule Axis requires some more. It is true this universe cannot exist without the four families but the families themselves have changed over time and where there is change there can be an opportunity but who am I to fathom the politics and the schemes of men. The battle Everly... I am told the defeat was.... unusual." Hayes quietly speaks and I nod solemnly as if his words make sense to me although I am curious to know why he thinks change comes for us.

"In what way?" I ask.

"The fighting was not...as your family would have normally fought." He begins "I am told it was as if you were all.... apart. No tactics were used. No allies we called. No more than the first wave of your family ran into battle. Can this be true?" He asks and as his words sink in, I realise he is right. We were ...separated! I cannot even remember seeing my father or brother move in the patterns of our formation. I cannot recall a single death at their hands. It was not until my father surrendered that I knew where he was, and it was not until my brother called to me that I saw him clearly.

"Your father never used his powers. Neither did you or your brother. Is this correct?" he continues when I don't answer, and I look up at him surprised.

"It was a very different fight. There was no power in the air, no shield, no shift, no strength. It was like drowning in blood and mud. There was no other choice but to continue fighting endless or die. The light and balance were gone. It was as if I fought in a void." I begin but don't know what to make of it. "Apart...we fought apart." I wonder quietly aloud.

"The ability to use light and balance is very powerful Everly.... as is any reason a First would have to surrender but light and balance are internal as well as external. Was there cause for surrender? For such an act of sacrifice?" he talks contemplating these thoughts as if he does not believe the information he has heard.

"A First would never surrender without just cause but I did not see any cause for surrender. I never saw my father raise his sword. I only saw my brother in the fight and even he moved away..." Is all I say feeling the sadness of those memories engulf me once again.

Hayes looks at me carefully as if he waits for an answer or further explanation, but I have none. I have replayed the battle in my head numerous times without understanding.

"Many years ago, there was an event that threw the light and balance of Axis into chaos. It was an explosion of light like no other, but I have not heard of any event such as this. It was the same the night of the battle. Your father surrendered, your brother and allies disappeared and then an explosion reputed across Axis." he tells me "But no cause or a reason could be found for the explosion although its effects were deadly. Have you heard of such a thing?"

"An explosion?" I ask innocently "So strange..." I add but say no more.

"Such an unexpected event. And you survived?" he asks.

"Barely. I was thrown against the mountain just outside Amara." I tell him truthfully.

"Hmmm." he ponders as if he is in deep thought "The same mountain that the dragons and soldiers were found dead. It is very fortunate you survived Everly. I thank Axis for such a blessing." He smiles kindly at me. "Perhaps it was your father's death that triggered the explosion? Or that was the reason for his surrender." Hayes continues.

"A First would not surrender without a cause. Did they say he surrendered and not captured?" I ask hoping he has more information.

"It is assumed as he could not have been captured," Hayes says matter of factually.

"You are right Hayes. Surrender must have been his only choice but only he knows the reasons for his actions." The battle was out of the ordinary and none of us noticed. The surrender was impossible. I need to find the reason, not the result. How could I not have seen this?

"Then he must have had a reason beyond our understanding so significant that it cost him his life. He would have known better than anyone what it would mean for Axis...for you. You are alone without any support now. Even your greatest force, the Aurelians and dragons have abandoned you." He quietly acknowledges and I can only nod in agreement.

"You are to stay the night Everly, to rest. Az has asked this of you, and I have prepared a room." Abella's voice interrupts our conversation before I can ask any more.

"Thank you, Abella. It would be very much appreciated." I answer gratefully.

"I will show you to your room. We have a bathroom you can use, and I will wash any clothes you need."

"It is very much appreciated," I answer suddenly in desperate need of a shower! I stand and follow Abella leaving Hayes to quietly contemplate our conversation.

I shower quickly and as I sit in the candlelight of the bedroom a quiet knock comes on my door and it opens with Abella and my lovely clean armour.

"Thank you, Abella. Thank you so much." I tell her and am glad when she looks pleased.

"It is an honour." She answers and I see her pause "You must protect yourself Alta Axian even when you think yourself safe, stay alert." She hesitantly says and quickly continues when she sees my surprise. "True Axians honour our ways even now. We cannot understand the burden of the First but be assured of my loyalty to the Alta Axians. I wish you well and will leave you to rest. My apologies Everly." And with that, she smiles and gently closes the door leaving me lost in my own thoughts.

Chapter 20

"You look at me with disappointment and it makes me angry."

"I look at you with sadness because you do not listen and think to disobey me."

"I do not disobey you! I am showing you a better way."

"You are not listening."

"This way could make it easier for you."

"Show me."

I watch as the younger warrior, my pride, my joy, stands, determined to prove their point. The ripples of light and balance roll towards the centre and I see the storm gather. It happens quickly but I am prepared and shield, so the explosion of fire is contained.

The young warrior roughly pulls at the light and balance again and again with the same result while I patiently watch and wait.

At last exhausted, frustrated and humiliated the young warrior stops for a minute. Head bowed and hands quiet I am curious to see their defeat.

"You do not listen..."

And within the space of a heartbeat, the young warrior turns in the air and lands behind me holding white fire at my throat.

"I listened and I obeyed but I also knew I could do better."

And as the young warrior stands behind me triumphantly, I change the air and the light and balance disappeared as to does the white light.

"You did not fight fairly."

"That is the lesson, little one. When you think you have won it can all be very quickly lost. Everything can be taken away from you in an instant and you can choose to fight or die. You can choose to fall or rise."

"I choose to rise." She tells me fiercely and my heart nearly breaks at her viciousness.

She is innocence and strength, power and peace, but she is also chaos and destruction...and may yet drown us in flames.

Chapter 21

It is quiet in the house as I lay in the dark thinking on my conversations with Hayes and then Abella's strange warning.

I am showered, clean and feed and am comfortably in a warm bed with clean sheets rather than against trees and take a moment to appreciate what may be a rarity in coming days. I have many miles of travel before I reach the border of Eos and can only then expect the help of the pAx.

Hayes is right, the battle was …different. My father surrendered within minutes of the first wave. We had allies at our backs that had not yet joined the fight. Our family always lead from the front and my father would signal as our strategy for the battle was applied. The enemies' fight was rough. It was group upon group, no single combat. They pushed up in waves towards us, but I cannot see a way they separated us so effectively.

The first wave ran towards us in three separate formations. I try to remember the faces of those I fought in the forest and at the tomb, to see if there is any pattern in their formations or fight strikes but I cannot find a strategy that would force my father to surrender. Although we fought within a void, he was powerful enough to survive.

I am deep in thought in the comfort of the soft bed when I feel the air suddenly vibrate. The vibration accelerates quickly, and sparks erupt brightly around the house before the light in the air splinters falling like rain.

The barrier! Someone has smashed through the protection around the house. I sit up alertly when I hear the quiet fall of feet outside. Someone is circling the house! I move silently, dressing quickly in my armour. I call my sword and open the bedroom door quietly walking through the house.

I look up and see Hayes walking towards me from the opposite end and watch as he signals that he hears the intruder as well. Together we take up defensive positions at both entrances and wait. I gently call the light and balance and hold it in the air around me. A significant strength is needed to shatter the barrier, which tells me this is not mere soldiers. This is a power that comes searching in the dark and I do not doubt what it seeks.

With Abella and the children, hopefully safely asleep the quiet is eerie as I wait for the next sign of movement. We wait patiently in the quiet and in this dark the peace seems to settle again. Silent minutes tick past and still no movement or sound from outside. It as if I imagined it and am thankful Hayes heard it too. I stand and search the air around me.

"Do not be fooled by those quiet footfalls. They do not ask for entry." Hayes quiet voice comes from across the room. "They shatter the barrier without a knock or introduction. Be ready this must be the darkness that comes searching for you because it seeks to destroy the light."

"It cannot be soldiers Hayes." I tell him certain "This is power, Hayes. I can feel it in the air."

" You are right, it is not many…. it is one." He answers and I can hear he is suddenly angry.

"Hayes? What do you mean 'one'?" But the world suddenly ripples in a very familiar way. I know the draw of this power, almost as well as I know my own but surely it is impossible. It cannot be, right?

Hayes stands and comes towards me. I can see he is worried.

"Be ready. We must defend ourselves." He speaks harshly, almost frustrated.

"I know who it is Hayes. I feel it. We will be ready for whatever comes with it, but this is no enemy." I reassure him excited.

I hear a flick against the front door and the shadows recede as the moonlight falls across the floor as it is opened. A tall dark figure steps quietly into the house and turns to close the door.

"Do not move brother." I hiss at him as I hold my sword to the back of his neck.

"Everly?" comes a familiar voice in the darkness.

"Are you alone?" I ask cautiously worried he might be a trap. "How many? How many come to capture me?" I ask him quickly, not trusting what I see and feel in front of me. He shakes his head, so I release him and wait for the rush of soldiers. Surely, they use him as a prisoner to capture me.

"Everly!" And he turns to greet me and grips me tightly, hugging me. "You must listen to me. We do not have time! I must tell you what comes..." He starts as he looks down the length of me as if checking I am still intact.

"Did you escape? You were captured? How do you live? Are you ok? What on earth are you doing in a little house on the east road?" I ask my brother. I am shocked speechless. He comes shattering barriers with no explanation. "How did you escape? Did you have help? Our armies are gone. The dragons are slaves. Our allies have disappeared. Yet here in the middle of nowhere my brother arrives." I look at him carefully, suspicion blooming in my mind. This is all too convenient. "Tell me, Tallon, where have you been? How did you find me?"

"Everly, you must listen! We do not have time for your suspicions. It's me! I have searched endlessly for you! Protected you. They keep me from you! I must tell you..." he looks at me and then realises we are not alone. He draws his sword and looks at me in shock as I step away from him. Hayes moves into the room alongside me and in the small house, space suddenly feels very cramped.

"Everly?" Hayes asks questionably although he does not take his eyes from my brother.

"Tallon how are you ...here?" I ask not knowing where to start. "It has been weeks since the battle."

"It doesn't matter Everly. I am here and that is what is most important. I come to take you to safety. You are not safe travelling Axis alone. I must get you to

Eos now." He tells me and steps closer, but it is the intensity of his gaze at Hayes that is unnerving me and maybe Hayes feels it too because he steps closer to Tallon as well.

"There is no safety for us Tallon, our world is destroyed, our family in tatters. There is nothing left but the Last. Go to the Aurelians. Save yourself." I plead with him.

"I will not turn from my vows, Everly. You are all that matters, and I can protect you. We must go to the pAx together. There is more at stake here than just the Last. I ask that you listen. Please. I come to save you from what hunts you. You cannot trust anyone and there are things we must discuss." He begs me reaching towards me as if desperate for me to hear him, but I step slightly towards Hayes.

His manner is strange. He looks frantic and afraid. I have not seen him so uncertain. I have thought about my brother every day since my father's death knowing our destiny. I thought our reunion would be at the Last. This is filled with suspicion and he looks at me with.... such sorrow! He looks at me as if the world is ending and he is trying to save me.

"Everly please it is me. They are trying to break you." he pleads, and I step towards him when I see his pain.

"Leave," Hayes tells him sharply suddenly stepping in front of me. "Leave now. You are not welcome here." He speaks quietly to protect the ears of the children who hopefully still sleep but my body stiffens with shock.

"No Hayes! He is my brother!" I whisper in the harsh night stepping past him to stand beside Tallon.

"I have no quarrel here. I only want my sister's safety. We will leave." He tells Hayes staring at me intently. "Everly, this man hides your light within his barrier. It is not for protection but to keep you contained."

"Tallon?" I ask and watch the aggression spark in his eyes.

"Everly, I would know the trail of your light anywhere." He answers quietly. "Just as you know mine; just as you know my loyalty to our Father. We need to move sister. We do not have much time and I fear your friend here has already betrayed you."

The tension in the small space is suffocating. My brother looks at me and I know he speaks the truth. He has always been loyal but before I can step away Hayes grabs my hand. Tallon raises his sword but it is too late.

"Why?" I whisper as my world spins and I feel his power hold me. I open my hand calling my sword. "You have betrayed us all." But I do not call the light quickly enough as Hayes grabs my wrist. I turn to shatter his hold, hoping I am wrong, but I feel the cold touch of metal wrap around my skin and look down I hear a click.

"TALLON!" I scream into the night and I jerk my wrist out of Hayes's hand to lift my sword and kill him but am blinded by a flash of white light and as the world around me suddenly moves and I brace for what comes next.

Chapter 22

"You must betray her in the battle."

"I understand."

"You must ensure my death. Do not let her save me. Save your people."

"They will think her weak." He agrees nodding and I watch the sadness grip at him.

"They must think we are destroyed, and they will be right. It will not be easy. Abrastos has seen what comes if it is not this way. She is strong and brave, but she is not invincible. She trusts so easily and finds hope where there is only death. We must force the light to rise, or it will never come."

"She will have my protection even as she struggles."

"We have planned for this day knowing the forces that gather to harm us, the darkness that comes to take what cannot be theirs. They will do all they can to break her."

"I know what you ask."

"It is no small request and you understand the enemy we face."

"I will not fail you just as you have never failed me. I will never forget the place you have given me, the guidance and care you have shown, against all odds we are here."

"Yes, my son...we are here. You may not have been born of me, but I have and will always consider you mine."

"I will not fail you."

"Be at her side, she will need you more than ever. Your place now is even more important. I have done everything I can to ensure you are ready."

I pull him close to me, holding my son for the last time as if he is a child. I feel the grip of his embrace as well and feel sadness and guilt. I am asking him to *betray the sister he loves to murder and kill in my name to save us all, to protect my greatest legacy and I know he will not fail me.*

Chapter 23

I hit the ground in battle position with my sword held high above my head. As the light quickly clears, I see soldiers surrounding me while I stand in the centre of what used to be my training circle in the centre courtyard of the royal house in the capital of Axis, Amara Arcelia which is lit up in dazzling white light most of which is focussed on the training circle I stand in.

I look around at the royal house, my home, savouring the familiar white bricks but it is forgotten at the sight of soldiers staring at me in anticipation from every window, ledge and wall.

They sit waiting as if they knew this moment was coming. Even in the darkness of night the lights of Amara seem tainted by the menace that lives within as they become quiet and I wait.

I can only guess the trouble that comes now and can only hope Tallon has the power to protect himself because I can do nothing to save him.

"WHO SUMMONS ME HERE?!!!" I scream angrily for I will not show them any weakness. "FACE ME, YOU COWARDS!!!!" I scream at them and am pleased to see hesitation. I am scared. I am heartbroken. But mostly I am angry that I was so foolishly tricked! This is not defeat! This is a betrayal of friendship and loyalty. To think I believed the kindness and care I was shown by Hayes. I am foolish and naïve I am! How stupid to believe in Az.

I turn, slowly aware that an attack could come from any side. I am in the courtyard of what was not very long ago my home, but I might as well be in an alternate reality! The area has been stripped of all banners of the First family and the starkness of the light bricks is all that shows…. except for the darkness of their uniforms. I recognize the colours that surround me, knowing that darkness of black we battled against and lost.

Right across the huge centre courtyard, the huge space is filled with soldiers who are gathered a dozen and deeper around the perimeter of white chalk that outlines this training circle. This is the training circle I grew up learning combat in and I am well used to the fray than happens here!

I look carefully around me to see if I can spot the traitorous Hayes. Hatred and rage fill me as I think of how he has used me, gained information about the battle and our formation but it means little now with my father dead and my brother.... I pray quickly to Axis to guard him if only so I can find him again.

Now, if only the gutless fool Hayes has the courage to face me, I will run my sword through his black heart when I'm finished with these fools who think to circle me like a prize!

If this is the battle to take back my world then I will embrace it!

"FIGHT ME!!! FIGHT ME NOW!!! COME BRING YOUR DARKNESS!! LET US SEE IF ANY OF YOU ARE GOOD ENOUGH TO BE FIRST!!!" I call out, smiling with my usual battle viciousness!

I am fed; rested and healthy so there is no better time than now to let them feel the end of my sword! I watch as they ready themselves. There is order in this chaos although they seem to want me to believe otherwise and as I turn within the circle showing them the shine of my sword.... they come.

They come towards me timidly at first, as if testing me, working out my strategy and I let them come. I only give what little I need to teach them fear. I move instinctively, defending and fighting, and I do not have to wait long before the real fight begins. They charge towards me in never-ending dozens all at once and rise to meet them showing them why I am feared.

I adjust my stance over and over as I battle a never-ending stream of these foolish soldiers. I was raised for this, trained for this, born to defeat those who thought to take my world. This only fuels my strength. The blood and sweat coat my armour but vanishes as it touches the pliant metal giving it strength and their deaths at my feet gives me fuel to fight on.

With careful blows I slowly push them back towards the perimeter of the circle, my sword moving in endlessly arches and stabs. I see the stone edge covering in chalk that surrounds the sand inside the circle and step again towards it, to take the fight to them. I lean forward as I reach the stones, always fighting, always focused but then without warning an invisible force grips my wrist where that dreaded torque sits and throws me back into the centre of the circle and I understand. I am trapped in the circle! I can only survive within the perimeter, but I have fought in worst places and at least the aggressive movement of throwing me into the centre each time can be used to my advantage.

Time and time again I battle them to the edge, killing their comrades, their dead littering the ground, disposable in their numbers before reaching the perimeter where I am thrown back once more. The edge becomes relief as I fight endlessly forwards. The throwback to the centre becomes a short reprieve before they attack again. It is endless, if not sustainable but what choice do, I have!

I cannot maintain this pace without light and balance and although I have tried over and over to pull the power towards me it has been blocked and it becomes a pointless waste of energy to try. I have no doubt this metal at my wrist is to blame but regardless, I cannot falter.

I use the perimeter as a break between fighting, a second of reprieve before it begins again. I start to hone this pattern and maintain this rhythm focused on the fight when without warning red hot agony explodes across my back and everything.... every breath.... every thought.... every movement is rendered helpless against the searing pain.

It is pure fire, a thousand hot needles across my skin, and for that second, I cannot function at all, let alone fight! I remain upright in the face of this agony and as I turn towards this fresh hell I watch the soldiers recede quickly to the edge of the circle dragging the dead with them, clearing the circle as silence reigns and I turn to face the monster, hooded in black, who destroyed my family.

"Everly Anise Signa Regla Mas Alta, daughter of the recently deceased First, the revered Alta Axian, welcome to my city." This fool tells me proudly while holding his whip as if to make the point, but I cannot see his face "Get on your knees and show the next King of Axis your allegiance!!" he bellows, announcing his great victory, and I smile viciously at him. He walks the perimeter of the circle as the soldiers cheer him on and I watch him carefully.

"Show me your face so I can look in your eyes as I kill you!" I boldly demand, "You are great enough and strong enough to defeat my father, yet you hid from a mere woman? If you want this world, to be King of this world, then fight me for it!" I tell him but still, he does not come any closer.

"You do not need to see my face to concede to me. You only need to bow in the dirt and declare your failure to Axis." The monster tells me as he readies his whip once more.

"Only a coward would stand on the edge of a circle announcing his greatness rather than prove himself in a fair fight."

"You are no mystery to us Everly and I certainly have no need to fight you." This monster laughs. "We know the truth of your light and balance, your strengths and weaknesses. You are nothing anymore. You have no one to save you. No one to stand at your back. No allies. Not even a single Axian or Aurelian has come to your aid. It is finished for you. All that is required of you now is to concede. I have already beaten your father, taken your world and captured you. I have no need to prove anything. It is done. I only need those words of concession to flow from your lips and then the universe will know who wields their fate from this moment on."

"You may have defeated my father. You may have captured me. You may even stand at the top of the royal house and scream to the world you are their king, but you will never hear those words you need from me." I tell him stubbornly but as I speak the whip snakes out across the distance between us and I am silenced by the pain.

As the soldiers in the circle smiling gleefully, I understand...there is no battle here; no fight for victory there is only torture, only pain, only the chance to watch me suffer.

My chest heavy with this reality I know I cannot die this death so I lift my head and scream to Axis for only she may be able to save me from the misery that comes.

"It is pointless screaming Everly. There is no one left to rescue you. No one coming to save you! Certainly, no mighty First is here to stand beside you. There is just you...the last Alta Axian.... and me...the next ruler of the realms." this monster tells me.

"You want to be First then at least earn your place and fight me. It is surely not much to ask surrounded by the safety of your soldiers and my powers gone." I respond and I am surprised when he laughs.

"There was never going to be a 'fair fight' Everly. This is war." He sneers at me.

"Then you know it is not that easy. You cannot stand up and demand to be First. It is a legacy.... our family..."

"Ah yes, the mighty Alta Axians. The First family of Axis. Do you think those legends are sacred? I know the line of succession. I know the truth of the four families of Axis. I know the four families struggle against the darkness but where are your pillars now Everly? Those mighty four who are meant to save us all?" he spits at me cutting me off. "Power and control are all that matters. Strength and knowledge are all it will take to rule this world." And he walks the circle perimeter while the soldiers retreat a little to give him space.

I remember my conversations with Az who has told me I am the only one powerful enough to save us, but did Az know our enemy knew the truth? I can easily defeat this fool but know he comes only to torment me not kill me. He comes for power. He comes to bring pain and suffering. He knows he cannot face me in the Last and I know he cannot defeat me unless I concede. I see for the first time his power as my enemy. He would rule our world with tyranny and pain, and I cannot let my world suffer regardless of the cost.

This band at my wrist makes it impossible for me to use my greatest strengths and for the first time feel the trickle of doubt bloom in the formidable face of torture and how I have underestimated treachery. I glare down at that thin metal circle angrily it is the only possible way I can lose and in that second, I look away, he strikes at me again. The crippling sting of spikes wrap around my upper thigh before scrapping their release and I stumble forward barely holding my feet.

"Bow before me, Everly! Bow at my feet like your father did when he knelt in the mud begging for your pitiful life!" he roars at me, but I ignore his taunts. I steady my breath and hold myself up, moving to stand in combat position again, showing him my sword refusing to let him succeed even in this pain.

The whip flicks out and towards me once more and I move aside to let it wrap around my sword. I have misjudged his strike and feel the pain as it scraps but a few strands across my face. The agony explodes and I quickly reach with my armour to wipe away the blood that begins to flow. He lifts his arm and in the space of a heartbeat, I am whipped twice more across my back and legs and fall to my knees.

"This will be your life Everly...every day." He calls to me as I struggle to breathe "Until you concede to me, I will keep you alive just enough so I can enjoy your suffering. I don't need you to be healthy nor fed. Nor can you escape. You can try to fight but this will be your end. The end of your line. The end of your father's legacy. I can promise you this!"

The pain is unbearable. With the light and balance gone my armour is soaking the blood as fast as it flows but does not seem to be strengthening and I am weakening rapidly.

"Take her sword." I hear him call and feel movement as they come and take the only defence, I have but I can do nothing to stop them. He thinks I am defenceless, defeated but it is clear when he thinks to take my sword that this fool does not know the truth of my power and as they carry it across the perimeter of the circle I smile as I watch it disappear into the light.

"I will enjoy this Alta Axian. Thought you were invincible, didn't you? The righteous Solomon and his treasured daughter. I have waited a long time for this moment, for our time. Our moment you both die at my feet." And I hear him laugh but I keep my head down.

The crowd moves away, and I am left within the circle. I stay with my head down on my hands and knees. I cannot sit as deep gouges bleed from my back to my knees in throbbing waves of pain, so I stay quiet waiting for whatever agony comes next. With the crowd gone I am left to swim in pain. My misery is bone deep as I repeat one name over and over. He hasn't heard my whispers as I call for Az.

My brother cannot help me. I have no allies left. There is only the one person who has saved me twice and if he cannot help me my doom is inevitable.

"Food." I hear from the perimeter of the circle and see a plate and cup placed just within the stones. I crawl over and quickly eat the bread and drink. It is little but I only have to stay alive. I only have to be strong enough to survive. I only have to survive but while he lets me live, I will never give him what he needs. I know the pillars come even now. I must have faith in Axis that this is true and only then can Axis herself decide my fate.

I am a prisoner in this circle and spend a cold night half laying on my shoulder, the rest of my body too damaged to rest and too painful for any pressure from the ground. My sleep is scarce and broken in waves of pain as the fresh agony of this torment continues. My armour does not seem to be repairing itself or my body and as I wait my agony growing along with my fear.

The warm light the next morning is like pure liquid gold against my aching body and as I hear a crowd come towards me, I use what little strength I have to rise to my feet. I am Everly Anise Signa Regla Mas Alta, the daughter of the First family of Axis, Right Hand of my father, Alta Axian, and not for anyone will I be found lying in the dirt defeated.

I am my father's daughter. I can endure the worst because I am the best of my father's training. I am the strongest of all Axian soldiers and I will die as I have lived...standing tall facing my enemies! I lift my head defiantly and see the surprise in his soldier's faces as I grin at him viciously.

But this stranger, this darkness, this terror to my people hides his face from me, and before I can even demand he fight me, the torture begins. He whips me for hours until I am bleeding and crawling and then I am given a small reprieve before it begins again.

Each time I rise and refuse to concede, and his anger grows. His demands to bow are screamed at me with such hatred. If only he could kill me and be done with it.

By the third day, I am slipping in and out of consciousness and so his tactics change. I am given better food; a medic tends my wounds and he when he sees the extent of my injuries it is clear he cannot sustain the constant whipping, so my reprieves are longer. I stay down and don't move to gather as much strength as possible in these moments. My body is battered beyond recognition and I am aware that escape is slim, but I am determined.

It is our royal medic that tends to me with kindness. I smile at him slightly when I see the pain and sadness in his eyes.

"Rise, Everly. Rise for us all child. Do this for Axis. Save us all." He whispers to me over and over; each time he tends to me he gently whispers his prayer.

I think of my father in the moments of greatest agony. I could imagine my father's explosive reaction at the thought of me tortured and it comforts me to know he is not here to see this. He would weep at the sight of me as I imagine with the swelling to my face and head, I am almost unrecognisable.

I am so badly injured they leave me alone for a day and night and other then the medic rolling me over I do not move. I cannot bear the agony that sweeps in burning waves across my body. I cannot breathe more than shallow pants as my back and front are both torn to pieces. My armour is shredded and peeling back and has long stopped absorbing my blood. I am weak and can do nothing more than watch the slow crimson drips as they pool in the sand. I have screamed and screamed in pleading waves. I have begged Axis for help until I can no longer speak scared, she has forgotten me.

The next day they gather and discuss my torn and broken state and I listen. They wonder if they have overestimated me and that I am weak and pitiful. They laugh and I feel the poke of swords as they make jokes over my condition, yet I live. Living is all my world needs for now and I smile.

I have lost count of the days and nights I have laid in this circle but today is enough. I will end this either way. I will not be tortured endlessly or condone the constant ridicule by this enemy. I will not lie on the ground waiting for death to arrive anymore. They will not let me die and they will not let me live so I will make the impossible choice for them. They have left me just enough, just enough for me to try the impossible, I hope.

When they surround me the next day, I am ready. I will stand and look at this faceless cowardly enemy who stands at the edge of the circle. I hear the gasps of shock when I slowly, painful get to my feet, my head high and turn to face him.

"Coward." is all I say through swollen, shredded lips and shattered teeth and I am happy to see his hand lift knowing his anger must flow. I brace myself knowing I will have only one chance to save myself or die and stand ready but surprisingly the whip does not move. Instead, he places on the ground some distance away before coming back to the edge of the circle.

"Concede Everly. I vow to give you peace. Concede for the inevitable and I will ensure you live a long and comfortable life." his voice gentle as his tactics change but I only remain standing in the face of his offer. "Let the medic help you and together we will eat and drink and plan the future of our realms." He continues but I do not respond. "I do not want to harm you anymore when I know it can be better if we work together. Consider the future Everly. We could ensure prosperity. You could control the light and balance and open the gates to the realms. I would ensure you have a good life, peace for Axis." He kneels slightly as he finishes as if his offer is true and I bow my head as if I am considering it.

I can feel the change in emotion around the circle. It is as if they are excitedly anticipating my acceptance. I raise my head looking directly into the darkness of the hood and smile before I spit on the ground.

"PARA AXIS!" I shout into the sky as loudly as possible. I stand defiantly in the centre of this circle of hell and let the rage burn in my every word. "Never!" Is all I say.

He does not react other than to stand abruptly. He calls for his whip, but his hood does not move from me. My attempt to smile at him is pitiful but I see he gets the message when he roars with anger.

Within seconds the whip flies towards me, those thousand threads of agony ready to shred my skins even more but instead of moving as he expects me to do, I stand still. The nasty coils snap as they reach me, I grab at those wicked strands wrapping them around my already shredded skin ignoring the pain that coils up my arm and, in that instant, I jerk the whip violently towards me bringing him into the circle. He stumbles forward struggling to keep his feet at the unexpected jerk and I am there to meet him. They have no knowledge of my ability to call my sword and before any can react, I kick his knees from under him and lift my hand. As the talisman moves across my broken body the blessed heat of it soothes my arm before it moulds into my palm, I call my sword and hold its blade across his neck. His whip is still wrapped around my other arm and he can do nothing other than kneel at my feet. I smile as the world outside the circle stops for a second before all hell breaks loose.

"Release me." I hiss at him through the pain and I feel him tense under me. He thinks me weak and is considering his options, so I pull the sword tighter, letting him feel the strength in my body behind him and watch his blood starts to flow down his front. Soldiers surround me with swords drawn but I ignore their demands to release him.

"STOP!" he yells but he is too late to negotiate when I am ready to kill.

"Release me." I hiss into his ear again as I push him down further towards the bloody dirt. "Who is in the dirt now you coward? At my feet."

I can hear the panic of his soldiers that are clearly worthless without their leader. I reach to rip the hood from his face but pause when I feel him grapple for my wrist and brace for a fight, instead, he reaches the torque and within seconds it is gone from my wrist.

"You may be able to leave the circle, but you will be hunted and captured before you leave the city." Is all he says, and I push him out of the circle but not before cutting him cleanly across his neck. They flock to help him, and I can see the blood flows as he stumbles but I know the cut was not deep. I stumble back as the light and balance hit me in waves.

A strange power wraps around me trying to stop the inevitable and I look back at the hooded monster with rage.

"You are nothing but a coward and a fool!" I spit at him as I rise, and he steps back into the circle.

"You will never leave Everly. It is over. Concede!" He whispers at me angrily while those around him smother his neck desperate to save their pitiful would-be king.

He faces me and I am sure he watches carefully thinking he can stop whatever my next move will be.

"Never." is all I whisper back through broken lips and the rage erupts across his face.

My strength is fading but with the torque gone the light and balance now flows into me. I draw it to me in shaky breaths focusing on my father's talisman as a chant for help, as I plead with my world to save me. I throw my head back and scream into the skies for Axis once more knowing only she can save me. The talisman burns warmly on my hand. My blood still flows, and I can feel it coat the talisman and the handle of my sword. I pull the power to me roughly, uncaring of the ripples it leaves and focus it on my hand holding my sword.

"NO!!!" he screams at me seeing the light break through the talisman and steps into the circle, striding towards me, uncaring of his injury but I do not look away from him. I can only think of Az at that moment and scream his name to the skies. He is all that can save me. As my legs crumble under me bight white flames rise up from my sword engulfing me and the world around disappears.

Chapter 24

"She is our greatest hope, Solomon." I tell him sadly knowing I do not have much time.

He sighs and rubs his hand across his face. "It is only us in this room who know the truth and I do not want to do this without you. Even you can see it emerging and I am afraid I am not strong enough alone."

"Yes, the truth of her origins will always be questioned but what we did was right. Do not be afraid. Only you can guide her because only she can save us."

"I need you." He pleads with me and it breaks my heart to deny him.

"No, you need her, Axis needs her. I have done all I can for Axis. We are surrounded on all sides and the darkness rises. I must bleed to ensure the ground beneath holds when it comes."

"We can hold it together! No one will question it, especially now it has been established by the pAx. There is no doubt given the clear lineage and Tallon knows."

"Tallon is loyal and loves. It is his right to rise alongside our future. Trust him Solomon even with this and know I have been grateful for our life together regardless of the challenges. I have always accepted the truth, accepted her but this must be done. It is the power of the Aurelians that will give her the chance to succeed, the chance to save us all."

"I disagree. It could be our future. I would rather have you on my side in this future than against me. This could so easily turn against us. She could tear Axis apart! We are stronger in partnership!"

"We both know what needs to be done. It has begun. She is your legacy and Tallon is mine. It is a bond between two that cannot be broken, I have ensured it."

"She has the power to destroy us all Sidra! She could take everything! It would be her right."

"Then we must ensure the future is kind that she grows surrounded by love and protection, that she is compassionate and understands her place."

"I vow it to you. She will be our greatest legacy. I do this for Axis and the future of the realms, that is all that matters. I will not kneel here and ask the impossible of you. I will not relive this evermore. It is done. The darkness gathers strength and we no longer have the power to hold it. Go in peace Sidra. Para Axis." And I watch as he leans towards me, kissing my cheek before walking away.

I look at the light that streams through the window knowing she calls me. I have loved and been loved, I have lived knowing this is my last, my destiny and I sink slowly, peacefully and with hope knowing my end is her beginning accepting my death with a final breath.

Chapter 25

The flame dissipates as I crumple in a heap unable to stand any longer and cry out in agony. I lay huddled on the ground unable to do any more. I have no sense of what surrounds me, only pain. Only the darkness of agony that shuts out light and drowns in terror. My breathing harsh and desperate, my body shredded beyond any feeling. I am numb. I cannot feel the light and balance. I cannot call for help or save myself. It is fear and finality; despair and frustration and I know without any doubt I am dying.

I don't know the minutes or hours that passed before gentle arms wrap around me.

"Tallon...." I whisper and sink into his embrace.

"Everly. Everly. It is Az. I am here." He tells me over and over as if desperate to offer me comfort when he knows there is only pain. When he knows I want to run away from him as I beg Axis for my brother in hushed pleading whispers.

I feel the gentle movement of running as I am carefully carried. I sob with fear knowing he has found me. I sob with agony at the state I am in, at the bitterness of betrayal, pity blooming, all ego gone in the face of my failure and at the fear for my brother.

"I am sorry, so sorry Everly. I couldn't get to you. I could not reach you. Everly." He coos to me constantly as if I believe him while cutting the remnants of my armour away. It is all too damaged. I am too damaged. My armour could not repair itself without light and balance and now it is too destroyed, ripped in shreds.

"It..is...too...late. It's...over...." I mumble at him through the pain knowing he cannot help me now anyway.

My body is a mash of torn flesh and rivers of blood and still, he tells me how sorry he is before gently touching my head pleading with me to sleep. I needed

Tallon; only he has the power to save me. I screamed his name for hours and now I cannot fight any longer. I have no strength to battle this pain.

"It cannot be over, or Axis is lost." He tells me his voice filled with violence and fury and I curl away from more rage.

"You...never...came...betrayed..." I whisper "I ...need..."

"I am here now." His voice quiet as he desperately tries to save me "Sleep Everly, know that I will keep you safe." Is all he says as I see the pain in his eyes as he looks over my battered body.

He gently kisses my forehead again reassuring me I am safe and telling me to find some peace in the inevitable darkness of my unconscious mind. I know I cannot fight or flee, so finally accepting the inevitable I close my eyes sinking into the darkness of sleep hoping that for a little while it can bring me a small measure of relief.

I wake slowly waiting for the spears of pain to come, for the torture to begin. It is when I do not feel the sand of the circle beneath me that I remember Az came.

"Az?" I call out carefully remembering my injuries as the stiffness grabs at my skin and I try to move as little as possible.

"Everly. I am here. You are safe. Rest." he tells me gently as he comes to sit beside me.

"You cannot save me this time Az. The damage..." I whisper, my face aching from the swelling that still remains.

"You will heal. I vow it." He answers gentle brushing the hair away from my face and my eyes stay on him until sleep takes me again.

I wake to screams, scrambling, waiting for the strike of the whip. The pain! My whole body screams with the agony of it and then a weight crushes me, holding me still, keeping me immobile.

"You will open your wounds, Everly. Stop" his quiet voice whispers next to my ear "You must lay still, please. You are safe here. I promise this. I will not let them take you again."

"Stay with me." I plead with him weak for protection, security when I am so vulnerable.

"I will stay if only to make sure you do no further damage." And the peace his assurance gives me makes the tears split from my eyes.

"Do not cry, Everly. Sleep and know that I watch over you." He tells me moving to sit in the chair beside me.

"You betrayed me," I whisper. "You sent me to Hayes, to be captured."

"I know what Hayes has done." He tells me "I tried to save you and I could not reach you no matter how I tried. I arrived at the house, but it was empty." He hangs his head as if frustrated.

"Am I dying?" I ask quietly.

"Not today Everly... but it was close." He answers taking my hand. The warmth of his palm against mine is comforting. I mentally check my injuries and am not surprised to feel he has healed the worst of them. I lay naked under a sheet on a bed and look around in surprise. I am not outside as I expected but, in a room, lying in an unfamiliar bed.

"Where am I?" I ask.

"Safe." Comes his answer.

"Whose bed do I lay in?" I ask knowing how evasive he can be with his replies.

"We are at a friend's house, a medical man." He answers simply and I can do nothing but trust I am safe. "I needed extra help to ensure you survived Everly. I could not save you alone. Your injuries.... were extensive." And I can see this has not been easy for him. He looks frustrated, agitated, and even angry but only speaks to me kindly.

"Lay next to me for a minute Az. Let me feel as safe as I sleep." And he looks at me in surprise before smiling sadly.

"Another time Everly, you are still too badly injured and need to heal. These lacerations across your body need to be carefully tended to.... the damage to your body was extensive. What was the torture that could possibly have torn your armour to shreds?" he asks quietly as if he is afraid of my reaction.

"He had a whip of some sort... with spikes on the ends," I tell him remembering the pain they brought.

"Who?" he asks, and my tears flow endlessly.

"A monster. My enemy. The man who leads those dressed in darkness. He hides in a hood and would not show his face." I whisper angrily but if he is shocked, I cannot see it beyond my tears. He takes my hand and holds it tenderly shaking his head.

"Did you recognize him? Did he tell you what he wanted?" He asks me gently but seeing my distress he leaves those questions unanswered.

"How often did he whip you?" he asks.

"Hours at a time...for days." I tell him and more tears slip from my eyes "I thought I would die. I couldn't save myself Az. He would not fight me. They only wanted to torture me until I conceded. He knew things that should have been impossible...about the Four families and the pillars. I am scared Az, scared that I have underestimated this enemy." The words tumble out, but I do not expect any answers.

He bows his head as if ashamed. "Your screams went for hours Everly...why didn't you just concede...Was the pain worth it? Was your life? Did he offer you more?" But he can't go on and grips my hand to his chest as if pleading for my forgiveness.

"Az....I cannot concede.... it is not that easy." I tell him sadly.

"Why can't you concede? Surely being First is not worth the agony of this pain?" he asks quietly, and he turns my hand and kisses the back of it gently waiting for me to continue.

"Does Hayes live?" I ask changing the subject and holding my breath waiting for the answer.

"It is unclear." He tells me "There was no one in the house when I arrived. Some signs of a struggle... but Hayes and Abella were gone. Tell me what happened Everly? Did you fight Hayes?" He asks.

My body stiffens as I remember Hayes and Az were friends. Maybe he does not know what Hayes has done so I do not mention Tallon's presence at the house. "I travelled down the east road and found Hayes as you told me too. They were kind...Hayes and Abella. They shared food and stories, cleaned my clothes and offered me a bed for the night, and I could not resist. It was late into the night when I felt the pull of power. It rippled across the room. Hayes and I prepared to defend his home. We stood together in the darkness waiting and then...well, everything happened in a blur. Hayes grabbed at my wrist and then I shifted and found myself in the training circle at home." I trail away shaking my head as if I've forgotten the details of what happened. I watch Az carefully. I want to know I can trust him, but I cannot see any emotion on his face.

"It is understandable you cannot remember the details of what happened at the house but hopefully you will remember more in time." He tells me as if to reassure me.

"I hope so." I agree quietly.

"You are alive and safe and that is all that matters for now. We can talk more tomorrow. Sleep Everly, rest. I will be here when you awake." He tells me and I stay very still. I am quiet as I watch him gently smooth my hair back from my face. Until I am healed there is nothing I can do so I close my eyes and lay quietly before the weakness of my body forces me to succumb to sleep once again.

Az checking my wounds wakes me. He is focused on cleaning and redressing.

"Are they not healing?" I ask seeing the concern in his face.

"They are. It is just taking more time. There must have been some kind of substance on the whip that prevented your armour from re-sealing, and it is also making your healing slower. Each day your injuries improve Everly. The world continues to turn while you breathe so give yourself time, let your body recover. You will be back in the fight again soon enough."

"Az, I need to ask you something...how well did you know Hayes."

"Well." He answers although he does not look at me.

"Are you even listening?" I ask annoyed that he seems unconcerned by the world around us.

"Of course, I am." He says looking at me with a frown across his face.

"Hayes and I spent time discussing the battle and the families. He asked a lot of questions."

"Yes. Everly" he looks at me, "He asked questions. Isn't it normal to be curious about such an event? It was perhaps the first encounter with your family for Hayes." He answers logically.

"But his knowledge of the families was..." I begin but stop when I see Az staring at me intently.

"Was what?" he asks, "What did Hayes say?"

"He said he was a son of Xiana." I tell him and as I watch he visibly relaxes.

"Well, that is a relief and would explain his knowledge. The Xianans number in the many hundreds of thousands."

"Are you a son of Xiana?" I ask curiously.

"I am a son of Axis." Is all he says firmly.

"The hooded man must be more powerful than any of us realised. Perhaps he was related to Hayes..." I stop when I see his face.

"Yes, Everly the hooded man is undoubtedly powerful, but your father was not the only powerful person in this universe and the hooded man, as you call him, defeated him, the strongest Axian. He captured the dragons now, somehow, he has managed to capture you, all of which should be impossible, so yes, he is very powerful. As for the legacy of the four families is of legends and where there is power there is always someone willing to take it. Who knows what his reasons for this attack on Axis? Maybe your father thought himself absolute? Untouchable? Regardless of why surely it is possible for times to change. Is it fair that your family alone be given the power of Axis? Not many people understand that the rule of the First is not a role of dominance or greedy it is a lifelong commitment to service and sacrifice but each of the other foundation families has served and sacrificed. The only reason the hooded man would try to force you to concede rather than kill you could be because he may not want to hurt you. The torque was specially made for you which means he must have known how to null your powers without harming you and the spikes in the whip destroyed your armour but did not kill you." He finishes and a snort at him.

"I am only alive because I saved myself." I tell Az "I could feel his hatred and rage. He chose to crush me, torture me before offering peace. Those are the actions of dominance, not kindness."

I watch him as he quietly finishes with the dressings on my legs leaving me wallowing in my thoughts. He is right. The hooded man may be powerful, and my father may have thought himself untouchable but Axis nor the realms cannot survive without the four families and the fact that monster knew their importance bothers me more than any torture.

Very few, except within the families themselves, know the value and the importance of their place within the realms. Our family Alta rules as the first family because we have the power of balance and light both of which are needed for the realms to survive. The second family Xiana are the givers of life and governance. A family who only produces sons except for a pillar of life, which is always a girl. The third family Ihava defend and protect the realms. They are the shield and the spear. And the fourth family of Aesi have the gift of sight.

Each family produces one pillar each time a First Alta is born, and these are protected above all else. Each pillar critical to the foundation of light and balance.

But this is also the time those that seek power and control just as the hooded man does rise. They think Axis weak and vulnerable, but they are mistaken. You cannot just take what can only be given and this is where the darkness and the hooded man will fail because I will never concede.

"He is not worthy," I say quietly. "He is not powerful enough to control the light and balance," I say aloud.

"Perhaps. There are few that have the power of Axis and not as you do but there are other powers that can balance these. This man has tortured you and hurts you. He has a powerful army at his back and controls Amara. He will find you again so and will likely not stop until you give him what he needs." He sadly looks at me. "Turn over Everly so I can do your back." And I turn in the quiet and close my eyes trying to work past the lump in my throat.

"It has always about the fight, isn't it Az? This life, mine, it was never going to be easy."

"To hold our universe together. No, not easy which is why Axis herself created the four foundation families. Most would crumble at the torture you endured not stand boldly in a circle challenging a monster for more. It sets you apart, this fight in you, it is your birthright and yes, and it is not in your nature to surrender. Even as much as you have begged Axis, you can do not less than face what comes for you head on...this destiny you worry about, regardless of the pain it will bring. It may be less about the fight and more about survival Everly; for this is not a fight for your life this is a fight that affects us all, billions! Without the light and balance, we are all doomed, none of us can survive unless you rise or concede so you need to be sure of your actions and do what needs to be done even if it means sacrificing yourself or conceding to an army that could destroy Axis to save us all."

"I fear for our future Az. For the violence and destruction that brings darkness and doubts. In all of this, there is only me the last Alta Axian that stands in their way."

"I am here Everly, you are not alone. You will rise; you will do what is needed for Axis. You can do no less."

"I need Tallon," I tell him hearing the truth of his words but still doubting my abilities for a task beyond my own comprehension. My father was all of this and so much more and I feel like I am failing for even trying to follow in his footsteps.

"Your brother? He has not been seen since the battle! So, you want what...a friend? An ally? Someone to do the work for you. You never needed one before Everly. Tallon was always second to you. You always fought alone even surrounded by all of these people you saw as your protection. You were always different. Stronger. Your brother saw this. Your father knew it. You felt it in every situation. Tallon has abandoned you, left you alone. He fled the battle and did nothing to save you. Is this who you want at your side?"

"How long before I am healed?" I ask, not wanted him to see how angry I am he could talk this way. He has forgotten the honour of our family and the strength in those bonds. I know Tallon.

"Maybe two weeks."

"How long has it been?"

"Three weeks." He answers continuing when he sees the shock on my face "Healing you was not an easy task Everly. Every cut on your body contained part of your armour as well as the poison that destroyed it. It has been a long and painstaking process to remove every trace. Together with your injuries, it was always going to be challenging regardless of your own healing abilities."

"And my armour is completely ruined I'd imagine?"

"Yes...but replaceable." He tells me smiling kindly at me.

"Az, what do you do when you don't know if you have the courage to rise? When you don't know how to be stronger? When the footsteps you follow in seem too big. When you've lost everything and just want to.... I don't need the fight that keeps finding me. I long for my father's advice. I need to know why? I believed in my father above everything else. I know Axis will have to choose a First, but it is not necessarily my destiny."

"Ah but Everly you will never know your destiny until you have to fight for it. The daughter of the first family of Axis. I'm afraid you are wrong. You cannot be born with such powerful skills and choose to never use them. You cannot be granted such talent and gifts and keep them only for your own purposes. You will fight because you care because it is no less than your responsibility! You care about people, you love your world, you can do nothing but honour your father and whether you agree or not this is your destiny. It is not in you to let people down, to walk away from a challenge or be anything other than stubborn and determined and fight for those who need your protection. You are allowed moments of doubt. And you are entitled to think poorly of yourself every now and again, but it will not change who you are or what you need to become."

"I need to get to Eos Nevaeh as soon as possible. This delay leaves the light and balance in disarray. The pAx will provide safety and shelter until the Last and whoever this crazy fool is in the hood cannot force it without their consent. " I tell him, and he doesn't react at all. I move my body carefully to sit. I know he watches making sure I do no further injury.

"I agree. At least you would be safe from capture. I can see you waiting for a reaction, but you will see nothing from me but relief as I too want this war at an end." He looks at me and gently smiles.

"I want peace Az."

"Peace...like the hooded man offered you?" he says as if he ponders it solemnly. "I would guess after a lifetime of war it is understandable, but would peace bore you after a while? It is in the fight that your vicious grin appears and your eyes light with fire. Would you compromise with your enemy to ensure peace for us all?"

"War is familiar, honest, but this battle is overwhelming, at times too big for me. Armies and allies and soldiers, not individuals fight a war, but this is no ordinary war. This is a fight for our future, and I know it will require everything I am. I know this Az; I have heard these words from my father repeatedly! But I will never compromise. I will never concede, and I certainly will not surrender." I tell him looking at him to ensure he sees my resolve.

"And when you face the impossible? When no one needs you? You cannot stand someplace feeling overwhelmed or worrying Everly. Neither Axis nor the realms need weakness. We need strength and leadership so choose who you are going to be or do as the hooded man says and concede to someone willing to fight for us all!"

"No one, not even those with power can hold the light and balance. I am the Alta Axian, First, a guardian of light and balance. But who are you Az? I wonder at your place ...your need to defend my enemy."

He chuckles as if I am a child who has said something amusing.

"I am a child of Axis." He answers again and looks at me as if he is amused by the question. "I only ask these questions as your friend. We face an uncertain future, Everly... all of us and you must be certain it is a war you want."

"It is a war that comes to me. I know my place in this world. I know what Axis needs from me, but you never answer my questions about yours. I have a right to know who you are." But I stop when he grabs my arm and silences my next words.

"Do you Everly? Do you know your place? It was pretty bloody clear you enjoyed your place in this world the whole time you were the precious little princess, right? People at your beck and call, every wish granted." I jerk my arm away shocked at the anger in his words. "Was it clear in defeat also?? When there was no one left to save you and you fell to your knees? Does your fate suddenly change when you lose? Does destiny abandon you when you give up? Where would you be now if I had not saved you...twice?"

"Can doubts come Az when every part of your body has been shredded into pieces and you realise how fragile this life really is? Am I not allowed to speak of my fears with a friend?" I whisper at him angrily.

"You do not see yourself. The power, the abilities you possess and beyond any expectations. You are extraordinary Everly. Your father knew it, I can clearly see it and I have no doubt the hooded man is very much aware of it as well. You should never have survived the battle or these injuries, never mind the length of time you endured them. You have always been extraordinary. I see the truth of all the tales told of the daughter without equal so decide. Axis knows you are extraordinary and maybe it is time you knew it too."

"Yes, I suspect I am... extraordinary. Extraordinarily lost, extraordinarily tired and extraordinarily alone. This is not just about me, Az. I watch the impossible defeat. I was captured easily, tortured without compassion. This monster of darkness wearing his hood has an army of thousands behind him. If he is willing to go to those lengths to be First, then how can I alone stop him? Do you hear what I am saying? I don't know whether any of this is even possible!" I tell him gesturing to my body and the damage that has been done. I look across the wounds and bandages that crisscross my body sadly. They are the scars and the marks I will now carry with me always. All that is left is a marked, mangled, girl with no allies, no help and barely a throne to defend.

These marks remind me angrily of everything I have lost. They have taken everything from me. Every word that they spit in my face. Every time that whip brutally scrapped across my skin, tearing it to pieces. It is as though I have lost the love this world sheltered me in. I have lost the confidence to trust Axis and scream her name in battle. The dust rises and the balance continues to unsettle, and I feel it. I feel it in my core. The weakness, the dustiness of the light, even the unbalance in my soul but I am struggling to find the strength to rise.

"It is getting worse. The unbalance. Can you feel it Az? Does it pull at your insides?" I ask not wanting to find misery in this conversation.

"Yes," he replies with his usual briefness and if he is surprised but the change in conversation, he doesn't show it.

"How long do you think before we are lost?"

"No one knows. It is not a certainty, not yet. You have triggered the pillars so who knows what happens now but there will be a First or we all perish. There is no other way, no other option, and no choice. If you do not reach Eos and complete the Last the pillars are lost too."

"There are no choices. I must get to Eos and complete the Last before he tries anything else. I cannot let this army of darkness do any further damage. I am going to have to end this and I can only do so by facing him." I say, more to myself than Az until I hear him inhale with surprise. "I'm not going to be able to defeat his army or call him to war but I know I can kill that man, one on one and make him bleed piece by piece until he knows undoubtedly I am stronger and more powerful than he could ever hope to be. I am going to show him the price of murdering my father, attacking my people and thinking he can take my world." I whisper my vow to Axis knowing she hears me, knowing even in my moment of pity and sorrow I will rise to fight for her. Sadness will not change these scars and being told I am extraordinary does not make it so, I do this to protect my home. He is right, I was born for Axis so I can do no less than save her.

"Yes, mighty Alta Axian you can lay here while you heal, plotting and planning as much as you like, just please don't injure yourself with all this untapped fury you have inside you." Az cuts through my anger and I turn to see him smiling gently at me and I know, I know he sees me and yes, maybe he even believes in the extraordinary but all I feel is rage and it burns violently like fire in my bones.

Chapter 26

"This power cannot be contained." He tells me looking sadly as if he pleads for my help.

"What was the trigger to the explosion?" I ask knowing but needing him to explain so I can understand his reluctance better.

"It is too powerful for us. We cannot contain it nor control it."

"The trigger?" I ask again waiting.

"There is no trigger!" he stands angrily and begins to walk the length of the room. "I am training the impossible! I am expected to protect and guide but feel helplessly inadequate. The potential is evident as is its origin, but it is causing dissension as well as...."

"It's origins?" I ask prompting him further.

"There is a power that is beyond the light and balance, but I cannot tell you what or why. I cannot figure out its purpose."

"You must continue with the training. You have no choice. It would destabilize Axis herself if you do not abide with our agreement."

"I know. You have my word, but I need help. Please." He looks at me as if he seeks more than just advice.

"There is no other able to do this. You have no choice. I have contained the power. You are only training the little that is left, and Tallon, in this I need your support...."

"I understand Father." Is all he says finally sitting down defeated. "She is difficult and strong willed."

"She will need to be." I smile at him and am pleased when I see his familiar grin.

"You are right. She will. I just wish she would not be difficult and wilful with me!" he responses a little exasperated.

"We will succeed Tallon. The potential is there."

"It is more than potential, it is potent. It is extraordinary."

"Dangerous?" I ask concerned at his choice of words.

"Not now.... not with guidance, structure, discipline... love."

"We will do everything we can to ensure the extraordinary.... together."

"It is all I can hope."

We have to succeed. I dare not tell him the burden he carries for if he fails Axis and our realms will lose what they have waited millenniums for and everything, every realm will drown in a firestorm like no other.

Chapter 27

I close my eyes and roll my head back, lifting my face up to the warm beams of light that pierce through the trees. It is one of my favourite things to do. So simple but I am content to just feel the sun on my face. It has been more than three weeks since I escaped the circle and with the help of the light and balance, I am, at least, physically healed.

It seems I will carry the marks of the whip on me for some time as a reminder of the torture I faced, and it is frustrating to admit that I am vain and wish them gone.

My face will bear the marks of that whip however slight and while my body has deeper scars it is the struggle within that tears at me. I refuse to let the marks consume me with hatred or define any part of me, I try to look at them uncaringly and tell myself they are just part of the cost of war. They bring me moments of grief and sadness, but I will not let them consume me or be constant reminders of all I have lost.

Acceptance of my destiny has not come easily. I will be ok I tell myself. These scars may remind me of that moment in time, the weakness that came with my failure, but I survived.

I find myself frustrated, waiting at Az's insistence, while no doubt chaos and destruction fall across Axis and the realms. I understand Az and his caution in making sure I am okay, but this time healing has given me too much time for pity. As if I struggle to recognise myself, struggle to find my balance amongst the confusion.

I brush off the darkness of my thoughts as I hear Az walking towards me, and I look up at him as he gives me a slight smile in greeting. I watch his approach and recognise the gentle care in his eyes knowing he comes to check on me. While I have raged and screamed at all that has happened, he has refused to make any plans until I am healed. He has patiently walked away from the arguments I have tried to start in my frustration.

He comes to stand in front of me as if he has guessed I am wallowing in pity. I glance at him dismissively but then pause when I see he looks questioningly at me. Stillness fills the quiet and the sunshine lessens, as the world seems to gently fade away.

"Still pitying yourself I see." He shakes his head at me, not in disgust, but more that he thinks my feelings of sorrow are pointless. "Feeling sorry you were fooled? Worrying that you are not strong enough for what comes next? Still living in the past?" He pokes at me.

"I am tired." Is all I answer, and I am relieved when he stops knowing I am not interested in fighting.

I am wary but watchful as his eyes gently trace the contours of my face, studying each feature as if considering their individual worth carefully before committing each of them to memory and then moving to the next. I am well used to stares and admiration. I have no doubt of the pleasantness of my face, but I wonder at its worth now covered in scars of fine white lines.

"You are still beautiful Everly, never doubt that," he whispers quietly, and I hold my breath suddenly not knowing what the next moment will bring. I study each of his expressions as they run across his face. I see his contentment to slowly study me, his face softening as he raises his eyes to meet mine. I stare, caught in those soft brown eyes as they carefully watch me.

"How can you look at me like that?" I ask in the quietness of the forest.

"Like what?" he asks whispering in reply as if he also does not want to break this spell.

"As if you accept what you see. As if you see beyond these scars." I respond slowly but the doubt creeps in stealing the peace and intensity of the moment and I look away.

"It is you, Everly." He tells me "You are still so very beautiful. Maybe the scars have softened those vicious features that terrify your enemies but to me, they show your character and worth, your strength and your depth."

"I don't need your pity," I answer quietly but forcefully, doubting his words.

"Perhaps not, as you've certainly spent enough time wallowing in your own." He answers and my anger builds. Does he realise what I face? What I have endured? It makes me feel as if I am a child not worthy of the truth or too fragile to understand when he dismisses my feelings.

"Broken, scarred, hunted, betrayed...." I spit out angrily turning the intent of his words over in my head. "I do not see myself as you do. You're blind to the truth that comes for me! The truth of what I must do! Of what is required of me! You have no idea what I am about to face!"

"Surely you mean all that has been given to you. All the skills you have to face an enemy such as this. All the training and skills taught to you by your father? The extraordinary gifts from Axis herself? Never mind the fact you were actually born to be able to do all of this...and more!" He tells me gently lifting my chin, so my eyes meet his again.

'No, I don't. My feelings are disregarded! Even when I am broken, I am still expected to fight! When I am abandoned by death I am still expected to fight! When I have lost all, I believed in I am still expected to fight! To the end! To save everyone else I must risk myself! So, what has this life given me? This wondrous birthright I was born into. Pain! Suffering! Betrayal!" I glare at him, so he sees my frustration. He does not realise what anger I hold on to. He has no understanding of what my future will be.

"Oh, here is the real Everly! The great and mighty Alta Axian that believes she has only felt the worse of this life but has truly been loved and cared for! You avoid the tough questions; you ignore the truth of your situation and worse of all you actually think everyone else is here to hurt you, but never do you bother saving yourself! You scream at Axis! You scream at me, but do you ever just get off your own arse and fight for yourself!!! WEEKS!!! Weeks I have put up with your pity and bitterness! NO ONE IS GOING TO SAVE YOU EVERLY!!!! Don't expect your hero to turn up and save us all. He is gone! It is all gone!!! There is only this destiny so stop this weakness and FIGHT!!" Az yells at me, towering over me as if to make his point and I snort. Does he really think I would be intimidated by the extra six inches of height he has on me?

My insides seem to boil in rage. I cannot think of anything other than his throat pressed against my sword. How dare he!! It is time to teach this man who is the Alta Axian here and without breaking eye contact I call my sword and in one swift movement step back offensively before swinging it towards his handsomely annoying head.

"Finally!" he yells at me "Fight Everly!! Feel the burn of your fury! Use it! Your anger is certainly a lot better than your self-pity!" I frown as my sword sweeps past him and he appears unsurprised at the rapid escalation of my anger. He steps back watching the swing of my sword and smiles at me before drawing his hands together and opening them to reveal a sword of light that burns as if on fire!

"You liar! You use the light!" I yell at him "You don't just know what it is! You know how to wield it!"

"As can you if you stop and listen instead of wailing constantly about how tragic your life is!" he replies but before I am able to consider what this means he steps towards me and sweeps across my body returning my sword strike and showing he is not intimidated in the slightest by my aggression. All the frustration. All the bickering. All the resentment. All the pity. All this rage I have been feeling bubbles to the surface in a single moment as I glare at him before grinning at him viciously and we begin circling each other.

"Do you really think you can fight me?" I taunt him.

"Do you really think you are able to best me? You do not know who I am," he replies smugly. I wink at him and am pleased when he blinks in surprise as I leap towards him with my sword raised and it begins.

No quarter is given as we move seamlessly, giving no reprieve, no chances, no easy shots or short strikes. We battle for dominance within this sliver of the forest with every strike, every clash, every savage sweep of steel and every scream of rage the fighting frenzy rises.

His sword of light is as fierce and frenzied as mine and he does not offer the gentleness or the kindness I have come to expect from him. He thinks is evenly matched against me and his skills are equal to mine in every way and it only increases his frustration and my determination to put him in his place.

With each strike of his sword, I feel the strength of his power as is sparks against mine. It is as if he knows every move before it is executed. I drop as his sword swings towards my head AGAIN and kick his feet from under him. He rolls and leaps back to his feet with such speed I drop my hand momentarily at the athleticism of his recovery. He sees his chance and leaps towards me, grabbing my hand and turning my body against his but I am no green soldier new to combat and smile with that viciousness I am known for as I elbow his face and kick my legs out and around him before flipping him wholly on his back into the ground. I spin again to stand, thinking I have bested him only to feel him mirror my movement coming to stand at my back as he wraps his sword around me and towards my throat.

I drop again to escape but I am bested once more when he drags me upwards, using his strength to move me. I lift my sword along the front of my body and meet his sword at my throat. We still. Both swords silently crossed between us. Mine points at his throat while his is poised across mine.

"ENOUGH!" he yells in my ear, but I will not. I will not concede. I am rarely unbeaten in single combat and he should know this. My adrenaline high but my hand steady I spin again, and he unexpectedly lets me go. It infuriates me to think he may be toying with me. I turn to face him, my sword held high and attack again. He insults me again when he only defends. He does not counter, and my anger increases at his insolence. He turns as I attack and whacks me across my back with the flat of his sword and I scream at him in anger! I attack again and as he passes; he flicks upwards and takes an inch of my hair close to my neck. He is humiliating me, and I am done. I lift my sword across my body and slash downwards into my favoured attack position as I run quickly towards him, dropping to the ground and sliding towards him to thrust upwards but as I slide near him he spins downward grabbing me around my waist and lifts me against his body before unsuccessfully trying to wrench my sword from me before pushing me away.

We stand across from each other panting with rage, but I can see he will not back down as he smiles at me just as viciously as I smile at him. This is impossible! He is impossible! But I know he forgets who I am. Without light and balance, I was equally matched against my father, but my power does not lay in the physical and I smile viciously at him and insolently wink as I quickly pull it to me. I see a slight hesitation in his eyes as he sees my grin and feels me draw in the light and balance.

This is when they all remember who I am! How dearly he will pay in thinking he can beat me! He has turned me into a weak soldier with nothing but a few misguided feelings he thinks he invokes but no more! I brace triumphantly as power fills me and as it peaks, I run again towards his smug face. I lift my sword and focus on its placement. As I raise my arm and feel the movement of the talisman. I sweep it towards him and bright with the strength of my power my sword lights as it reaches him. I hold firmly as our blades meet but without warning my whole body is blown back by a blast of blinding white light. Struggling for breath, I find myself looking up at the sunny sky, my entire body sparking with light as I battling to move! I can feel my sword still in my hand but the light from it is gone. My power drains. My body is batted and....

"Everly?" I hear and open my eyes as his concerned face appears above me. "Are you ok?"

"What. Was. That?" I ask between hisses of breath as I sit up gingerly on my elbows and look at him. "And why do you look completely unharmed?"

"Let me help you up." He answers extending his hand, which I brush away, annoyed.

"This is the exact reason we fought Az! You ignore my questions! Treat me like a child!" I raise my voice angrily. "I can hear just as well from the ground, so answer me. What. Was. That?"

"Get to your feet and prove you are okay!" Eyebrows raised he grabs my hand before I can respond and hauls me to my feet. "Come on Everly. Peace. Food and then conversation. You are right. It is time we talked and not that vicious 'talking' you enjoy with swords." He smiles at me and I only grunt in response, partial because he is annoying but also because my bloody body feels as if it is overfull with light!

"We need to talk of the future Everly. It is time we started planning." He says and steps away from me.

"And what future would you have me talk of?" I ask after a while, once I can breathe properly again.

"Yours and mine," he answers simply but I know this tactic of his now. Simple answers to provoke bigger responses and I refuse to fall for into his sneaky little trap. Yet he still frustratingly waits, patient and I wonder if this is the second part of trying to start this conversation, exhaust me or just infuriate me until I become annoyed and comply.

"Just say whatever it is you need to get out. I am tired of trying to get the truth from you. Tired of you treating me as if I am a child. I am sore and hungry and too beaten to stand here while you decide what is best for me to hear." I finally say.

"Do you understand the talisman?" he asks, and I look at him in surprise. It is unexpected that he asks about this when he has refused to answer my questions about anything for weeks.

"All these weeks you have given me no information about anything, not a scrap. You tell me to concentrate on healing, to rest; recover and now you want to ask me questions? No, it is time you answered some of mine." I face him with my hands on my hips, scowling in an attempt to intimidate him.

"You are right. It is time. Come, Everly, we will eat and talk away from our swords!" and he smiles as he turns towards the little house and I watch him go, happy to hopefully be getting some answers to my mountain of questions.

Chapter 28

I hold my shield steady and begin to draw it in. The power is incredible but dangerous and cannot continue it destroy this world. It is as if it crackles with energy far beyond light and balance and I am in wonder at its beauty and brilliance. It can't be just Axian, is it ...more and in my question, I see my shield slip as I struggle to retain control.

The power explodes out of the shield and I am thrown back meters. I lay on the ground feeling the scorch of fire ripple through my body and gasp in the agony of it. Fire leaps up behind me and on both sides in flames that form a circle from the detonation point, and I see the source, calm and quiet in the chaos.

I smile reassuringly and move again. It is more than I have seen in all these millennia and I must call on Axis herself to help me save us. I draw my shield wider and calmer as if I must lovingly encourage and kindly ask as I draw it in. I keep my face gentle knowing it is this reassurance that is making the difference. My shield continues to draw in, but I cannot force it. It is as if I ask permission not demand compliance and I understand. I understand the force that rages in my shield as much as any can by understanding the core of its power.

I step closer and calmly but the uncertainty of my actions and the feel of my power causes it to push at my shield, fighting for freedom and I call to Axis desperate for help. If I cannot do this all will be lost, and I am relieved when the flow of light and balance fills me, and the shield holds steadily. I kneel quietly and see the peace that settles at my kindness. I watch fascinated as if it is able to understand but surely this is impossible. My shield tight and reduce the flow small enough to tether it to the source binding myself.

It will hold. For now.

Chapter 29

"Are you a child of Xiana? A senior member of the family I would guess." I poke him curiously when we are washed and ready to eat. It is an honest question and would explain his abilities to use the light. It has been many years since the Xiana have come to Axis and I am suspicious of the ties that bind this family given Hayes's admission that he is a son of Xiana.

"I am older than you and yes a son of Xiana, so I am able to use the light." Is all he says shrugging his shoulders and I look at him in stunned disbelief.

"Az, please, be serious. Tell me the truth." I say as I sit down at the table. "I am tired of answers I don't understand or cryptic replies. I just want to have an open conversation. No riddles. I need to plan, to know what your part is in all of this. To understand where you fit in my destiny."

He looks up at me and nods as if he agrees before walking to the table with plates of food.

"I was actually only coming to get you for dinner." He says gesturing to the now cold food on the plates. "I didn't really expect to end up in a sword fight." He says smiling as he approaches, and I nod.

I feel the weakness of my body after our sword fight but don't want him to know how badly I feel. I am too tired to make a smart comment about his sudden sense of humour or the cold food so sit silently as he settles into his chair and I watch ...and wait. I can see him searching for a beginning. His dark features focused on eating as he works on his words.

"I know the talismans represent more than the power of each First. A talisman also represents their ...strengths but beyond this though, they were destroyed at the death of a First. I was as surprised as you when you told me they were missing from the tomb." He begins, and I sit up suddenly surprised that he has dived right in, answering a question I have been wondering myself.

"My father's power was shift and shield but it doesn't necessarily mean that this talisman does the same. It's likely to be more decorative than anything. I can't imagine what use they would be to anyone else." I say wanting to encourage him to continue and am pleased when he nods.

"His power enabled you to both shift and shield when you left the circle, but strengths are not hereditary they are individual and that should be your bigger question because it should have been impossible for you to do either." He looks at me pointedly and I stare back as if I am fascinated by his observations.

"I assumed it was the talisman. Do you know how I used it? Are they all able to be used? Can others use them?" I ask him.

"I have wondered the same since seeing the way the talisman has moulded itself to you. I cannot work out whether your powers are your own or due to its power, but it is almost as if your powers are growing." He looks at me thoughtfully and I smile a little because I am pleased to hear he doesn't know everything.

I stand abruptly realising the implications of the talismans "If the talismans were able to be used by others they would have been stolen long before now."

"But only the First family knows the location of the tomb." He points out.

"Another First has never held the talisman of a previous either and Az, you know the location of the tomb now so luckily all those talismans are gone hey?" I jokingly tell him, but he doesn't laugh. He is deep in thought.

"It may not be that simple. It may be blood, or it could possibly be power." He responds and runs his hand through his hair as though he is struggling with this conversation. "Light and balance are Axian. These two elements are the basis of our entire universe and flow through to all the worlds within the realms. Axis is the core of all life within this. However, light and balance can become unstable, can be spread too thin, or be too much so must be managed because light and balance are finite. They are not a never-ending resource. There is only one-way light and balance can be sustained or replenished is..."

"By each line of the families through the pillars," I answer, and he looks at me in surprise. "My father taught me the importance of each of the four families Az."

"Yes, by the line of Four but there are also limitations to this. The first to rule, the second to bring order, third to protect and the fourth to guide. For example, the first family are only able to have only one child to keep the light and balance stable so that child is generally born with great power but also because one so powerful does not affect the flow of light and balance across our worlds it strengthens it. The second family only have boys because of...." But his words are lost when he sees my face and I become still as I see his caution, reeling at the implications of his words.

"How do you know all of this?" I say quietly, watching him. "These are the secrets of the four families, most of which is not common knowledge."

"Maybe more people are aware of these things than you realise Everly. Maybe we have become lazy in our protection of Axis. There are three other families of Axis all of whom have the right to succession under the right circumstance." he answers and the shock and anger even horror at this realisation sweeps through me leaving a cold dread in its wake. I stand and move awake from the table to pace the room while I think. He sits patiently in his seat as if he lets this information settle knowing questions will follow. I wonder if I really want to know the answers to all my questions so decide instead to take the easier route.

"The talismans Az. This must be the reason why they have been stolen. If you are right, it could be any of the families except the last. " I say frustrated with all that seems to be happening.

"Who knows...? This may be why the dust rises so rapidly. You must feel the pull and stretch of power in the air it could be that whoever has them is attempting to wield them." He tells me elusively.

"The light and balance.... he needed more...the hooded man. Does he have so little? No, he certainly did not feel weak or look uncertain as he whipped me...." And it is then I understand and my heart drops at the heaviness of my thoughts.

"Who is he?" I ask quietly. I turn to face him and see he rises from his chair. I am afraid. He stands in front of me. He looks at me such seriousness etched across his features.

"Maybe it is Tallon...he is strong enough to wield the talismans." is all he says.

"Impossible!" I respond immediately.

"He is not your brother Everly, not by blood anyway. Who knows what resentment he holds towards you? Where has he been all this time? He has disappeared without a trace!"

"Tallon loved our father and me. He would never..." I trail away seeing the determination in his face.

"People change Everly. You would be surprised the lengths a person will go to when they have a chance to change their destiny." He tells me quietly. "Where has he been all this time? Why wasn't he captured, and it would make sense when your enemy will not show his face. Sit Everly and listen." Az breaks through my rampaging thoughts abruptly and I stop to stare at him. He gestures to the chair I was sitting in and waits.

"If it is Tallon then the only way to stop this is to get to the pAx. He will hunt the other families to ensure succession." He continues.

"This is why you have been trying to protect me, to keep me safe?" I confront him placing two hands on the table and leaning my weight towards him "This is why you have healed me and saved me so I can get to the pAx to save your family? So again Az, who are you?" He looks at me without expression and I glare back at him.

"It is complicated." He answers.

"Well un-complicate it for me!" I raise my voice in frustration.

"Whether you know or not does not affect what happens next. Whoever killed your father does not realise the danger we are all in if Tallon is using this as an opportunity to seize power. We need to leave. If you do not get to the pAx soon the realms will begin to become unstable. You have an abundance of light and balance, you are all that balances the realms at the moment, it is true Everly you can feel it. You know the truth of who you are. Whether you fight or whether you accept a different future Axis and the realms is all that matters now." he tells me "So what other choice do you have Everly? Do we have? Tallon must be stopped."

"People never surprise me Az. Did you know this?" I smile at him sadly, stepping away from him as he looks up at me in surprise "There has not been one person I have met who hasn't wanted something from me. My father wanted me to be the perfect daughter, to represent him and dazzle people with my abilities as it reflected on his greatness. My brother trained me in the hope I would be invincible. Realms wanted more trade, more riches, and more alliances that benefited them. Friends wanted status. People at their core are selfish, even the kindest of them look at the world through their own perception of reality. It makes people, sadly, incredibly predictable and easy to anticipate. It was easy to meet my family's ever-increasing standards because they were expected, and I was loved. It was easy to be the daughter of the First because I knew what people expected when they saw me. I knew they never saw ME, and I don't think you do either! I think it is time I continued my journey to Eos, alone. I am well now Az. I need to finish this." I smile as I stand. "It is the strength in myself that defines my destiny. I will not be manipulated or manoeuvred. I will not be hunted or captured. It's enough. It is time my enemy saw me and realised what he must face and understand that I will not go without a fight."

He watches me intently as if waiting for me to surrender to what he thinks is right, but I continue.

"No more running Az. No more hiding from the truth. I will go to Eos, face the Last and defeat this imposter who thinks he can rule my world and I take my place as First. With all that has been done, I can do no less than protect all that matters from the destruction this war brings."

"Do as you must, Everly." Comes his quiet reply "The inconceivable has already been done when your father surrendered to his fate and for now, it is enough. There is more Everly, much, much more at stake here but you are right. Now is not the time. I will travel with you. You are not alone on this journey; I will protect you from Tallon and accept the future you choose." He finishes and I look at him surprised.

Hope floods through me. He has been the only one to help me and I cannot ask for more. In this life, as I struggle with this destiny, I will face what comes knowing Az stands at my side, for now, hoping it will be enough.

Chapter 30

I need time to think so before Az can say anything else, I walk quietly out of the house and back into the peace of the forest. The tops of the cool, green canopy move in the breeze and it makes me long for the wind on my face. That feeling of freedom would be bliss, right at this moment when I know destiny has finally caught up with me and there is no whisper of escape in the wind or from the truths that drum repeatedly in my head.

I stop walking when I feel the talisman move unexpectedly up my arm and across my shoulder. Its pressure light against my skin, it moves as if in waves before stopping across my heart. I stand still waiting, not sure what it means.

I've mostly tried to ignore any movement of the talisman even when I have accidentally used it. It is not an uncomfortable sensation; it more prickles with energy as if it is almost alive. I have avoided even looking it, other than an occasional glance. I try to ignore the talisman, but I cannot ignore the memories it evokes. It is a representation of my father and I feel as if I am a fraud for even attempting to think I would be strong enough to be gifted with something that represents him so powerfully.

The talisman is the colour of Firsts, the shimmer of pearly alluvial white gold with royal blue deepening to purple at its edges and I trace the outline as it sits over my heart. The talisman seems to have no defined shape since it contacted with my skin. When I took it from my father's pyre it was similar to a flat bracelet but as it touched my hand it moulded and moved, forever changing, almost as if bonded to me, but two things about it never change; its colour and the symbol of my father's power.

His stamp remains constantly at the centre of whatever shape it makes. It has almost become part of me as if an extra limb, although it is an oddly moving one.

It stays mainly on my sword arm so this movement across my heart has made me hesitate and for the first time, instead of ignoring it, consider its purpose.

At Hayes house, I did not see any sign of the talismans on Tallon. I do not believe it is Tallon who works against me but if it is really him that has stolen them, he must surely be naive to their power. My brother is very smart and resourceful, but he is also loyal and powerful himself. Tallon's origins are not known off Axis and it sparks questions of Az. If Az is truly Axian as he claims he would know the truth of Tallon. He would recognise his vibrations, but he is blind to the power my brother holds and it is perhaps his greatest revealing truth yet. I have no doubt whoever has the stolen talismans is studying and learning them even as I stand here staring pointlessly at mine.

I trace the symbol as it sits at the centre of my chest and sadness washes over me. I remember the pride I felt as I child when my father explained the meaning of his symbol. I was forever in awe of his greatness and wore this very symbol on my own armour with pride.

My father taught me the power of light and balance and what was required of me to be able to use it. It is strange to think that this talisman is all I have left of my life with him and I feel foolish to have ignored it. The light and the balance. These are two things weaved intrinsically into my very soul. I stand in the quiet and feel the world around me. I am safe here so can let the light and balance gently flow through me without the fear of capture. The flow is soothing and comforting as it fills and strengthens me in familiar waves.

I draw my sword. If Az is right, I should be able to use the talisman to protect myself. I draw the power gently towards the talisman; softly it comes, wrapping me in such familiar strands. I focus this energy on the talisman and hold my sword upright but tightly. The talisman moves to bond with my sword and I try to clear my mind. I focus the light to the point where the sword and talisman meet, and a spark of white light ignites! In my excitement I push harder, wanting more, but it only sparks again and then disappears!

I try again and again, each time holding the light with greater strength but never am I able to push it harder or brighter without it exploding in my face. I drag the light in the air towards me roughly again and I watch it race up the handle of my sword until it is completely covered. I smile pleased with myself before pushing at it with force again only to have it explode in epic fashion blowing me off my feet this time. I sit on my butt annoyed and frustrated.

"Maybe stop trying to force the light Everly, it's within you anyway. Let it bloom instead of trying to control it or demanding more." A familiar voice calls and I stand up quickly, brushing the dirt from myself before turning to face him, watching as he steps closer. "The white flame is the light of Axis in form Everly, work with it, in harmony, in balance."

"I have always been able to draw it to me without effort but never to hold it or use it, more to just strengthen me," I tell him.

"Those who are of Axis are able to draw the light and balance to increase what natural abilities they are born with, but it is impossible to enhance what isn't already there. It is the same as the light. It is within you and for now, you can call it in waves but with practice, you will be able to manifest it in physical form. But you need to be quiet and patient, to work with it not against it."

"My father never used the light."

"It takes practice." Is all he answers but it is as though he only tells me half the truth.

"He was the First." I push unsatisfied.

"And his gifts were extremely powerful." He responses.

"But no light?" And I see the frown form on his face when he realises, I will not give up.

"We all have our strengths, Everly. Your father held the power to shift and shield but no, he did not have the strength to form the light. You seem to have always been driven by the light. This is likely your strength. Come on now Everly; show me the strength of your power. Work with the light. Maybe in the next ten years, you may master it half as well as I have!" He finishes, as he winks at me.

He is so conceited! I roll my eyes at him before trying again. I call the light and hold it at my centre feeling to grow quickly, focusing gently this time on the talisman but as I hold it, I sense a difference. The talisman does not strengthen my powers or give me more it shields the fullness of my light. It protects. And I begin to understand. I watch Az thinking he is the master and I am the student, so I hold it back not wanting to reveal the true power of my strengths or the purpose of the talisman.

"You are forcing it, Everly. Wait. Feel it. You cannot demand it obey you or force it to do your will, you must be calm." Az instructs me not knowing that I easily hold the light close. "Gently," he says again, and I breathe in deeply letting him think once again he is more powerful than I.

Perhaps I will give him a taste of the power that has grown steadily since the battle. I have kept it contained, hidden, close, knowing that with such power comes fear. Slowly I run the light down the length of my sword and see him smile as if I am a child and he is a great and masterful instructor.

"Stay calm Everly, centred and peaceful." He repeats, over and over and I remain quiet. I allow the light to be, breathing deeply before it settles, and I can hold it along the length of my sword. It is the weave of my soul, such pure light, and as it shimmers its luminous whiteness, I find peace settle and purpose rise.

In the stillness of the moment, I study the light within me and its physical form along the length of my sword. I am in awe. I know it intimately, and at that moment, I understand the purpose of the talisman. My father's gift is an internal shield. Enough for me to contain the strength of light, to give my powers structure, to protect from catastrophe, to allow me to learn them and I smile through the tears that quickly gather.

He knew!

I hold a gift far beyond my capabilities and would have brought me terror and pain. His talisman does not give me his gifts. Its only purpose is to temper mine. A gift he could only give in death. My father knew his sacrifice would protect more in his death that was possible in his life and I understand. His life of sacrifice, his actions. He trusted me, believed in me and I will not fail him!

I begin to train in slow motion with the sword until I can feel the shield without so much concentration and although Az does not realise my practice is its use, not the light. As my confidence grows so does the pace of my sword.

Satisfied but exhausted, my face covered in sweat, I rein in the light using the power of the talisman and watch pleased when it dissipates this time rather than exploding in my face.

"Of light above to surrender below..." I hear him mumble as he runs his hand through his hair; his expression shadowed in..... rage. Such an odd expression. He guides and councils me has become frustrated at times, but he has never looked at me with rage. I hope it is not a disappointment. I have come to understand his ways. His personality has grown on me and I am struggling to think of continuing my journey to Eos alone regardless of his motivation for helping me.

"Az?" I ask smiling at him, breaking him from his strange mutterings "When do I leave?" I ask and am pleased when I see him roll his eyes at me.

"Eager to go now you have a new skill hey?" He asks as he smiles.

"I do not have the half of it mastered yet, as you would know, and I haven't even asked about the shift.... how do I master the shift of the talisman? Is it even possible?" I ask eagerly hoping he thinks I am a willing student.

"The shift may come as you become stronger at holding the light. You can hold the light steady now but shifting is a power that takes years to master and requires significant balance. You will be lucky if you can move yourself let alone others within the first few years." He answers and I nod knowing I will never have the power of the shield.

"How long did it take my father?" I ask casually hoping to continue this deception. He seems excited as if he has cracked the secret of the talismans and it only peaks my suspicions.

"A decade," he answers, and I whip my head up at his response.

"You knew my father! I knew it! I have seen you before! I have the memory of your face in my head Az!" I smile pleased with myself for tricking him but curious as to how he will react, but he only shrugs his shoulders at me and starts to walk away.

"I suggest you start packing, Everly. You have a long journey ahead of you." Is all he calls to me.

"Az!" I call to him "Tell me the truth!" Knowing he will likely ignore me, but I watch in surprise as he stops and turns around to face me.

"I have always been part of Axis as are you. It is only natural you would know my face, recognise me even." He concedes carefully and I look at him sceptically as he smiles gently at me. "You wanted the truth."

"So...son of Xiana, child of Axis...you are all these things? Yet you come in peace, as a friend, with no allegiance?" I poke at him.

"No, it is not like that. No one sent me." He begins and I can see he is trying to be truthfully, although struggling to find the words. "The light and balance of Axis will continue to fade and turn to dust unless your place within Axis is settled. I can do not less than protect all that is precious to Axis. I must ensure those who determine her destiny fulfil their purpose. With you Everly it is.... different.... perhaps even complicated. And yes, I want to protect Axis, probably because you tend to get yourself into so much trouble but also because Axis is the centre of our universe and its importance should never be underestimated."

"I think you tell me half the truth." I tell him "But your actions give me clues. The manner in which you fight tells me you're clearly skilled in combat."

"Our lives are long, with many challenges." Comes his response and I laugh unexpectedly. I have certainly been a challenge for him but am pleased to see he at least believes in my naivety.

I drop to the grass, sheathing my sword and gesture to him to join me as he continues.

"You may not want to be First, Everly but you don't have the luxury of choosing an alternative without dooming us all even if it means you risk yourself and have to fight for it. This is not some game were a worthy opponent is going to bow out and wish you well. The bravest, most fearless, the one prepared to sacrifice everything is the one that will prevail. The first family of Axis is a powerful bloodline but there are others and the fight.... well, that's all on you. I am sure this is not how you pictured your life, but it is the path you have been given. A path that includes murder, betrayal and sacrifice."

"I know." Is all I answer, and he looks at me sadly but thankfully stays quiet.

"It's not going to be easy," I tell him.

"Definitely not."

"There's a strong possibility of failure."

"Yes, that's true. It's not as if billions of lives lay in the balance."

"What will happen if I fail?"

"You will die. We will all die. Our universe will cease to exist. It will be armageddon and there will not be one person left who can save us."

"The plan?"

"Safety. The pAx. Then... the future." Is all he answers

"Eos Nevaeh." I acknowledge knowing it is my only option. "When do we need to leave?'

"Immediately. We will start our journey tomorrow."

"I'm not to travel alone?"

"You cannot be trusted alone it seems. It will be safer together." He smiles and I am pleased. Travelling alone is awful but keeping Az close is also important.

"Do you know the truth Az? Of who I am?" I ask and can see him thinking about how he will respond.

"You are Everly, Alta Axian; the daughter of Solomon. The possible next First. This is all that matters ...for now." Is all he says.

"Possible? Who would stand in my way?" I ask.

"There is power within our universe. They may not be as strong as you individually but if some chose to rise together then your place may not be certain. But who's to say...will it change your destiny to know?"

"No."

"Will it change who you are as a person?

"No"

"Who you will fight for?"

"No"

"Will it make any difference to you to have such knowledge as you go into this fight?"

"Probably not but it is a question that echoes in my head. You are right. It is distracting and there is undoubtedly a very long, very justified story of betrayal and traitors that will accompany any information. And to be honest I really don't care. Let them come. Let them fail. Let me hunt them down and show them the price of their treachery."

And I see the frustration in his face. "It may change if they have the power of the talismans."

"Can they be used to destroy us?" I ask curious to hear his reply, but my question goes unanswered as he stands and brushes his clothes off before extending his hand towards me to pull me up.

"Come, Everly, we need to pack." Is all he tells me, and the conversation is not forgotten but pushed aside as the urgency to leave is implied. It is time to face what comes regardless of my questions, his intentions or who searches for power.

Chapter 31

"It was the light that spread as if a fire in abundance. The extent of it reached the outer limits. I have never seen anything like it."

"It is contained. For now."

"It pains me to have asked of you, but you must be the shield to this.... light." She tells me and I see such pain in her eyes before anger creases across her features. "How could you do this? No. I know how... but how is it possible? It should be unthinkable! And now for this to be required of me." And the pain comes again but I know she is strong.

"It is done. I can shield the fire. Find peace with this knowing I will do all in my power to ensure our legacy. They have no understanding of her truth, you know this."

"Yes, you are right, this sacrifice was necessary. Do what you must but there is no telling what may happen without balance. You must ensure our safety."

"I understand."

"And I understand you must make an impossible sacrifice to save us, but I am afraid it will cost us more in the end. We do not yet know the consequences of this folly. We must proceed with such care. The light has always been the more volatile, but it cannot surrender to the darkness that comes. Tallon will need the talismans."

"The talismans? Why?"

To ensure we are protected. I have prepared and planned not knowing how I will be needed."

"It is not just us. Everything we have built together, the realms, we must not fail in this. Go, Solomon, ensure it thrives...for now."

Chapter 32

We barely spoke to each other during dinner last night, both of us aware of the uncertainty of this trip and my head is full of a hundred questions I do not have the courage to ask.

It is in silence that we clean and pack the next morning and as I look around the little cottage, I know this may be the last of any peace or solace on Axis for me until I have completed the Last. This place has been a sanctuary, a place of health and healing and I am grateful to whomever it belongs.

I can only imagine the rage of my enemy at my escape. I know very well his fury; I wear those scars and know we will meet again with swords drawn before too long. I don't believe Az. How could it possibly have been my brother? I shake my head in disbelief. Az certainly thinks this may be the case, but I cannot shake the words Tallon spoke, the way he begged me to trust him. I know he had something to tell me. I feel his urgency, his worry, his fear but I did not feel rage or hatred or betrayal. I still wonder why I did not tell Az about Tallon but maybe it is fear that he is right, and my brother is the monster in the hood.

I pack lightly, only the basics I have been given and cry out with joy at the sight of new armour! I'm not sure how he has done the impossible but as I run my hands across its familiar surface, I am relieved to have its protection again.

I am ready to leave. I know I am still not as strong physically as I should be but with the dust rising there is not much time to waste. Each day we delay gives our enemy more time to grow stronger and more time to whoever thinks to master those talismans.

Now that the decision to go to Eos has been made, I feel almost agitated to get it started or more likely to get it over with! We have been sheltered by the reality of the world in this place and the journey ahead will not be easy.

To travel to Eos Nevaeh, we must navigate across the Aurelian plains and it will undoubtedly be the most difficult part of the journey. The alternative would add weeks and take us back along the dreaded east road and through the mountains making the journey nearly impossible given the terrain. I am not prepared for the plains, as I am aware of the former allies that live beneath them but will face whatever comes.

It is in the cool light of dawn when we walk to the door of the little house and both pause. I turn to find Az looking at me and smile at him with uncertainty. I reach for his hand and am reassured when he doesn't question why and wraps his larger hand comfortingly around mine and smiles.

"Smooth sailing from now on hey! I guess our adventure begins." I tell him cheerfully, sounding more reassuring than I feel. He smiles wider as if I am funny before giving my hand an unexpected squeeze and pulling me with him as we step out of safety and into reality.

I follow without pause and stop beside him to look around as the breeze blows wisps of hair around my face and the power of Axis wraps around me. My beautiful world is so achingly familiar that it troubles me to know that, for now, it only feels danger and destruction.

My hand drops away from Az's and opens ready for my sword. The feeling of exposure after so long begins to creep up on me. Suddenly I find I am on edge, nervous, almost afraid. I am aware of my plight and cannot shake the memory of the trap I was tricked into last time. I become angry with myself, stubbornly refusing to let these feelings bloom and fight to calm such pointless thoughts. If this enemy's plan was to make me scared then here, at this moment, he has succeeded, and I cannot let that happen!

"We need to move Az. I cannot stand here waiting for someone to find us. I will not be captured again." I tell him aware of the enemy that will constantly hunt me, knowing they will feel the ripple of light from me leaving the cover of the forest and will quickly begin the hunt for me once again.

"Be patient Everly. Wait." He replies but I cannot control the terror that continues to rise. I rub my hands down my sides as my mind replays the feeling of the whip that dragged my skin from my body once again.

"I cannot Az. I am shaking with fear." I tell him confused but angry with myself that I am looking to him for reassurance.

"Everly..." he gently says my name and I turn towards him. My eyes lock with his and he raises his hand and traces the side of my face. "I will not let them take you again." He reassures me sounding so certain and I turn away. I may not be alone but that does not necessarily mean I am safe.

"Do not fear. Do not fear." I chant ridiculously to myself while trying to breathe. "You are right. This is right and we have to start somewhere." I say turning to Az "I will not let them win even in this. They will not take me again." I tell him, faking my fearlessness and he smiles as he sees me force my vicious grin, which to be honest probably looks more like a painful grimace but nods his approval anyway.

"You're right. They will not take you again because you would never allow it. You are stronger than this fear Everly." he laughs at me and I see clearly his fearlessness and faith in me. My moment of unreasonable terror begins to slowly ebb away, and I stand, still desperate to leave but patiently waiting as he has asked.

He is different, this man. He challenges and questions me, demanding nothing less than my best but he does so with such confidence. He doesn't obey my every command and most of the time snorts at me if I try giving orders. He expects me to pull my own weight whether it is fighting or doing the dishes after a meal. He is such a puzzle. With him, I do not feel like the Princess or even the mighty Alta Axian. He does not treat me with reverence but rather expects more of me, demands I be accountable for who I am and to be my best and although most times it makes me feel frustrated strangely enough it also makes me feel stronger. It is as if he is my equal. I strangely relax around him even though I do not trust him, almost letting my guard down.

I am deep in my wonderings when I hear a sudden and fast approaching sound of hoofbeats. I call my sword and step forward ready to fight but as I step past Az, he grabs my wrist and laughs at my immediate reaction as he pulls me back to stand again beside him.

"Relax Everly. I have called them. They come to me." And as he finishes two unusually patterned horses appear through the trees and I watch in awe as they race towards us before coming to stop in front of him, snorting and stomping. They are almost a coppery black with blue edges at the end of each patchy pattern with white splashed in between. It is a rare and wondrous sight to see them and I grin with excitement.

"Your admetos! They are so different...not the black of our royal horses. They are almost the colour of the ground and sky...of white gold and dark storms." I murmur as I step towards the closest and cannot resist running my hand across its coat. The shimmer and shine of the staggeringly luminous hair are almost blinding. It reminds me of...

"It is as though the light of Axis shines within their coats... horses of light!" I say.

"It is said the admetos are of Axis herself." He proudly tells me as he gently strokes the nose of the horse in front of him and I stare at the sight of the legendary admetos.

"Am I able to ride them? Do I have to prove my worth?" I ask excited at the possibility of being able to ride one.

"We'll see." Az smiles and leaps up "They are wild and free. They cannot be tamed so you should get along just fine I think!" And there it is again his strange sense of humour! So, ignoring him I vault up on the horse who's coat I studied and turn to see if he follows.

We are Axian born to light and balance. Our light and balance are protected above all else and because of this entry to our world is through gates that do not accept any form of technology including weapons, devices or electronics of any kind.

Most other realms have advances but here, on Axis, we are born loving the thrill of horses and riding and have celebrated the simplicity of our way of life for generations so riding for me is as natural as breathing.

Az laughs at my excitement.

"I forget sometimes how fearless or more likely sheltered you are! It's fine! They are mine so of course, you will be safe. Let's ride!" he smiles and leans forward as his horse surges past me. I do not wait a second before I follow and just for a minute, I forget everything else laughing with pure joy at the pleasure of riding an admetos no less!

Chapter 33

A circle of royal blue gently outlined with the darkest of nighttime purple watches me carefully as if knowing what I must do. They are identical to my own eyes and I know the truth of her origins.

The truth must be hidden from the billions but not from Axis herself. It is the Alpha and Axis above and below will fear it's coming while Axis herself will cry tears of joy and celebrate.

It brings blood and death, destruction and chaos. It must destroy before it can be rebuilt. It will insight fear and anger. Wars will be fought for it. Millions will die. Men will seek to control and possess such a gift, but I will ensure its safety. I have bound the fullness of its light deep. I have hidden it in plain sight. It is my greatest joy and most feared treasure.

It will forever own me, and I will be tied to it for eternity regardless of the cost.

I will ensure the safety of the light for Axis because the darkness comes, and my death will ensure she rises.

Chapter 34

Disappointingly it is only hours before we reach the edge of the plains as Az has us riding at a cracking pace. The gait of the admetos is flowing and smooth and I admit I am excited as a child and am enjoying every second of our journey with them.

We have navigated our way to the far south corner of the plains as it is furthest away from Amara, our capital city, which is where I was tortured.

We will be exposed as we cross the golden expanse from this side and expect nothing less than a battle or chase but as we start from this point it will give us more time to get further across.

We have discussed every possibility and are confident of reaching the opposite side if the attack only comes from the city. The dust is still light, and balance still flows easily giving us the greater advantage, but it is those that live beneath the plains whose intentions are unknown.

"Az?" I ask looking at him questioningly as he stops and studies the golden expanse in front of us.

"We must be prepared for an attack above or below." He answers knowing my hesitation and the frustration of having little choice but to cross into what could be capture or worse.

The glittering carpet of pure gold lights up luminously in front of me and I stare at it angrily! Our supposed allies the Aurelians live beneath the plains and it is certain they are now my enemies. They fled at my father's surrender instead of fighting for us. They are safe from any attack hidden beneath the plains, inaccessible to those above unless invited from below.

It is betrayal I feel as I watch the perfect flowers of gleaming gold that cover the entire surface swaying in harmony with the gentle breeze. This beautiful place only brings up the resentment and anger that comes with the helplessness of hindsight.

"Your emotions are clearly showing on your face Everly." I hear Az's voice come from beside me. I turn to see him studying me with concern. "It is likely we will be summoned during our crossing but please do not leap straight into battle mode. They may not be our allies, but they also may not be our enemy. I would not be surprised if the Reine Fee has decided to remain neutral in this conflict so do not fight your way out against the Aurelians unless there is no other choice."

"I can defeat the Aurelians...." I glare at him in response "But I will not start the fight. I will not let them see my pain even if all I want is their throats on the blade of my sword, but they are more likely to remain beneath like the cowards they are." And he nods as if he understands but that sour taste of anger still sits in my throat. The sight of these golden fields only reminds me of their betrayal and encourages the rage that simmers in me.

It is within minutes of setting out across the plains that I feel the earth move beneath us. I don't know whether to move faster or stop because I know what comes towards us. I keep my pace and so does Az as I watch a dust cloud forms meters in front of us and within seconds rising from the plain are about fifty soldiers who are looking right at us and suddenly run purposefully in our direction.

"Ahh, we are to be enemies then." I smile gleefully calling my sword to my hand.

"Everly. Be still. They come but let us wait and see what action they take before we start slicing them into pieces. Who knows, they may come for a friendly conversation." Az and his warped sense of humour gently tell me. I can see he is watching me carefully and probably hopes I don't start any trouble so is no doubt relieved when I relinquish my sword back to the light.

I glare at the traitorous Aurelian soldiers of the Reine Fee, Queen of the Aurelians who I have not been seen since the battle. I can only cling to the knowledge that although Aurelian soldiers are extremely dangerous in their ethereal form and are known for their assassin skills, they are no match for me.

They are dressed in the same iridescent gold as the flowers and move in an athletic, rippling way as they flow towards us almost like a death driven ribbon of light. Their strength lay in unity and their ability to move in harmony across a battlefield. I know them well. My rage burns as I remember all of the battles, we have fought side by side, the alliance strong and our world protected, but in that final battle, I wonder if all those years were false.

I look back towards the edge of the forest and see we are too far into the plains to turn back. I don't want to sit here pretending we are amicable when nothing but treachery lay between us but can do nothing else but wait to see why they come for us so I sit as straight and tall as possible braced for a certain storm, gently drawing the light and balance to me while I glare fiercely at the soldiers who do not falter in their relentless stride.

I notice a shift in the flowers in front of them and at the hooves of the admetos. The flowers around us start to flatten and turn into cobblestones making a path that runs towards the soldiers. I know who comes with this display of power and there is nothing left to do but wait. The soldiers get closer and as I study their formation, I see in the centre is the Reine Fee rising from the plain hovering about the heads of the soldiers.... looking right at me.

I watch as the soldiers' part in the middle allowing me to clearly see her face as she flows regally in my direction. She walks towards me gracefully covered from head to toe in spun gold which falls to the ground in silky swirls, her hair so golden it almost shimmers white in the sunlight and she looks as serene as always, completely untouched, poised and regal as if her world has never changed!

Her gaze is unwavering, daring me to submit but I will not look away. As she comes within speaking distance and inclines her head and I make absolutely no movement, I only continue to hold her gaze. I see the uncertainty gather in her eyes and continue to watch unmoved. She stops in front of both horses and bows respectfully to me, but I am in no rush and sit silently knowing no one can speak until I have acknowledged them.

The silence stretches and the rustle of unease increases. I would dare her to speak as I sit above her on the admetos and glare down the space between us from my greater height but know she will respect the old ways until her last breath. Her gaze has not faltered, and I see her determination to speak with me. At least they do not come as enemies, although I am not certain they are friends either, so I decide to find out why they bother to come at all.

"Signa" Is all I say using only her given name without any acknowledgment of her rank or royalty and hear the shock reverberate through the soldiers, but she is older and wiser, and her mask remains emotionless as she addresses me.

"Sovereign" she bows as she uses the correct address. "Welcome Everly Regla Mas Alta, Alta Axian, daughter of the First."

"What reason do the Aurelians have to come to meet us? We only ask to cross the plains peacefully." I ask, poking at her by refusing, still, to acknowledge her position in our world.

"I felt your vibrations above the plains. We have heard rumours of your survival, but we're overjoyed to feel your presence ourselves. We offer only a haven and hospitality Alta Axian. We would be honoured if you ate with us, rested, before continuing your journey." She answers and I only grow angry at her complete dismissal of everything that has happened and the destruction that continues as well as the battle in which my father died. I open my mouth to respond until Az gentle touches my elbow.

"Reine Fee, we are honoured you greet us personally and accept your offer of hospitality. I am Azul, companion to the Alta Axian." Az tells her and inclines his head respectfully. I look at the Reine Fee in anticipation, waiting for her to tell me who he is by the taint of his power, but there is no recognition of him, and her focus is clearly on me. There must be magic at play for which no doubt Az will refuse to acknowledge when I try to question him about it later. For now, I will wait. His truth will be revealed in time along with his intentions I am sure.

For now, we will seek the safety of the underground city and I will find out what I can from Reine Fee. Although there is little hope thinking she is my ally and I am exceedingly aware of the trap we could be walking into I am sure of who I am and know the Aurelians would do nothing to harm me when they need me to live.

The Reine Fee signals to follow and her soldiers fall into line at our backs and we dismount. I watch as Az sends the admetos galloping away before turning and following the Reine Fee. It is within meters we rapidly start descending into the ground on the gold cobbled path. I look at the sky above and wonder at the worth of my enemy, the exposure of the plains makes us all vulnerable and no doubt we have already been reported to our enemy at Amara but cannot understand why they do not attack.

"I will not be captured nor imprisoned," I whisper quietly to Az.

"Understood." Comes his reply and I am relieved to see the intense set of his face giving me assurance he will keep his word.

The further into the plains we go the deeper below the surface the path descends but it is not darkness we walk into; it is gold and light. I look at the walls of the path that are cut from the earth and glimmer with light and before long see only a glimpse of the sky above the plains and the golden flowers until eventually they too disappear, and we are deep under the ground beneath the Aurelian plains.

The walls of the path we travel on are covered in intricate gold swirls that run in each direction throughout the walkways. We follow this pathway for some time descending into the ground before entering the main platform that sits slightly away from the main path.

I look around at the familiar space, the shimmer of the walls, the golden cobblestones beneath my feet and step forward in wonder towards the edge of the platform curious to what changes, if any, have affected the Aurelians since the battle. Beyond the edge of the platform, which is made of the same gold cobblestones as the path, there is an entire golden city. It is buildings reaching up to the ceiling of the dome of the plains that protects them all. It is just normal noise and bustle of a busy community. This city has always been so magical and like a fairy tale but with the dust and unbalance I can only imagine the same destruction here.

I reach the edge and grip the rail with shock, looking across the city beneath the Plaines des Fees, home to millions, all I see is a celestial revelation of gold proportions, which to my utter astonishment, remains completely untouched!

I watch as Aurelians go about their daily business in the streets below. The buildings still function, and commerce still thrives. They live here so ignorant and so removed from the realities of the chaos on the surface. All the death, all the destruction, all the pain that reigns above does not touch this place.... and it makes me shake with anger.

I do not know that fate of those who called Amara home. Axians above live in fear of the unknown, the destruction of towns and imprisonment, the dust rises as the realms wait for the balance of the First and all the while these so-called allies safely continue their lives beneath us.

I am shaking with rage, I feel such injustice for those above, and the anger of my father's death coils up and the agony of all the suffering, all the destruction and all my failures hit me. It matters to no one down here! They know their safety is assured if they remain hidden. The underground can only be accessed by those already beneath.

The houses, the people, the children, the shops, the flowers, the paths between buildings all luxurious, untouched and most of all safe.

"You hide from the truth of what comes Signa. Huddled beneath the dirt. Never facing the terror of above. Never have you tried to save those who suffer." I calmly tell her.

The Reine Fee does not respond, nor does she move. She only turns her head to look at me, waiting as if expecting this so I give her something to think about and release a little light in a rough wave through the air around me. I watch as the soldiers' step protectively towards the Reine Fee sensing the danger, although, she does not move.

"Everly, I did not greet you to fight. I do not want war or pain or any more death. Please do not test your power on me. I am too old and have seen too much conflict to be intimidated by such things." she tells without fear "You are young and yes powerful but do not think I will allow you to show such disrespect even in your suffering. You may have frustrations and questions but let us at least respect our bond in Axis...for now...until ...things are settled." She finishes carefully.

"I earned the right to stand against you the second you betrayed our world." I scowl at her. "You deserted my family in battle. I think you watched my father die and didn't intervene out of fear for your own life. Fear you would also be defeated. I think you bring us here now to either pretend we are still allied or in the hope of protecting your people from my rage, so by all means Signa show me your strength. You are right. I have no armies at my back, no allies to call for help and yet I will ask you...Do YOU think you are powerful enough to defeat me Signa? To protect your people from my rage?" And I watch as she steps towards me.

"No Everly. I am not powerful enough to defeat you... but I will tell you, as Signa, Reine Fee of the Aurelian I will always remain loyal to my people...and my blood but above all of this my first loyalty is and will always be to Axis." She tells me calmly.

"I have no doubt of your loyalty to your people but explain why you bothered to breach the surface at all when your loyalty to me, the daughter of your First, is in doubt?" Is all I ask.

I am surprised to see no rage, no hatred in her eyes. She is calm and her words ring with the truth but what is more surprising is the sadness I see in her and it is this that makes me stop.

"We have much to talk about and I will guarantee you safe passage across the plains. I only wish for you to listen to me Everly, and for you to reach Eos because we both know our worlds, above and below, depend on it." And with that, she turns and walks away gesturing to us to follow.

It is the pain in her eyes that leaves me subdued. It drowns out my rage and makes me wonder at her words. We follow the Reine Fee without argument along a path set higher up from the city. It follows the edge of the hollow in the earth, still with the gold pattern running the walls and I glance continuously at the bustle of the city below watching, waiting for reality to hit.

We reach two very large, very familiar ornate doors with two more soldiers guarding them and I know we enter her private quarters. Upon seeing the Reine Fee they step to the side and open both doors for us to enter.

"Everly, come and sit." she motions as if we are welcomed guests and I look around noticing that nothing has changed in the living area filled with beautiful furniture in creams and golds and aqua.

I am covered in dust and dirt and wonder where in this pristine palace I should sit as she motions to the seats placed in a comfortable sitting area at the centre of the room.

I look down at my armour and back towards the Reine Fee before walking over to the lightest, creamiest chair and sitting down heavily on it. Imagine how much grim will be covering this thing when I'm done, I smile proudly at myself but as usual, she does not react.

"I'll be back shortly." is all she says and then disappears around another intricate corner while we sit quietly waiting. I look around at the untouched beauty of the room that seems so far away from war and violence and I feel angry at everything I've lost while it seems beneath my feet life has carried on as usual.

"There will be no peace here for us Everly, not if you insist on trying to provoke her." He begins with the admonishment I knew would come.

"It is inevitable," I answer simply.

"But it may be wiser to listen to what she has to say. Find out what it is she expects of you. Did your mother not bring you to see her? To form a relationship with the Reine Fee for the future?" he asks.

"My mother? Oh, you mean Sidra. She died when I was only a baby." I tell him and seeing his nod I continue. "Sidra is Tallon's mother not my own. I do not know my mother. The Reine Fee does not know my mother. Only my father knew the truth of my origins as far as I know. The truth of me is not a secret within my immediate family or our close allies including the Reine Fee." I tell him simply turning to watch his reaction.

"I don't understand." He responds spluttering and I smile when I see the shock on his face "You are the daughter of Solomon but not of his wife Sidra? This was never revealed. Not even to the other foundation families. I cannot fathom your origins. You are unknown. This is unheard of. There is no blood between you and Tallon... maybe this is the reason he has deserted you. Maybe she knows where Tallon is? He is her grandson. I cannot believe this!" he finishes running his hand through his hair and I watch him begin to pace as this knowledge sinks in.

"I have known for, well...ever. It was who my father was that was important not who my mother is." I tell him simply for it is the truth but do not acknowledge his comment about Tallon. "I do wonder, however, if the truth of my origins is somehow related to my father's destiny."

"Your father's destiny was his own Everly. It could never have been tied to you. These are the actions of others but there are so many other unanswered questions about this whole situation." He finishes as he continues to pace.

"Yes, I am sure you have many questions but none of them are important right now. The only truth that matters is where the Reine Fee fits in with the whole invasion and then the question is who? It is strange that this enemy comes with no banner, no name only darkness and destruction. Is that not strange? Are these not the real questions that need answers right now?" I look at him waiting for agreement.

"It was your father's choice to surrender maybe he knew...." Is all he tells me his words lost, as he looks exceedingly anger and I suddenly become very, very still.

"My father died at the hands of the enemy that attacked our home." I answer him "He surely fought until he had no choice. There was no light nor balance in the fight Az, maybe this is the reason he could do no more." And I frown as the memory of the battle replays once again in my head. I cannot reveal the truth of the talisman without betraying my father, but I know now the reality of his death.

"Maybe you are right." He answers and I turn quickly to look at him wondering what nugget of wisdom will come now. I am surprised that he has left the conversation of my mother alone when I can see how shaken he is by this revelation.

"Which part am I right about?" I ask calmly.

"Maybe the light and balance were the reason your father died but he had fought to victory without both throughout the realms many times. He was not captured...he surrendered...and I, for one, have yet to work out why." And as he finishes frustrated and suddenly walks across the room to study a painting on the other side away from me.

"What other reason could there be Az? He was invincible." I ask and turn back to wait for the Reine Fee.

"No one is invincible Everly." He answers me quietly and it immediately regains my attention "Even you were defeated when we fought. Previously invincible right?" I smile as he tells me this, but I do not deny his words.

"And why is that I wonder Az? Could it perhaps be the thousands of years of combat experience you have on me? Or perhaps it was that you watched me over the years learning and remembering the way I fought? Either way, I'm quite comfortable with that." And he looks at me in surprise as I continue, "Because even though you had the advantage of experience and studying your opponent you also didn't beat me. You let me walk away." I finish only to watch in astonishment as a strange smile breaks over his face and I wonder if he was fighting to his full abilities as well and take note to remember to find out sooner rather than later.

"There was no light and balance in the training ring Az when I was captured thanks to that torque," I tell him. "I have only felt that sensation once before during the battle, but it was not the same. The void during the battle was of significant power, although it was not a gift, I recognise so how is it possible? How is it possible to create a void that is powerful enough to defeat the strongest on Axis?" I ask him and see the seriousness in his eyes.

"It is a question that has also worried me, Everly, to starve air of light and balance would be a very powerful gift indeed but I am sorry, I cannot give you an answer. I have never heard of it before now."

"It is yet another question that has no explanation. We need to be looking at the bigger picture, as there are obviously others involved. This attack took time and planning. The fact our enemy does not identify themselves tells me there is more to come, more to learn about why and how." I say walking towards him.

"I agree Everly, but it is also the reason we must tread carefully. We do not know what others may be involved even those you considered family. All that matters right now is getting you to Eos." He assures me. "It is likely many of your questions will be answered in time when you face the Last and are ready to be First." He smiles at me and I know he is right.

"Yes. They are for later. Not now." I tell him walking away so I can gather myself for what the Reine Fee intends to tell me. I understand the importance of gaining any information we can from this visit under the plains if only to ensure I am able to defeat them later but I want to have this conversation because it has never made sense that our closest allies fled at our darkest moment.

Chapter 35

We do not wait very long before the Reine Fee re-enters the room and Az turns, politely acknowledging her entry, while I walk back to that beautiful cream coloured chair and sit back down.

"We must talk Everly." She announces regally as she glides towards me and I wait as patiently as possible while she settles herself, fixing her skirt until it sits perfectly, in the seat across from me. "There is much to discuss. I was relieved to feel your vibrations above. I waited patiently knowing you would need to cross the plains to travel to Eos. There is hope..." She begins and I am interested to hear what she would think was pertinent to me. I study her as if I see her properly for the first time. I always saw her so golden and white, graceful and regal. The perfect Reine Fee. Now I see the lines in her face, the tension that is evident in every gesture. It would seem the Reine Fee struggles with the chaos of Axis as much as I, but I cannot move past the moment the Aurelian's did not send in the second wave during the battle and then fled at my father's death.

I study her familiar face seeing the strength in the Aurelian line that was evident in Tallon's mother, the Reine Fee's daughter Sidra and in Tallon himself. It is the beautiful golden hair, the glint of gold in the brown of their eyes that they all possess. They are of below while I am the image of my father, not gold at all, only the midnight black hair and eyes of blue and purple of the First family that rules above. It is a constant reminder that there can be no mistaking my parentage or even my destiny.

"Are we to discuss your betrayal of my father?" I ask abruptly and am pleased when she stills before quickly collecting herself.

"Of course, if you wish, we can start with accusations but Everly, there is a lot you do not understand. A lot your father sheltered you from Everly that you should know before you jump to conclusions. I did not betray your father, to betray the First would mean betraying myself and my world." She finishes drawing herself tall and strong as she makes her point.

"If you did not betray my father then where was the second wave during the battle? Why did the Aurelian's flee once my father's head was taken? How could you stand and watch our world destroyed? It makes no sense!"

"Any action taken during the course of that battle was with the approval of your father..." She answers as I look at her in complete disbelieve.

"You lie! My father would never have betrayed Axis or her people by allowing the destruction and defeat of our world. He would NEVER surrender! I am not a child he sheltered Signa, I am the daughter that fought at his right for years. I have fought the battles and celebrated the countless victories my father led with you and your people at our side. Did you harbour resentment against your ally, your friend, and your son by marriage by abandoning him to this enemy and dooming us all? To think, all these years you must have despised him when you demonstrated such a facade of loyalty and love. This is the greatest betrayal to us all. You stood by and watch traitors drag the sharp edge of their sword across my father, your First's throat, and in doing nothing you betrayed Axis yourself. It was you who gave them the sword when you did not stand with us." I tell her directly and forcefully, my voice filled with rage.

"Everly, you have this all wrong." She begins as if to placate me. As if I am a child who does not understand the meaning of her treachery.

"No Signa, you are right we have much to discuss and I am interested in listening to what you have to say but do not think to twist and manipulate the truth with such lies!"

"Everly...please..." she pleads but I only snort scornfully at her ploy.

"How long did you and Tallon plan such treachery Signa? And Sidra too no doubt when she was alive. I know the binds of blood and family." I say angrily, beyond reason. "How many times did you meet to work out the details of my father's death? To think you would take such a risk and leave the realms so vulnerable all for greed! And now he is dead you sit here blaming every action on him!"

"Everly enough," Az says suddenly laying his hand on my arm and I turn towards him. I look at him surprised he has intervened. I should be angry but, in this world, when all I see are traitors and betrayal, I need him. I need to trust he is here for me regardless of his intentions, so I look at him and nod understanding before continuing with a little less anger.

"Signa?" I turn back to look at her. She has no emotion, no reaction to my accusations that I can see. She has sat quietly while I have demanded answers, yelled and screamed and accused her of the worst of actions. She is the first of our allies and is tied to me to protect Axis, should I become First she will be sworn to me by right if never by blood and I stare at her in the quiet, my anger subsiding quickly as her mask cracks and I watch a tear fall to her lap.

"Everly, you are right. We met many times to ensure our success." She begins sadly and I sit silently in shock "but the meetings were between your father, Tallon, Abrastos and myself." She pauses as if to make her point, but it is pointless for I hear nothing more! I struggle to function beyond the pain that grips at me. She cannot be implying that my father's death was planned.

"I don't understand! What does that even mean?" I ask rising from the chair to pace across the floor.

"Everly, there is so much I need to tell you. That your father wanted you to know but couldn't. Had you known..." She tells me quietly and it has more effect than if she had shrieked and screamed it at me.

"My father...And Abrastos...Tallon? And my father's death was not surrender? Was it not defeat? But the dragons? I cannot believe they would submit to such torture!" I raise my voice frustrated that she speaks in riddles.

Signa stands and faces me making sure she has my full attention. "You were ready Everly and we could all see the truth of your destiny and the power you hold.

We have fought so hard to push back the dark and save the light and balance. We have raged against the impending storm that threatens to destroy us all, but we could never find its source. We could never destroy the heart of the darkness and because of our failure, it overwhelmed us all. Without the strength of the light the darkness affects the realms, brings instability to Axis and we can do no more, we have no more to fight with, none of us has the power of light that is needed and because of this Axis is dying. Solomon knew this was the only way, Everly. "She pauses as if in pain before continuing. "We all agreed that it was time. Your father knew you were ready, but we made a mistake Everly. We gave the darkness too much time while preparing for their attack. We thought we knew this foolish enemy that they were only filled with greed, but the wrong information was given to us. We were told they attacked to only take Amara and the gates. We were fooled. It was deception but before we could stop it had already begun. To stop the battle would have meant losing everything...you...Tallon...my people. We thought we could defeat them in the aftermath but then the dragons.... they knew. They knew our strengths and our weaknesses and before even your father knew their plan we were doomed. My people barely escaped only thanks to Abrastos who paid the price for our freedom by submitting so we could reach the plains. He sacrificed the dragons. I have not seen or felt his vibration on the land since the battle and I fear the worst. We have had no word from any dragons and only see the torture they endure and in all of this.... I cannot find Tallon who fled at my side broken with the agony of loss. He left soon after searching for you and we do not know his fate. I am so sorry Everly. I am so sorry you have lost so much in losing your father but know he did what was needed in an effort to save us all.... to save Axis and the realms."

"My brother.... Tallon...oh no!" I turn realizing what I've done "Signa I left Tallon! I abandoned him! I should have told you sooner. I was captured and he was trying to save me, but I didn't listen...." I say quickly before remembering Tallon also told me not to trust anyone; that the enemy is close. If all the Signa has told me is true, then why isn't Tallon here? Even I cannot fathom all that she has said. The dragons. My father. Tallon. They all have such power but are now all missing or dead.

I sit quickly on the lounge closest to me and Az comes closer to stand next to me.

"You saw your brother?" he asks angrily.

"Everly, where is Tallon?" Signa asks at the same time, and I see guards enter the room quietly.

"I don't know," I answer her honestly. "I thought he had been captured during the battle and then he found me on the east road, and I didn't understand how or why he appeared. I was captured...he tried to save me...he tried to tell me something, but it was too late. Oh, Signa! I left my brother! I am so foolish, and I need to find him!"

"We will find him, Everly. Trust me. Let me find him for you. Know my love for Tallon. You have too much already to do. Let me do this for you." She tells me firmly.

"It has been weeks Signa. Weeks since I saw him." I tell her sadly.

"We will find him. I only need a place to start. We will follow his vibrations across Axis hoping he chooses to answer my call below." She tells me before walking quickly towards the soldiers and I watch as she gives them her orders.

"Everly, you are tired and need to rest." I hear Az's voice next to me and turn to look at him beside me. I have almost forgotten him with all these revelations. It is as if the whole rotation of this horror has changed and if this is all true then my brother Tallon knows the truth.

I have known only love and protection from him and he would never harm me I knew this, and I am angry at myself. If only I had listened to what I knew was true and trusted those who have always protected me I would not bear the scars that line my body and face.

"Everly, listen to what you are told but think on all that has happened. Do not let a few kinds words from someone who is familiar let you believe in the impossible. The light still flows, and I cannot see this darkness she speaks of. Think on what the Reine Fee had said but look at it from every angle." Az quietly counsels from beside me as the Reine Fee gives instructions across the room.

I watch the Reine Fee come back and sit across from me.

"I will answer all your questions, Everly. I am loyal to you. We are Axis above and below. Bound together and you know our alliance has always been honoured and cherished." She tells me and then reaches across to take my hand. It is warmth and light and I look at her face and only see the truth. She has only been kind to me, loyal to my father and it is this history that makes me want to believe what she tells me.

"My father..." I begin but she stops me.

"Your Father had faith in you Everly. He knew that if he sacrificed himself you had the best chance of saving Axis and the realms. He couldn't. He tried. He gave everything of himself in trying and in the end gave his life knowing that is what it would take."

"The light," I say nodding.

"Yes. The light. It was time. Solomon knew this however he did not anticipate the strength of the darkness that swept in through those gates. He knew his death was going to be painful, but he also knew you would rise. What he underestimated was us, his allies. What was done to the dragons is beyond Axis and not even the power of below can free them although we have tried."

"Abrastos is free," I tell her smiling as her face lights with joy.

"How?" she asks with such eagerness.

"My sword...and the light," I tell her honestly and as I do; I remember the talisman. I am hesitant to share the information of my greatest treasure so decide to wait. Maybe tomorrow I will have the courage to tell her, but I need time to think, to trust her a little more.

"I am so pleased, but we have not heard from him! No message declaring his freedom! Why hasn't he saved them all? The dragons fly in formations across the plains regularly." she asks.

"Abrastos does not have the strength without a First. They seek refuge in Eos knowing I will come."

"I am pleased." She says nodding. 'It is the safest place on Axis for them until we can save them all."

"Everly needs to rest." Az interrupts abruptly and I look at him angrily he would embarrass me and imply weakness.

"I am well." I smile at Signa reassuringly when I see the concern clearly in her face.

"Where you injured?" she asks as she checks me over worriedly, and I know she cares.

"I was ...captured.... tortured." I tell her and she places a hand across her heart at the shock of my words, so I quickly continue "But I am healed." I smile at her.

"Oh Everly, I am so sorry. The lines...on your face?" she asks gently.

"Yes, but they will fade." Is all I answer, and I am gratefully when she asks nothing further.

"I understand but you are here now, and I will give you my vow. The Aurelians are loyal to you Everly but yes, rest, we will talk again in the morning." The Reine Fee responds rising from her chair. "I have prepared the apartments Everly so you will have the familiarity of the First family's rooms. Anything you wish will be provided you only need to ask." She finishes and turns towards me touching my arm. "We will talk more tomorrow. I have so much to tell you and a message...from

Solomon. We will make this right Everly. Our world depends on us...above and below...we will not fail her." And she leans forward to kiss my cheek.

"Thank you, Signa. You have my word too that I will make this right but for now, your hospitality is very much appreciated." I smile at her, all my frustration and anger gone. I am grateful for her honesty even if the truth brings sadness. I take her hand kindly ensuring I have her attention "Please Signa, send word immediately if there is any news on Tallon. I am so worried I have failed him."

"You could not fail him, Everly." She tells me kindly touching my cheek "Your brother loves you. We will find him, and you will have his protection before the Last." And I smile at her words remembering the number of times Tallon and I spent discussing the Last. Wondering at the mystery of the sacred event and now, when it is time, it would mean everything to have him beside me.

"Be at peace Reine Fee. I will be waiting impatiently for your call in the morning as I am eager to receive my father's message." I tell her as I lean in and kiss her cheek. I am pleased to see her smile.

"You are not alone Everly." She answers and I become still as I study her face. These are the same words Az has said to me and I hesitate at such a coincidence. Maybe I constantly look lost or alone so on that slightly miserable note I incline my head in acknowledgment before starting the walk to the apartments in silence. Not trusting the questions that gather with increasing momentum in my head.

Chapter 36

It is failing once more. My shield has slipped, and the source has grown beyond my control once again. It is becoming more frequent now; the time is drawing nearer, and I must prepare for what comes. The darkness is becoming increasingly dangerous and soon there will be no other choice.

I move with hast, Axis at my back pushing me towards her greatest salvation. The pain cutting through me tainted with the sour taste of humiliation and shame.

I find the source and see the destruction. It is surrounded by so many this time. Questions will not easily go unanswered as I see the accusations and opportunities grow and take seed in each person's heart.

I cannot hide it. I cannot destroy it and I cannot stop my enemies from plotting and rising because they see what I have hidden.

I slowly move towards it. The blue of endless oceans watches me, knowing me, understanding why I am here.

This cannot keep happening. There must be a way to protect it, even from itself. It is my only hope.

I will hide it in plain sight, at my side. I will encourage strength and training beyond all expectations.

It will rise without knowledge or understanding of its origin.

It will gain everything, and I can only hope it will not destroy us all.

Chapter 37

"Get up Everly! Move!" I hear Az yell at me from the doorway of my bedroom and I leap out of bed at the urgency in his voice. I can hear screams in the distance and explosions. The walls shake slightly with each rumble.

Without asking any questions I dress as quickly as I possibly can in armour, and it is only moments later I run into the main living area to find him pacing, dressed surprisingly in battle armour himself.

"How do you have the armour of Ihava?" I stammer at him surprised, knowing this armour is especially made by the third family for heirs and is the same as I wear.

"The city is under attack." Is all he says and before he even finishes, I am moving out the door. I will find the truth from him later. For now, there is only war.

I run along the top of the passageway towards the Reine Fee's apartments knowing I must protect her. She holds the balance of Axis below. She is formidable and fierce, but the underground has never before been breached because of the protection of my family. Now all I see is scurrying Aurelian soldiers and hear screams of terror from those who call the city home.

From the walkway above I can see out across the expanse of the underground. The plains above the city have been torn apart and enemy soldiers descend on ropes into the heart of Signa's stronghold.

Like ants, they come in never-ending waves and my heart races at the familiar sight of the same soldiers and sheer numbers of those who battled and defeated us at Amara, those soldiers who watched eagerly while I was tortured.

It is within a dozen strides the first soldier drops onto the path in front of me and without stopping I call my sword and plough through him. Let them come! I tell myself as I gather my wits to fight. My fear clawing at me, my doubts threatening to drown me, I run into the heart of this battle. I will never stop protecting my world.

I draw the light and balance to me leaping off the side of the path onto the nearest rope that descends, full of soldiers towards the city streets. With my sword high, I hook my leg around the rope while attacking those above and below me, but they are no match. I turn my body around the rope cutting and stabbing everything with my swords distance before leaping to the next rope and doing the same. Over and over I leap across those ridiculous ropes until I reach the centre of the below.

I watch as soldiers endlessly scurry down the ropes, hungry to destroy us and I call the light down through the talisman to my sword. I watch their faces turn toward where I am suspended on the rope and smile at them viciously before releasing white fire in an arc of sparks outwards across the roof.

Now they will taste my power! Their cries soon turn from excitement to terror as the ropes burn with the light, and every soldier clingy to them falls to their death below. I smile viciously as I watch their flaying bodies drop into piles of darkness beneath.

I turn as another explosion rocks across the city and see more of this scourge streaming in never-ending waves of black through the tunnels on the east side closest to Amara.

Their tactical advantage with the ropes lost, I descend quickly into the city where I can see families running for cover throughout the streets. Explosions rock the city as I hit the ground running, moving quickly through the main market area screaming at people to head south.

Soldier after soldier attacks, coming at me over and over and blood quickly coats my sword. I am never afraid death waits for me in battle. The blood and sweat and fury of defending my world only increases my strength, knowing I kill these destroyers who think to bring terror and continue to invade what will never be theirs.

As their numbers increase, I suddenly turn within their midst and release light. It sears and burns in an explosion outward leaving nothing but ash in its wake until I use the talisman to shield its power within.

I cannot see Az in the chaos but have no doubt he is quite capable of protecting himself as it would have been impossible for him to follow my erratic fighting.

As I run towards the south tunnels which lead to the safety of the mountains, I see the captain of the Aurelian guard surrounded by gold soldiers running in the opposite direction and signal to him to stop. The relief in his face when he recognises me is evident as he comes to a halt in front of me and drops to his knee.

"The Reine Fee?" I ask urgently.

"She is protecting the people as they flee into the tunnels on the south side away from this invasion." He tells me.

"And her guards?"

"The numbers are too great. She has sent her guards to protect the people, as there are too many! We cannot hold against these numbers! Once the enemy has crossed to the south of the city the Reine Fee will seal the tunnels. We do not have much time and not every Aurelian has been evacuated. The below has never been breached… " He tells me desperately.

"I will do what I can to assist. Move all your guards closer to the south side of outer walls and defend the safety of the tunnels until everyone can be evacuated. Leave the east entrances and city centre undefended. Let them flood that area and give your people and the Reine Fee time to ensure their own safety. I will do what I can to hold them in the centre as far away from the south as possible. Now go!"

"Thank you, Alta Axian!" he tells me and takes my hand.

"Enough. Rise. Let us save who we can! This enemy can have hollow buildings and burnt homes but never our people!" I call out and the guards cheer as I turn and run back into the city centre ready to hold the line.

I will draw them to me with the light I tell myself as I race through the streets to reach the pavilion in the central gardens.

Within minutes I see the white bright dome of the central gardens and the beautiful, meticulous grass. I run quickly to its centre and as I do, I lift my hand in the air letting the light flow towards me, rippling the air and sparking like splinters of white fire. The light blinds the air around me as I continue to run in a shower of light. I hear the excited shouts of soldiers and I'm pleased when they scream my name, celebrating in their foolishness, thinking they have found me.

I leap onto the pavilion; my hand still sending light through the air and watch as their numbers mass around me. They gather like stupid rats smiling at their own cleverness until I jumped into their mass, watching with glee as they are turned to dust, ashes in the light.

Still, stupidly, they come. They relive on sheer numbers as their strength, but it is only death that gathers around me now. The glass flows with red as my sword leads the charge. I see only white fire in the air as soldier after soldier attacks. This is my fight, my place in this world is protection and defence and they come to me now stronger than I have ever been, and I relish the feeling of death at my feet.

They attack as if a child with sticks and soon the grass is littered with bodies and blood. It is not long before they realise their foolishness and the cry to retreat sounds, but it is a doomed cry of desperation because I will ensure no one leaves here with air in their lungs as I send the light behind their retreat.

Satisfied no enemy stands within the centre of the city I run using the balance to speed my pace, finding them desperate for escape now their fate is clear, but I am unforgiving. I am rage and light. I am vengeance and destruction. I am what I need to be for Axis at this moment.

I know they will regroup, and I will be waiting for them. They will realise I am power and light but when they do my sword will greet them again to show them the price of their failure.

The shock on their faces as I continue to cut off their retreat is bliss. This is not the easy battle they perhaps thought to dominate beneath the plains. I will not let them think their vast numbers make them invincible. They will know the force of my bloodline, the power of my destiny. And if these soldiers are unable to grasp this message, then I am sure their leader will feel it when he counts the bodies at his feet.

It is only minutes before they lay in a mass of death at my feet, but I am already moving, searching, hungry for more as I run back towards the south tunnels.

I am confident the Aurelians will be saved. There have been no signs of civilians the closer I get to the tunnels. Let them have the city, it means nothing without the might of the Reine Fee and her people anyway! I will reach the Reine Fee and do what I can to assist with the evacuation.

Determined and deadly I flow through the streets fiercely cutting down any sign of the enemy as I head towards the tunnels pleased with the lesson they have been taught today.

"ALTA AXIAN!" a familiar voice suddenly booms out across the city. "ALTA AXIAN! SAVE THE AUERLIANS! SURRENDER!" It demands from high above.

But I do not stop running.

I know that voice which has called to me in my nightmares. That muffled voice of rage and darkness he always obscures by the cowardice of a hood.

He calls to me as if he expects me to submit but I am not captured, neither do I have any kind of torque on my wrist so all he will find is that I will fight against whatever comes. I will kill whoever thinks to support him. I will do whatever it takes to bring him and his army defeat, but I will not surrender so I scoff at his words, ignoring his rage as I continue towards the south side of the city.

I can only hope the Reine Fee has had time to save her people. That my distraction was enough to secure their escape before the rage of this madman catches up to me.

I hear the pounding of my feet as I move and draw the light and balance for the strength; I know I'll need when the fight finds me again.

I am relieved when I see the south wall looming up ahead and have not come across any enemy soldiers within the last few neighbourhoods, but before I can reach the outer wall a scream pierces the air across the city and I stop as the sound of pain fills my veins with icy dread when I recognise who cries.

"EVERLY! DO NOT LISTEN! SAVE THEM!" I hear her pain-filled scream and I turn and look up at the royal platform above the city knowing what I will see.

Even from this distance, I can clearly make out the gold of her gown along with the iridescent shine of her hair. She is such golden magnificence made all the more emphasized standing surrounded by those dreaded black uniforms of darkness.

I see they span out across the upper walkways as they search across the city below for me knowing I cannot ignore her plea.

I am enraged.

Their numbers seemed endless and chaotic when I fought them unexpectedly but now, they appear organised and I realise my delay may not have given all the Aurelians time to escape. My delay was their ploy and clearly gives them time to capture the Reine Fee.

I glare frustrated at the platform above. I have no choice. I can do no less than save her and as I glare at the platform in the distance, I am furious they have outplayed me.

I look around carefully, watching for some foolish ambush, as I begin the walk back towards the centre of the city. I move quickly away from the south hoping that I have not given them the location of the tunnels. Hoping the Reine Fee has let herself be captured to save her people.

When I am closer to the centre, I send a pulse of light into the air, so my position is clear and within seconds see the black armour of my enemy's soldiers amongst the rumble as they track my steps. I look in every direction for Az fearful he might try to save me. I can only trust he will do all he can to protect the Aurelians.

My head held high, I walk the rest of the distance to the centre of the royal gardens and stand on the platform I know will rise to meet the large one above. My sword in my hand, I look fiercely towards the roof and breath in deeply, gathering myself as the ground begins to move.

As both platforms touch, it is clear they come in great numbers, as soldiers stand ready in every direction. At least they are wise enough to show some respect, I think pleased to see the fear in many of their faces.

I see the Reine Fee held tightly within the centre of the platform, so I nod slightly as she lifts her head to meet my eyes. I see sadness sweep across her face at my sign of respect, but she does not utter a word.

"Ah, the beautiful Everly." He begins and I look into that dark hood that looms just beyond the face of the Reine Fee. I stand resolutely on the platform not moving at all and then decide to yawn as if I am bored.

"And here is the nobody who thinks he is somebody I see. At least show me your face so I can have the satisfaction of knowing who threatens me." I tell him but his only response is to laugh.

"Such confidence in the face of defeat!" Is all he says before making his demands "This is an easy exchange, Everly. I simply ask you to save the Reine Fee's life...in exchange for the crown. You only have to concede."

"How predictable! This again?" I smile at him insolently. "But foolish. The Reine Fee deserted us during the battle that cost my father his life. I have no intention of saving her now." And I wipe my hand on my pants hoping to make it glaringly obvious that I have better things to be doing.

"Choose." He says quietly and I do not respond. "Always the hard way with you." He tells me angrily and before I can move, he raises a knife into the air above the Reine Fees heart.

"I will concede...." I say uncertainly. "If you beat me in single combat..." I say quickly but forcefully hoping my fear isn't strangling my words.

"I have no need to best you or anyone else on Axis. I have defeated the First and now the Reine Fee. I don't need anything from you but two little words. A short, sweet 'I concede' is all our universe needs to hear."

"It is not that simple! You are asking the impossible!" I spit at him angrily "You do not understand! With these two little words, I could destroy this entire universe! Billions! It is not mine to give away."

"I know exactly what I am asking. I have been tied to Axis, my entire life Princess! I have done her bidding for too long! I know the sacrifice, the light and balance! I will control our destiny! Our history! NOW CONCEDE!" he screams at me.

"You are Axian?" I ask surprised.

"We are all Axian. Every one of us within the realms bows down to the great will of the light and balance. It doesn't make you special." He tells me calmly, but I can see there is more. He spits rage and destruction, darkness and revenge. He demands the impossible as if it is his right...

"But I am Alta Axian," I tell him quietly knowing the importance of my legacy and hoping this will prompt him to reveal his.

"And you will be the last...." Comes his hissed reply and before I can move, he brings the knife down stabbing the Reine Fee in the stomach.

I do not react. I stand watching as the gold of her blood blooms across her gown and flows to the floor. "You can still save her Everly." He promises but I remain still. There is no winning here, no losing, no compromise. There can only be one certainty...and that is death.

"Everly." Her voice catches me by surprise, calm and composed and I lift my head to meet her eyes. "It is you, Everly. Only you have the power to save us all. Your father, he shielded you, hid you but you know the strength of what you possess." She smiles at me and I see her decision. "You are enough."

I know what she is about to do and jump towards her, but soldiers intervene, and I am too late. I step away understanding her loyalty, her honour to Axis above all else.

She is the distraction. The reason the Aurelians will be safe. She is the reason I will survive. Without her, there is no more for me here and once she is gone, any negotiation will be over, and I knowingly bow my head respectfully.

"Para Axis." Is all she whispers.

I stand blocked by the mass of black armour but hold her eyes watching sadly as she smiles at me and without any other warning a shard of the ground rushes up piercing her in the heart, killing her instantly.

He jumps away from her body. Screaming in rage as he grips his shoulder in pain. I am frozen as I watch blood, the colour of the night, flowing down his arm and onto the gold platform.

"Seize her!" I hear him shout and I look into that hood as I move. The soldiers are too slow, and I am already gone. I leap from the platform to the city floor and run. I move rapidly towards the east, towards the capital city of Amara, purposefully avoiding the south. I am only strides away from the first tunnel on the outer walls when I hear his voice and stop. He runs towards me fanatically and I fall into his arms.

"Everly!" is all he says before stepping back to check on me.

"She is dead Az, she is dead," I tell him sadly.

"I know." He answers me.

"And her people?" I ask desperate to know.

"Evacuated to the mountains. They are safe." He reassures me.

"We need to leave. NOW!" I tell him urgently knowing they will find us quickly but before I can move, he steps towards me. He holds both my arms while staring intently at me before gripping me almost angrily and pulling me close. He is warmth and safety and just for a second, I melt before stepping away hurriedly and checking the area around us.

"We need to move," I whisper urgently to him and he nods.

I can hear the rush of soldiers coming towards our position and know we do not have much time.

"We cannot leave without exposing the tunnels!" I tell him. "We must find another way." I look around the area frantically.

"Wait Everly!" is all he warns as he steps back into my space. He clasps my hand lifting it with his towards the roof. "Draw the light Everly. Draw it roughly NOW towards your sword!" He shouts and without hesitating I pull at the air around me in waves. The light blooms rapidly within me and sparks ignite above us from the talisman. My hand, which holds my sword, ignites in white-hot flames and I watch fascinated as Az raises his sword alongside mine and the white light of mine consumes his. His light is different, but the power I yield becomes electric as if it is fire and flames.

"Push upwards!" he screams above the firestorm. And I draw the balance around me and push upwards watching in awe as we rise towards the roof. I look up to our swords to see his is completely obliterated by the light of mine and he is hunched next to me, clinging to my waist. The white light flows down and around us as we rise. It is as if a firestorm falls in our wake covering us in pure white flames.

"The roof!!" I call in warning, but he does not answer as we punch through the surface without any pause or resistance into the sky of Axis above.

"Let it go Everly!" he screams, and I let the light recede gently, watching the gold plains rise to meet us as we sink back down, and my feet touch the ground. I watch in wonder as the flames fall in every direction before I release the light and they dissipate without a trace.

I turn to look around me dazed with everything that has just happen and see we are close to the edge of the plains on the side of Eos. I look back to Az and watch horrified as he collapses to the ground.

"Az?" I ask concerned as I quickly crouch next to him.

"I'm fine Everly. Just give me a minute." He grunts and I watch him close his eyes as if in pain.

"What's wrong?" I ask but he doesn't answer. "Az please, are you ill?"

"I will be fine." He answers between grasps "Your light is unexpectedly powerful…." He finishes, looking at me as if he is deciding something. "I thought you only learnt how to use the light days ago yet…it doesn't matter." He quickly finishes and pushes himself upright. "We need to move."

"Az, the Reine Fee?" I ask worried "The Aurelians are unprotected. We must wait for Tallon! There is only Tallon left!" And I see confusion blanket his face.

"What do you mean…there is only Tallon?" he asks stepping towards me "The Aurelians are defeated. They are without a ruler. They will be ruled by the darkness…" He begins but stops when he sees me shaking my head.

"You are wrong…Tallon is the Heir below. The Aurelians will never be ruled by force or defeat." I tell him and he stares at me with his mouth open. "You can close your mouth Az. Heirs are protected, hidden, for their own safety. Tallon will feel the death of Signa and rise. It will give him the power to find me." I smile at him pleased, but he almost looks…furious.

"Yet another mystery of Axis revealed." He barks out in frustration, running his hand through his hair.

"There are mysteries of Axis that are kept for her safety…" I begin but don't bother continuing when I see him getting angrier.

"It is one thing after another with you Everly!" He begins. "Mysteries, riddles, call it what you will but it doesn't make Axis invincible! It makes you all liars! Thieves! Selfish even!"

"Selfish! Because we protect what is most precious to our universe? That's ridiculous!" I snarl back at him, annoyed at this unexpected outburst. "You pepper me with questions constantly wanting to know more and I have told you more than I should and yet you stand in front of me calling my family liars and thieves?? What does that make you? Whoever you are! I do what I am born to do, and it is only Axis that matters to me." I finish angrily.

"You foolishly trusted the Signa and everything she said just because she said it was from your father! You think your precious brother, who know just happens to be the heir of the Aurelians is out there searching for you! Even after all the battles, the torture, and the clear fact you are completely alone you still think you can save Axis??? Everyone has left you or is dead! She is gone, Everly!! Tallon will never reach you! You have lost!" He finishes screaming the last part in rage.

I stare at him shocked not knowing what he expects me to say.

"With everything that has happened it is more important than ever we get to Eos." Is all I reply and with that he stares at me for a second furiously before he turns abruptly and walks away.

I watch as he struggles to control his rage gripping his sword arm angrily, but I am glad when he finally whistles across the plains for the admetos.

Chapter 38

"It is duplicity, isn't it? Betrayal?"

"Yes, and I am not innocent."

"I know."

"There is always a price that must be paid for these things. Things that cannot be undone the cause pain which festers and grows. This was not a small slight. What I did tipped the scales for eternity for us all."

"Do you know what they come for?"

"Yes."

"Me?"

"No. They do not know who you are. It is her." Is all I say as I see the pain flare clearly in his eyes. She is my greatest treasure and he is sworn to protect her. "Can she be saved?"

"It is possible."

"What is the price to save her?"

"Everything."

Chapter 39

It is as if a hurricane chases us, the wild, angry, unpredictable storm that makes the air electric with tension and builds with pressure before unleashing destructive havoc. The energy increases the closer we get to Eos Nevaeh. They know we travel to the pAx and we know they track our every move. They circle our rear, following through the day as if they hunt us. Both Az and I have retraced our steps numerous times disappearing to watch as they search frantically for us.

We know their purpose is to constantly provoke us and we have battled with them throughout the trip, but it is as though the formations are used to poke at us and wear us down rather than try to capture or kill. It is frustrating and unnerving. There is no rest on this journey, no safety, no protection.

Our enemy must know what lay in Eos. He is Axian and I struggle to understand his origins if his purpose is to destroy. My family, Alta Axian protect the core of our universe and ensure we thrive. It is the harmony and legacy of each of the four foundation families that is our past, present and future. He is a fool in his quest for Axis, but he is relentless. I know his next challenge will come when he thinks he is in the greatest position of strength. I can only pray to Axis for guidance and hope that whoever he is he does not succeed before I reach the pAx.

This hooded conqueror reveals more and more about himself, but it only makes his identity more troubling. I have seen his skill in battle and know he is trained in elite combat. He understands the ways of war and has gained such knowledge of my strengths and weaknesses having captured me and seen me fight against his soldiers twice now but yet he knows he cannot kill me.

The trip to Eos from the plains is five days of travelling and until we cross the border, we will not be safe.

So far it has been four days of riding and fighting and we are both tired and in need of food and rest. We have camped each night in shifts, protecting each other and keeping a watch for these regular attacks but as we travel closer to Eos, they have become more and more scarce. We have barely spoken, both of us angry at our words on the plains. I wonder why he travels with me if he hates my family so much, but he is all I have and am glad he is here. I am not my family and maybe he will understand that in time.

It is on the fifth day as we prepare for our final run to the border of Eos it all changes.

A faint rumble echoes in the distance and Az steps protectively in front of me. I step beyond his protection, glaring at him, reminding him once again that I am Alta Axian but then turn to in horror as the dust warps into the air with such violence it is as if the ground of Axis herself breaks apart...and in that moment I know.

"The plains have collapsed," I whisper to him horrified. "He has destroyed the Aurelian city. Such folly. Now I must save above and below, and don't have much time anymore." And he looks at me but says nothing before quickly moving to the admetos.

"Everly, what do you mean you must save above and below now?" He asks as I mount.

"The Aurelians are our protectors. They are the balance to the power of our gifts and are bonded to Alta Axians are protectors, Tallon is mine, Signa was my fathers. Always opposites, always balanced. They were created not as a foundation family but solely for the protection of my family, which is why they fight at our side. Should the Aurelians fail or be lost it all falls to me and with such power and no balance there is only isolation and chaos. The pillars are for the realms. The Aurelians are for Axis."

"I didn't realise...." He says looking shocked at yet another revelation.

"It is knowledge such as this that gives enemies more power. The First family and the Aurelians have always ruled side by side. There must always be balance Az." And he frowns at me for a second.

"You knew this and let the Reine Fee kill herself?" He asks and I stop to look carefully at him.

"Yes." Is all I say before turning to move away. The Reine Fee has an heir. She knew this when she sacrificed her life. She also knew that I would do whatever it took to save her heir and the cost of her life was my freedom, the hope to save us all.

I see the admetos are ready and quickly mount eager to reach the pAx. I must push forward knowing what is required of both of us and hope he will find me soon. Tallon will understand my urgency to get to Eos, to survive this journey because his life truly began in earnest when the Reine Fee took her life. She understood her actions and with the Aurelian plains crumbling the dust will rise quickly and I can do nothing until I reach Eos and become First.

It is my greatest worry and has been throughout our travels. Walking away from the plains was heartbreaking. Knowing that destruction and chaos would erupt once my enemy realised there was no one left to harm or capture or use against me. My only consolation is at least the people will be safe within the mountain stronghold until Tallon is able to reach them.

Axis cannot balance the realms unless there is harmony above and below. We are both born of her will and this is the core of our power but what will it cost us when the Reine Fee is dead and Tallon is missing and we have no First?

I have felt the guilt of my actions even if she gave me no choice. I have foolishly thought I had found hope in our alliance but once again I have no army, no allies and Tallon is lost. I can only hope to reach the pAx and seek resolution.

We ride relentlessly on towards Eos as the dust gathers on the ground. The dust that was a gentle mist from the misalignment turns to a sandstorm at the disintegration of the plains and the loss of its Queen.

"We cannot sustain this pace Az!" I call to him as he rides slightly in front and I see he hears me when he nods. The dust is beginning to choke and the admetos slow as it becomes harder for them to breath and still Az pushes them forward.

"Az!" I call to him again and I watch as he drops his pace and falls in beside me. "Let them go!" I tell him but he shakes his head.

"We will not make it without them." He replies. I see the concern in his face, but he rides them to death if we continue and I will not see the admetos die for my sake.

"They will not make Az. Let them go. We will face what comes but I will not ride these animals to their death just to save myself." And I see the pain of the decision on his face. "Az! Please..." I beg him and I am relieved when he finally slows the admetos and once we stop, I slide to the ground and watch the indecision on his face.

"Release them," I beg him again and he doesn't answer. He dismounts reluctantly and stands beside the closest admetos. He places his hand reverently against its neck as if remorseful for the pain they have endured. He and the admetos stand together for seconds before the horses turn and run on towards Eos without us. They move rapidly away from the dust and I am relieved.

"Everly..." Az looks to me " You have given us little choice now." He tells me sadly and the pain in his face makes the moment all too real.

"It was inevitable. This is the moment Az. The darkness gathers and all my allies are lost. This is what Axis asks of me, the possible against all impossibilities." I gently tell him lifting my hand to press it against his cheek. His closes his eyes as if to savour the moment. "Thank you, Az. I can feel your anger and frustration growing and I am sorry." I tell him knowing he would have run the admetos to the ground to save me. "I will never forget all you have done for me, but I will not concede so easily so let's run towards Eos. We are only a short distance away; the border must be close. I will not stand here waiting for the storm to catch up, breathing the dust as my world falls apart. I will run to my salvation and hope the heart of Axis guides my path." And he smiles at me.

"So extraordinary..." he all he says as he takes my hand and squeezes it. " You are right! It is not over for us yet Everly. This fight for Axis just begins." He tells me looking at me carefully. "I will ensure you reach the pAx. You will not be alone." And at those words I nearly break as I realise, I cannot bear the thought of this life or the next without him.

"Destiny does not always give us want we want Az but if she hears me, I will only ask for you, in this life and the next," I assure him and as Axis crumbles around us and the dust blinds our path, I gather the light and balance in the air around me and I run into chaos with Az by my side.

Chapter 40

"They know who she is now."

"Yes"

"Then it is nearly time."

"It is."

"They will destroy her."

"Perhaps."

"And you."

"I can do no less than ensure they try."

"The other families?"

"This is the price, Tallon. It must be our secret alone. The other families must rise to support her, or they will fall."

"Will she?"

"That will be her choice."

"I am not strong enough to save her."

"No, she must save herself to save us all because what comes for us only contains darkness and she is the only one who is able to fight it."

Chapter 41

"It will be safest to camp at the border tonight Everly, as it is likely we will not make it make further before sunset." Az's voice breaks through my concentration. "And it will be safer with our backs against Eos Nevaeh ready to greet the pAx at daybreak." And he looks at me questioningly, so I nod in agreement.

"Are you ok?" He asks tugging at my arm until we slow to a walk. He draws closer, looking at me seriously.

"Just tired," I answer smiling at him, reassuring him that I am as stubborn and strong as I need to be although I worry about the ever-building tension that increases with each step towards Eos.

The dust has become thicker as we reach closer to the border and I am hopeful that without the admetos we are harder to track and have brought ourselves enough time. Any advantage we had at the beginning is long gone now and this thick, suffocating tension that rises warns me that the real trouble is not far away.

We walk in silence side by side. I am not willing to stop unless absolutely necessary. Every step closer to Eos brings me closer to the Last. I wonder at how this journey would have been alone and if I would have made the same decisions. Az has taken the lead the entire trip and I am happy to let him do so as long as it is in my interests.

There are no longer any expectations to be my father's daughter, Tallon's sister nor Alta Axian and with all I know gone, defeated or destroyed. I am struggling to recognise my place in this world, but I will not let Az's cruel words make me doubt what I know is true.

It has been a difficult day as we run against the thickening dust and I am relieved when we finally see the peaks of Eos Nevaeh rising in the distance. It has been nearly five long days of fighting and travelling and although the admetos were swift and carried us most of the way I feel the exhaustion of the day on foot and the ache in every bone of my body.

It is in those final hours, those moments when relief is close that I feel the desperation rise. The terror of this life grips at me angrily as if it demands my attention and I know my greatest battle is yet to come in the Last.

I know the hope of Axis and our realms depend on me, and I will rise. I am my father's daughter; I cannot fail Axis. The light floods through me as if in warning pushing at me, firing dangerously close to release but thankfully the talismans shield holds it for me. I cannot shake the feeling of doom that engulfs me. It is as if all my fears, all my doubts and all my future converge here, and I can do nothing but wait for destiny's next move.

As we search for a place to camp near the border of Eos, I hear the familiar slow, careful slide of metal and signal to Az who nods. This has been our constant, these skirmishes and I am tired of the endlessly, pointless conflict that continually comes our way. I have been careful to fight according to the abilities the enemy expects of me. I know in my heart the power of the light has grown in strength and I can use it easily, but I am not willing to share the extent of it, not even with Az. I don't know what it means and wonder if it is just a part of the unbalance.

"I am going to face them alone," I whisper to Az knowing this time it will be different. We are close now and the air sparks with energy, light blooms in me. "Can you feel it? The tension in the air? It is as if the light and balance lay heavily mingled in the dust. The spark and saturation fill me, and I am tired of these games. It is time I fought rather than just defend. They need a reminder of who I actually am." I finish smiling at him.

"I feel the increase in power Everly, but we are close to Eos, too close to take any risks. Why would you want to fight them alone...now? And what do you expect of me? Do you expect me to sit here idly while soldiers surround you; just to make you feel better? Everly please, wait. I feel the rising tension too, but you cannot face them alone. It is too much of a risk especially this close to Eos it could trigger the Last and you don't know what waits for you at the end of that sword." he pleads with me desperately, but I know I am right in this. I watch him struggle to convince me.

"I must face them alone. The tension is.... different. It is power. I can feel it in the air around me as if it surrounds me. It flows through me as if it is seeking more. It is almost as if Axis has been waiting and watching for this moment. It calls to me. It blooms with the fullness of light in my chest. It is time I faced what comes for me. Trust me in this Az. It is time they remembered who I was born to be." And when I see his frown lessen, I know he will concede.

"I only want you to be safe Everly. I want to stand beside you in the Last. The pAx will protect you until it is time, but we must cross over the border into Eos before they can intervene. Listen to me please..." He pleads with me.

"There is no future for any of us Az if we sit in the shadows waiting for the right moment, a weakness in our enemy that may never come. I can feel this as if it beats in my chest. The talisman glows Az look at it. The light and balance are almost concentrated at this point and it only makes me stronger." I smile at him "It is time to fight back." But as I step forward, he grabs my arm turning me to face him.

"You cannot defeat the darkness, Everly." He says quietly staring at me intently. He thinks I need him! That I am a helpless girl in need of protection and will not let me fight alone!

"Let go of me Az," I tell him angrily pulling my arm away. "What do you mean...I cannot defeat them? Az? They are yet to defeat me! Capture! Fight! Throw soldier after soldier at me! Kill the Reine Fee! Destroy the dragons! But me.... no...they have never defeated me." I tell him angrily.

"Everly, listen to me." He replies coming to stand in front of me. "Their numbers are endless. They have already defeated the two most powerful cities on Axis, the city of Amara and have destroyed the Aurelian city below. You have no allies left. No way of reaching the realms. Even if you complete the Last you have no way of reclaiming your throne!"

"I don't need to be told it will be difficult..." I begin to reply but Az cuts me off angrily.

"It wouldn't be difficult Everly. It is impossible! The Axis you know is gone! It is all over! There is no First, no Reine Fee. No dragons. No armies. No Tallon. There is nothing left for you to fight for!"

"It is not over," I say firmly angry at his doubts.

"You cannot win this fight." He begins and I see the air thickens and grows dark. "You cannot defeat what comes." And I do not move. "Everly..." he steps forward and whispers in my ear. "Concede.... we are too powerful. We have won. Don't force me to kill you." And I know the truth, so I step back and smile at him as if we are old friends. He waits tensely, knowing he has finally revealed himself.

"Az...." I begin softly and see hope light in his eyes as I do not seem to fight him anymore, but he is wrong. "NEVER!" I hiss into the air and let the light spark blinding him as I turn and run.

I will reach the border! I must. The tension increases and although I always knew the possibilities my heart is torn in two. How could I have been so blind? All this time he has been with me, healed me, and helped me only because I was the one person who stood in his way! Every betrayal! Every battle! I have been foolish! It is my fault! The Aurelians are my fault! Everything is because of me!

I cannot help the tears that stream down my face. The humiliation and anger that boils and bubbles torments me with every conversation, every time I trusted him, and the price has been...everything...for my world, my family, my people. It is me who has betrayed us all but it not over and will never concede.

I run. Push forward knowing, even now, he will be searching for me. I am nothing but his naïve prize that will lead him to the Last. I wonder at his tactics and then I feel them before I see them. The air thick with dust and tension but I force calm. I can only stand tall to face the enemy I have brought to this place.

As I reach a cleared area, I see they wait for me. There come in force now, formations of soldiers and although they look ready to kill, I smile at their foolishness. This will be the battle for my world. He must have planned all those skirmishes all the while increasing the numbers of soldiers at the border. If this is his final play so I can do no less than rise and face it.

I step into the open, bloated with the increasing flow of light and balance, to face those who think they are strong enough to defeat me.

While watching the soldiers draw closer to my position, I hear the cry of dragons close and know they must be chained only a short distance away.

After each fight, I have used my sword to release the chains and send the dragons ahead to Eos. Wild with fear and most times covered with injuries it has been frustrating and disheartening to see how they have been treated yet satisfying to know I now only save what all Axians revere but gleefully cripple my enemy's forces too.

I am happy to continue to face soldier after soldier if it means after each victory more dragons are freed. If Az will not face me alone, I will find him at the end of this war when his soldiers lay dead at his feet and take everything from him just as he has done to me.

I smile my vicious grin at the enemy that surrounds me, but they do not move any closer. They stand quietly, holding their position, as they wait, and I watch them cautiously. This is not what I was expecting. Each time I have stood ready to attack and they have run towards us but this time they remain still.... and I know they wait for him.

A strange heaviness gathers, and I watch as the dust around the perimeter of the clearing thickens before it turns black. More tactics and tricks no doubt and I wait not knowing what comes next, but I am ready all the same.

The soldiers stand quietly for a moment before fanning out into a semicircle around my position. I cock my head and raise my sword but still, they do not attack.

The dust sweeps through the area and then stills but nothing else happens, no one moves. The ground stops rumbling, as it has in intervals, and still I patiently wait. The light and balance itch in my chest and the energy around me intensifies but still, they do not attack. I step towards them, but they step back out of my sword's reach.

"What game are you fools playing at now? Or are you just waiting like dogs for your master?" I ask scornfully but not one moves.

The air suddenly charges with light but it is not pure like mine it is dark and murky, and I push back. The light pushes at me again as if it tries to obliterate mine, but it is slimy and falls away as if repulsed. He is testing me knowing there is no more to gain with his false friendship.

I turn and look behind me knowing it is him that brings this darkness. It has always been him. Every tactic, every betrayal, every battle, every conversation, and every time he pretended to help, every slash of that whip. It has all been for the power of Axis and now he finally reveals himself when he understands he cannot have it.

Chapter 42

Lightning cracks in the air almost breaking the darkness apart and I stand ready to fight when I see the familiar form of my brother step towards me.

"Tallon!" I cry out in relief and then stop. He is covered in the eleven missing talismans! "WHAT HAVE YOU DONE?" I scream at him.

All golden and handsome, my brother is tall and board and looks every inch an indomitable soldier. He strides towards me confidently before stopping out of striking range. I look across his body at the talismans he wears, and they sit like pieces of metal strapped to his armour rather than melded to his body as mine but as our eyes meet, I have no doubt he greets me for war as he returns my smile.

"I come to save you, sister." He tells me as he pulls his sword from his back and holds it ready as his steps into his position beside me squeezing my shoulder.

"To save me from who brother?" I ask looking around the circle at the soldiers who have not moved.

"The Heir of Xiana. He is the Heir of Xiana." He simply states focused on the circle but gesturing to Az. Surely, he is mistaken. He is acting strange and it is bothering me so without thinking I turn towards him and grab his sword arm.

"Tallon, what the hell is going on?" I ask angrily "Do you realise the danger you are in?"

Tallon turns towards me "I know exactly what I am doing, and I know all that you have done but together we will stand and fight for Axis sister. This was not ever going to be a fair fight so stop expecting them to be honourable! You are all that matters Everly! Everything you are is worth every sacrifice for only you have the power to save us all!"

"You know who we fight?" I ask shocked and he turns to me with such anger in his face.

"The Xiana. The Heir of Xiana is the Hooded Man, your companion Azul Alta Xiana." He spits out angrily and I step back in shock. He cannot be right. The Second family of Axis! I have triggered the pillars. I have called for salvation and in this single stupid foolish moment, I realise all I have done.

"His name?" I ask as the bottom begins to fall out of my world. I knew he was my enemy but not their leader.

"Az," he says, and my greatest betrayal is revealed.

I cannot let my brother die because I have been so blind to the truth.

"Tallon he has revealed himself as our enemy but not as the Xiana! It cannot be!! I have led the Xiana to the Last! They have betrayed us all!" I tell him quickly knowing we do not have much time. "He is powerful Tallon."

"I know who you travelled with Everly. I could not get close but be assured I have watched you, tried to protect you this entire time. " He tells me sadly touching my cheek "I should have tried harder to save you, but I couldn't. Every time I came close, they intervened. I have cost you just as much as you have cost me." And we both know the truth of our failures. "Father knew it would be impossible to save you from the darkness. He knew the power they had. I could do nothing, not until you stepped out of his shadow and I am here now. Now we are here at the Last I will stand with you to fight for the light and ensure our legacy." And I grip my brother tightly knowing he speaks the truth.

"I am so sorry, Tallon. I have been so stupid. If only I had trusted myself." I sadly tell him.

"Ha Everly, they outplayed us all. They found you in the forest before I could get close and burnt the area so I would not be able to reach you. Since then they have shrouded your steps in darkness. Even Signa could not save you from him although she tried. It is why he never left your side. But know I am here, no because you need saving but because I leave you alone for two minutes and look at the trouble you get yourself into!" My brother smiles at me and I grin at his familiar face.

"I have missed you, Tallon," I tell him.

"Ah, I'm just in time for a touching family reunion I see!" A familiar voice interrupts and my insides turn to ice as I turn hearing his voice behind me.

I look into the face the monster who is so achingly familiar. A face that has made me laugh, who I thought protected me, foolishly not knowing he was the source of all my pain.

He smiles at me, taunting me. "And caught dramatically.... again, I see or even better...two for the price of one." Az mocks me but I only return his smile. He is dressed in the black leather of the Xiana. He is every inch their leader. The hooded enemy that has tortured me, deceived me, earned my trust only so he can tear my world to pieces for his own gain.

"Finally, I meet the real traitor of Axis...or is it just Az a servant of Axis ...or just a lowly brother of the Xiana? Who knows with the games you play Az, but I'm pleased to say I haven't missed you at all! And sadly, for you... no torque this time." I respond flicking one of my wrists in the air.

"Ah yes, how I enjoyed hearing the scrap of your flesh beneath those spikes." He stands across the way assessing me. "And no protection for you yet again. No allies, no armies nothing but the pathetic sword of your lost brother. Well, having him here will certainly save me the trouble of hunting down the Aurelian Heir when I have finished with you." He finishes with a shrug of his shoulders and I refuse to show the fear that is blooming so quickly in my chest so instead, I smile as if I am unconcerned.

"What do you want Az? Do you come to try weakening me a little more before the Last because we both know you are no match for me? Or do you want to murder me as you did to my father?" I ask and he looks at me thoughtfully.

"I only want what is mine." Is all he says.

"Sadly, for you, I stand between you and your precious treacherous dreams so that's never likely to happen," I respond with way more confidence than I am actually feeling.

"The Alta have had their time and failed!" he spits at me and I laugh knowing it will only increase his anger.

"It's so strange, that you demand the impossible, fail at all these schemes and games for power that does not belong to you. Face me Az instead of expecting me to concede. Face me in the Last and then this will be done. And when I bleed you to death at the end of my sword the Xiana will no longer be second to the Alta and I will ensure every one of your family is banish at your death."

"Everly, it doesn't have to be a battle. I do not wish to cause you pain." He changes tactics. "You are the last obstacle in a very exhausting battle. There is no one left for you to save so save yourself, take your brother and concede what little is left to those who were powerful enough to bring Axis to her knees. Our numbers are endless, and we hold the power of Amara and the gateways already."

"You may hold Amara but the second my father died the gateways closed. Only the completion of the Last will give the next First the power of the gateways. The time of the Xiana will be over. Axis gave you power and you turned against us all." I remind him angrily "You used me to breach the plains! You used me to enter the tomb! I have been nothing other than a pawn in your power hunger game but now, when it comes down to this moment there is nothing you can offer me. Nothing you can bargain with. I stand between you and the throne you think to take from me. You chose to murder and torture and schemes all for greed and power forgetting the sacrifice required and you've placed all of Axis at risk because of it! You cannot rule Az.... it is not in your blood." I finish with frustration.

"Listen to what I offer." He tells me quietly and I watch him carefully but do not respond. There is no bargain I will make with him. He has broken my heart. "I want to offer you peace. You cannot win this fight, Everly. Not even you. We have planned this since your birth. We have watched and waited knowing Solomon would sacrifice himself to save you and we were right. You were his weakness and once we understood his vulnerability our plan was complete. He laid down his sword the second he thought you were going to die. He placed your wellbeing above Axis proving it is time for a change. Time Axis became powerful and conquered the worlds around us instead of maintaining peace at no cost and allowing other realms to become a threat to us all. Yes, yes, we may have underestimated your abilities, but we still will achieve our goal. You cannot escape. The sons of Xiana surround you on all sides. You know you cannot best me in battle, so I offer you a quiet life in any corner of this world...forever. It is that simple. You only have to agree to concede and this will all be over."

"And why would you offer me peace? Now? After you have tortured and hunted me all the way to Eos." I ask not because I care but because I want to understand his motives.

"It is the price of war, the cost of victory. Call it what you will but know I will do everything in my power to ensure you concede."

"Or you kill me, in honest combat, at the Last. Fight me for the right to rule. Show Axis you are worthy."

"I would rather you concede Everly. I have no desire to see you dead."

"But torture, attacks and increasing violence are acceptable? Murder? Theft? All these things you have already done are okay. My death is the only line you will not cross to be First?"

"EVERLY! ENOUGH! You do not realise all that is at stake here! You foolishly think this is a game!!" he yells at me frustrated. I watch as he runs his hand through his hair and wonder at this man who stands in front of me, the friend I thought I could trust above all others but clearly did not see.

"Why won't you face me at the Last, Az? At least show me you have some honour left and fight me for the right to be First or is it beyond you now? I mean, you stooped so low, got so desperate... If you want to rule so badly then earn it instead of trying to steal it!" I yell back at him "You think you deserve this because your family got tired of always being second? You want more power? Think this will enable you to conquer worlds beyond ours? Is Axis, the centre of our entire universe, wrong to ask you to prove yourself? To ensure you can lead the billions?? To be granted the full power of her light and balance? Who knows, maybe I would have given it to you when I foolishly thought perhaps you cared for me but not now! Not with everything you have done! Not when you have betrayed all that we are born to protect! And Az, you may have accomplished much of this deceit with your brothers at your back but this, the Last, this thing you want the most!! You must do it yourself and you can be assured I will stand in your way!! There is no agreement we can come to! No bribe you can offer! Nothing that will ever make me concede! I do this for my people, my father and for Axis!"

"YOUR FATHER??!!" he screams at me, the rage exploding in the space like spikes against my skin "The last true First, the great Alta Axian, Solomon the perfect!" And the anger in him grows as he spits angrily on the ground. "This man you think was so worthy...He had no choice your stupid girl! YOU GAVE HIM NO CHOICE! He was a fool and because of his foolishness...he died!"

"My father was murdered. He was respected and loved. You stand in front of me and think you are good enough to take his place! You fight without honour and in this, this treacherous path you have taken, you only lessen your worth even more. You have proved time and time again who are you, the leader you aspire to be, and what you are is no First." I push and push at his pride. I see his face darken and his fists grip at his sides. "My father fought tirelessly for the balance and the light. He was the shield and the shift of Axis. His abilities were beyond compare. He would never have done what you did.... to our people, our world.... the dragons! He..."

"ENOUGH!!" he explodes and draws his sword "He was not what you thought he was Everly! He was nothing without the dragons and for that, they paid the price as well. There was no other way. Hear me, foolish child. He was not true nor was he righteous. You saw him as nothing but pure and right, but you have no idea, Everly."

"I know he was everything you will never be! You will not stand in front of me and say such lies about my father. You couldn't defeat me chained in a circle, so you certainly won't defeat me shielded either. Come fight me because my father may have surrendered so you could kill him, but I will never yield." I stand ready as he explodes, just as I knew he would, and runs to me with his sword.

We clash in a mighty clang of steel, Tallon at my left, and Az's dark deadly power explodes around me, but it is fighting the familiar and his power has always felt like icy rather than my fiery roar. So, I push it back roughly and the shield shakes from the impact. I do not falter as I move. I see as he battles fiercely, he understands at once he faces the impossible with Tallon at my side. With a call to his army soldiers' storm into the fray and Tallon moves to protect my back.

"Para Axis!" I hear Tallon scream at them and it fills me with pride. I know he will protect me; in all these years he has been my protector so with confidence I focus my energy on our greatest threat.

I antagonise Az and belittle him, as he did to me, with slaps of my sword and pokes that draw streams of blood. His temper increases and he hammers me with blow after blow, but I rise after each one only to smile at him viciously once again. He is relentless and uses the darkness as much as I use the light, but he has forgotten my greatest ally is Axis herself and the air around us is unusually saturated with light and balance making me almost invincible.

He uses his strength against me, battering me with punches and slashes until I am pinned against the shield wall and look into the face of his rage. The talisman moves across my body and connects with my sword and white light explodes sending him backwards until he slams against the opposite side of the shield. The light and balance are flowing in waves towards me now. The power that has been ever-increasing fills me continuously and I begin to glow.

I laugh viciously at the uncertainty on his face. He recognises I am stronger, and I watch expectantly, gloating him to weakness as he runs towards me although slamming his head against my face in anger nearly drops me with the pain.

Blood pours from my mouth but I rise, and this dirty, desperate fighting only shows he continues to spiral out of control. His rage increases as he stabs at me in short strokes that do nothing more than infuriate him when I remain untouched. I move around the circle and he follows. I watch carefully, waiting in anticipation for him to use the darkness with greater force. He is strong but I have had enough of this pretence. It is time all the Xiana understood my place in this world regardless of their dreams. I have played my part for too long. Let this pathetic battle continue way beyond his hopes. He forgets I know the taint of his darkness when my light consumed his sword at the plains.

Screaming in rage he runs at me again and as he reaches me; I rise over his head while running my sword across his throat and within that single heartbeat he stops as I surround him with light using the pull of darkness to keep him trapped.

Everything stops. He knows. He understands. He has never been my match. Not now, not ever but only now does he understand the price is his life.

I have the traitor who has hunted me, tortured me, tricked me, destroyed my world on his knees with my sword at his throat I am ready to finish this fight.

I stand behind him triumphantly and look at the soldiers who have fought my brother furiously at the edge of Az's shield. Shocked at the defeat of their commander they stop and Tallon steps back from the fight. They scream at me in rage, threatening and gesturing but I do nothing.

My talisman crackles with power and it is as if my whole-body shines with white light. I can hardly see this traitor's face for the light seems to blend between us. I raise my hand filled with his hair in my grip and snarl at them before releasing a pulse of white light that rushes outwards towards his soldiers and kills them out in an instant and finally, I am left alone with my brother and Az.

"Is this what you wanted? Is this the end you searched for? Is this the price of thinking yourself worthy? Your army destroyed and you on your knees with my sword at your throat?" I scream.

The air around grows heavy and I look at this man who sweats and bleeds at my feet. He shakes with rage and fear knowing he will die and glares at me rather than respond.

"You gave me the power to destroy you the second you touched the slimy darkness of your sword against mine. You are not of Axis anymore. You are tainted with greed and power. I can assure you; you will never be First. You will never rule my world. Even with all your schemes and lies here you are with your throat against my sword exactly as you did to my father." And I lean back ready to slice his head from his neck, but he speaks.

"You cannot kill me Everly I am the Heir of Xiana. If you do, you will lose Salvation. Axis cannot survive without the four foundation families." He hisses threatened me with loss of the most vital pillar. "Without Salvation you cannot regenerate the light or balance. I hold the pillars."

"Everly?" I heard Tallon ask from my left.

He has me! I kick his knees from under him and he falls face forward into the dirt. I do not know what to do!

"If we cannot rule Axis, we will rule the Aurelians." I hear him gasp from the dirt and I turn in shock.

"You only ask this because you now know the power they hold." I spit at him in disgust.

"It is a simple choice, Everly. You can have the pillars and be First, but I will rule the realms beside you." He adds from the outer edge of the shield.

"I would not give you this even if I could." I simply tell him.

"I know.... which is why I will challenge your brother." He replies and I see his game. He knows he cannot hold the power of Axis but can control our destiny through the below! Again, I have told him this! He only knows this because of me! I turn to Tallon and see the understanding in his eyes. He knows how foolish I have been, and I am ashamed. It is all because of me. If he accepts this challenge, I can save Axis.

"It is a life of sacrifice, my sister. Father told me to save you would cost everything. We both understand all that is at stake. It is not for you to feel the weight of destiny. It is for me to fight for my own." Tallon whispers beside me.

"I have been so foolish brother. I have opened the door to our enemy. I have sacrificed father and now..." I cannot continue as my tears fall without any shame.

"I am not sacrificed yet." He replies smiling but I know the strength of Az. I know he is powerful and crafty and will not fight fairly. "You must save the pillars, Everly. You must save Axis. You are strong enough." And he looks at me with such pride, but I do not deserve his love.

"I am forever grateful for your love and protection brother. You have never wavered in your loyalty and kindness. Your strength when I am so weak." I tell him crying shamelessly.

"She knows you face your death." Az snidely remarks from the opposite side of the shield. "She knows it is her fault chaos finds her. Her powers only come to destroy even now the light grows within her beyond the possible ready to consume us all." He taunts Tallon but my brother ignores his words and turns to me.

"It is a worthy destiny, Everly! To die for what you have loved." He smiles and holds me close before stepping into the middle.

"I accept!" he boldly answers and from that moment I cannot intervene. A challenge must be fought in complete isolation. An intervention will result in death and as I turn to ensure his safety, I see the shield fall and look into the solemn faces of the pAx.

It is Tallon's Last not mine! They come to judge his greatest challenge and before I can scream in protest it begins.

Chapter 43

As if I am suspended in a nightmare I watch as my brother runs towards our enemy. It is violence and destruction, power and presence, blood and chaos.

Their battle is fierce, and I am helpless. I am no more than an observer of death as I watch, with horror, as the destiny of my universe unfolds.

I do not acknowledge the pAx. I want to scream my denial of this! I want to blame them for allowing such sacrilege, but it is beyond even them now! They stand there to judge combat instead of weight the worth of each man to rule! How foolish that they value strength over right and wrong.

This is all wrong! I cannot look away.

It is fierce and filled with anger and resentment.

It is a battle between dark and light even in the rising dust of our doom.

Az has the power of the light but Tallon is the balance and they are surprisingly evenly matched.

I have always fought beside my brother, never have I stood on the sidelines watching and it crushes me each time Az strikes at him. Makes me boil with rage that I am expected to stand aside for a fight to the death when it is within my power to save him.

Swords of light and steel clash repeatedly filling the air with sparks and vibrations.

Blood flows from Tallon's face and arm.

I cannot see any injuries on Az who wears dark armour, but I know his blood runs black and am pleased when I see it drips steadily on the ground.

They circle and strike in a fight that seems endless.

The pAx do not move. I cannot watch this injustice! I scream at them to intervene, to judge them on merit not on combat but it is pointless. They have been blind to all the destruction of Axis to the ambitions of the Xiana.

They watch carefully both combatants with equal intensity as if they are excited to finally serve their purpose.

"*You will have only one chance Everly.*" I suddenly hear the deep rumblings of Abrastos, the Dragon King, in my head and I quickly glance beyond the circle searching for him. In all the fighting I had forgotten my greatest strengths patiently waited for me in Eos.

"*Tell me how? Tell me what I must do to save him? To stop this?*" I beg him desperately.

"*You must intervene. The pAx have been swayed by the darkness. They have lied to us knowing the Heir of the Xiana comes. This fight is unsanctioned as Tallon has no heir. If there is no heir, he can only give up the throne through concession but not combat. The pAx know this but support the Xiana.*" He answers and I turn back to the fight. "*I am here Everly and I will save what must live, but It is time you trusted those who have always proved they are loyal to you and Axis.*" He tells me.

"*It is my fault. All of it!*" I tell him. I want him to know the truth before he helps me.

"*I understand but it was a lesson you needed. Your journey was never meant to be easy. The power you possess needs tempering with fire as painful as it may be.*"

"*I risked us all. It could cost us everything. If Tallon dies we lose the balance. If Az dies, we lose the pillars.*"

"*Even after all of this you still care for him. You cannot save them both.*"

"*You are asking me to choose?*" I ask him but feel the sadness of his loss all the same. "*He was supposed to be my friend! To care about me! But Tallon is my brother. There is no choice.*" I tell him angrily.

"*You trusted him.*"

"*Yes, but he betrayed me every step of the way.*"

"*Quickly Everly his death comes. Choose between them. Choose between the pillars and the balance because fate creeps up on us even now and we do not have the time to wait.*"

"*Tallon! I choose Tallon!*" I quickly answer and I wait for someone to save him, but nothing happens.

"*Abrastos?*" I ask but get no reply.

I turn back to the fight and watch as Az slices my brother across the chest and the pAx lean in with glee.

It is too late. I watch in horror as Tallon falls to his knees.

I scream in agony to the sky pleading with Axis to save him. My chest seems to fill with light. I cannot bear this agony. Not after this. Not after all I have done. It cannot be Tallon. The pAx nod and Az raises his sword for the final time.

Within this moment I see my father. His surrender. His faith in me and I know what he hides. I move quickly across the distance and call my sword regardless of the pAx I will fight for the destiny of my world, so I run and raise my sword calling the light in waves right from my core.

"I knew you would try to save him!" he snarls and lifts his sword to fight.

"I knew you would try to destroy him to hurt me." I spot back at him. I feel the anger of the pAx at my back and as they begin to chant and raise their hands. The ground shudders at Abrastos lands between them and Tallon protecting my back.

"*NOW EVERLY!*" he screams in my head and I raise my sword as if to fight but pause. Az looks at me confused. He thinks he knows my tactics. He thinks I am easily defeated but I am the light. I am the white fire that consumes and burns back the darkness. I have brought this destiny to my world and it is me who will destroy it and as I gasp a final breath of tortured agony, I shatter the shield my father placed within my chest and the world around me detonates in pure white light.

Chapter 44

This power is beyond what even Solomon thought was possible. It is of the origin of Axis in every way and I can only protect those who are meant to live as the world around me burns in a falling firestorm of white-hot flames. My scales burn white hot in the onslaught, and I cannot see beyond the blinding light.

I have little choice but do what Axis has asked and it pains me to think of what this means. I know the destruction she brings. The agony of the moment, of what comes grips at me, and I stop, pain clenching my chest to watch. She will destroy to bring hope.

Solomon spoke true. She is everything. She is the future. Fearless. Unafraid. Broken. Born of energy and pure light.

She is not the child they expected but she is the child this world waits for. She will bring destruction and freedom. She will wipe the slate clean for now and into the next. She will experience pain beyond measure and drive our world into the light with her fury.

It is not fate nor destiny that brings her it is Axis herself. She is the child of my world and I am forever tethered to her as the white of her fire coats my scales and sears my soul and I recognize her origins.

As the flames recede, I look at the destruction she brings. She has completely obliterated the pAx and wiped out half of Eos. The fire spreads out rapidly to cover Axis but it is not only destruction it is life and I see the truth of its purpose.

She is our hope...our salvation.

And it can only mean life as the fire still burns.

Chapter 45

"Do not give in to the light daughter. Rise! The end always comes before the beginning. Harness the light and let it recede in peace." he whispers softly to me knowing I cannot bear the pain he brings. "The agony of it tears your soul apart. The broken, wrenching pain that shatters your heart into pieces . . .. The others...those who think to counsel, to judge, to see you fall...they are nothing. They are the ones who sit on the sidelines of life...the ones who betray you, the schemers, the observers, those with opinions and theories who avoid the risk, and the gossip mongers looking for scraps in a reality they would never dare to imagine for themselves. It is in this agony you change, not grow, just change.... Hear me Everly.... hear my call.... feel my arms wrap around your heart holding it together when you are shattering into a million pieces and know I had no choice. This is their end, not yours."

"You left me!! Our world is destroyed. You forced me to fight...you forced me to choose and I have lost it all!" I scream in my father's face looking around for Tallon and Abrastos. "It is all gone! Signa is dead, the underground destroyed, they have taken Amara and now...." I cannot continue at the thought of Tallon death and fall to my knees in agony.

"I know...I know the betrayal that brings the darkness of the Xiana. Abrastos saw the fall of Axis sometime before this day but he also foresaw our salvation." He says gently and I look up at him surprised.

"When?" I ask.

"We have had many years to plan. If I had fought in that battle against the darkness, they would have wiped us all out.... our family, the Aurelians, the dragons. Our realms would have disintegrated." He tells me sadly. "The Xiana had grown too strong. Their numbers are numerous. We had only one chance at salvation and that was you. I trusted you, Everly. I did it...to save you knowing they needed your concession and having faith you were too stubborn and loyal to betrayal us all." He looks at me pale and drawn, pleadingly "The darkness had already taken the light! You saw it in his sword! The core of Axis was poisoned. Only you had enough light to restore it. He craved your position. He befriended you, hunted you, and tortured you. He cared for nothing other than what he could never have...the power you held."

"I am not enough." And I cannot look at him anymore. This pain. This is worse than death. "I let them in. Opened the tomb. I gave them the Aurelians. Forced the death of Signa. I even told them secrets and lead them to the Last. It was me, Father!! I did betray us all and with such foolish naivety!" I raise my voice at him in frustration, but he does not show anger or regret. He quietly comes and sits next to me in the sunshine. I cannot bear to look at him, but I cannot bear the thought of him leaving me again.

"I trusted him. I thought I cared for him, but instead, he took everything. He broke me more than I thought was possible. The pain tears at me, scarring me in ways that are irrecoverable." I tell him quietly.

"You loved him." Is all he says, and I lean against his shoulder.

"I was so stupid, so blind," I tell him. "I want to scream at him, punish him, hurt him but this agony leaves me helpless and, in the end, after everything else he took from me he drew his sword across my brother's chest." I finish and he waits. He lets me cry the tears I was too ashamed to cry in front of anyone else. To feel the pain that breaks my heart.

"Why did you leave me? Why couldn't you tell me all that was coming? Face it together?" I ask him.

"It was all I could do to save you." He tells me sadly "To save Axis. Without the talisman, you had no control."

"You didn't save me, you destroyed me. I cannot feel the light and balance. I cannot find peace even in death...." Is all I answer, and he is quiet.

"You are not ready for peace yet Everly. Not when you have a war to fight." He answers quietly and I lift my head to feel the warmth of the sunshine on my face and let the tears gently fade away.

"This is not death Everly." He tells me gently "Destiny is not finished with you yet. Yes, you were tricked and betrayed but, in the end, you knew loyalty and honour. These are the lessons that cannot be taught. They are the qualities that come through pain and sacrifice."

"I'm not done," I say knowing the truth.

"No daughter." He smiles "You are far from done. Your power was beyond the possible and in this small window of time, you have done the impossible and given Axis new life. You were never just destined to be First. You were always more but where there is power there is darkness."

"The talismans?" I ask, "Why did Tallon steal them from the tomb?"

"They protected him from the light. They will meld with him now. You have given him protection. He is the only one who is strong enough to stand at your back now. You shattered the shield at your core and the light could have killed him."

"So, they can be used?"

"Not by Tallon. They are only his protection. Yours is different." he answers honestly.

"So, I can use them?"

"No. I ensured you couldn't by bonding you to mine, which held the shield. They are dangerous Everly. Too much power can corrupt and affect the light and balance."

"Does Tallon live?" I ask sadly

"I don't know." He answers honestly and I see the pain in his face "Everly, it was Tallon who was tasked with your protection. I trusted him above all others with your life. He was all I could risk in case the darkness knew our plans. He shadowed you and killed again and again. He only intervened on the east road because he knew you were grave danger and it cost him dearly."

"I should have searched for him. I should have trusted him. I was so blind to lies."

"He knew you would go straight to the tomb and he planned to meet you there. We underestimated how quickly the Xiana would find you and when Tallon saw you at the tomb with Azul he knew just how much danger you were in."

"The explosion during the battle.... well, both battles...it came from me."

"Yes. I have protected you as long as I have lived. I shielded the power within you so others would not be threatened by what you were. Only Tallon, Abrastos and Signa knew the truth."

"I am a bomb...clearly," I answer and watch him laugh.

"No, you are light...so much light ...in such pure saturation it is like white fire." He tells me "You can feel it gather but control has, at times, been an issue. It is a blessing and a curse. The fire within you can destroy but also renew. I knew it would happen at my death during the battle, but I used what little time I had left to contain it. It is why Tallon and the Aurelians disappeared. The needed to protect themselves."

"I need to go back," I tell him suddenly standing and calling my sword. "I need to find Tallon." My father doesn't answer instead he stands facing me, looking at me sadly.

"Yes, Everly. Go save the world." He tells me before leaning forward to kiss my cheek and as he steps back and smiles at me gently the world around explodes once again in pure white light.

THE END.... for now.

Connect with Emmerson Allen

If you got this far, I'm hoping it's because you enjoyed reading First of Embers.
If you would like to find out more about coming releases and events here are my
social media coordinates:

Friend me on Facebook:
https://www.facebook.com/Emmerson-Allen-2289983351024561/
Follow me on Instagram:
https://www.instagram.com/emmerson_allen
Visit my website:
http://www.emmersonallen.com/

www.ingramcontent.com/pod-product-compliance
Lightning Source LLC
Chambersburg PA
CBHW070102260626
47160CB00004B/1282